RICHARD

Ben Myers was born in Durham in 1976.
He is the author of several works of fiction,
non-fiction and poetry. His writing has appeared in
a number of publications including *Melody Maker*,
NME, *Mojo* and the *Guardian*. He currently
lives in rural Yorkshire.

BEN MYERS

RICHARD

PICADOR

First published 2010 by Picador

This revised and corrected edition published 2011 by Picador
an imprint of Pan Macmillan, a division of Macmillan Publishers Limited
Pan Macmillan, 20 New Wharf Road, London N1 9RR
Basingstoke and Oxford
Associated companies throughout the world
www.panmacmillan.com

ISBN 978-0-330-51704-1

The publishers are grateful for the following permission
to reproduce copyright material:
extract from 'Welsh Landscape' by R. S. Thomas
reproduced by kind permission of Bloodaxe Books;
extract from *Naked* reproduced by kind permission of
Mike Leigh, Thin Man Films and Faber & Faber.

1 3 5 7 9 8 6 4 2

A CIP catalogue record for this book is available from
the British Library.

Printed and bound by CPI Group (UK) Ltd, Croydon, CR0 4YY

For Adelle Stripe

CONTENTS

PREFACE

Richard James Edwards was born in Blackwood, Wales on 22 December 1967.

In 1989 he joined the Manic Street Preachers with his childhood friends James Dean Bradfield, Sean Moore and Nicky Wire. During his time in the band he was also known by his stage name Richey James or in the press as Richey Manic.

On 1 February 1995 he left a London hotel and was never seen again. His car was discovered two weeks later at the Severn View service station on the M48 motorway, near to the old Severn Bridge. Many sightings of him were subsequently reported, some of which are considered more plausible or credible than others. The most notable sightings are those which occurred in the two weeks following his disappearance. In referencing these I no way suggest them to be true.

Richard Edwards was legally declared dead on 23 November 2008.

This novelisation of his life features characters based upon certain real people and fictionalised interpretations of real events and reported sightings. Other characters and situations are entirely fictional and this story does not purport in any way to be the truth. It is instead one outcome out of an infinite amount of possibilities and therefore artistic licence has been duly exercised. This account is written with respect to all concerned.

1

'He was a man, take him for all in all,
I shall not look upon his like again.'

(*Hamlet*, 1. 2)

BOMB THE PAST

Room 516.

A turned-down bedspread, a screwed-down TV and a locked minibar.

Frost on the window. London dark blue and dormant.

Five storeys up, encased in brutalist concrete and alabaster. Up in the air. It's all up in the air. Everything. Everything.

Trapped up here in the room where someone has removed the doors. Concreted them over. Filled in the gaps. All that's left is this window. A window that won't open. They've nailed it shut. Nailed me in.

Nailed me in, five storeys up. Up in the air.

It's all up in the air.

*

It's not blackened slag heaps or eternal grey skies, but the sun's rays shining through the inch-wide chink in your floral-print curtains turning your golden hair nut-brown.

This is what you remember.

The floral-print curtains. The sun on your face. A box

of crayons upended on the worn olive-green carpet. Sugar paper.

The sun on your face.

The smell of baking. Margarine and sugar. Burnt Golden Syrup. The clatter of pans. Mum in the kitchen. Radio 4.

The sun on your face.

Dust dancing in shafts. A cloud that looks like a cat. The rattle of keys, Dad in the doorway.

This is what you remember.

The sun. Your face.

A warm glow of happiness.

Because the human mind continuously edits and self-censors. It writes its own history and romanticises events in order to make sense of a life. The very earliest memories are buried so deep they rarely rise to the surface of the conscious, yet you definitely remember the day Mum and Dad bring home your baby sister. It is 1969. You are two years old.

You don't remember clothes or the weather or even sounds or smells. All you remember is an image and a feeling.

The image of the three of them behind the cobbled glass of the porch door that fragments them, turns them into abstractions. You are on the floor, playing with a toy car on the olive-green carpet. Your world is knee-high; everything above is an alien landscape.

Then the feeling you get as the door opens and the

abstractions become something real and tangible: Dad smiling, with a white bundle in his arms and a night bag hanging from his arm, Mum behind him, looking tired, but flushed with rosy joy.

— Richard. We have someone here to see you.

You stand, your toy car in hand.

Mum and Dad coming into a huddle and bending over the bundle.

— Look who it is.

You don't know whether they're talking to you or the bundle, but they crouch down so that you can see too. You can see the tiny face with the closed eyes. The tiny fists and the gurgling mouth.

— It's your new baby sister, Richard. She's called Rachel.

Maybe you have imagined this. Maybe photographs and retellings of the moment have helped you build a mental picture, but you know the feeling is true.

*

Outside, across the road, Kensington Palace Gardens is framed in the half light. The city home to generations of blue blood and international embassies, stately homes and multi-multi-multimillionaires' mansions. The playground of the super- and the stupid-rich; people with more money than the entire town of Blackwood. The most expensive street in Britain. A home to wealth and intrigue. Sex and power.

And pain too.

They kept torture chambers in there during the war. Right across the road in those beautiful buildings. MI19-owned, they were. I read about it. The London Cage, they called it. All very hush-hush. Down there in the basement was where they tried to extract information from German prisoners of war. Hundreds of them, maybe thousands. Physical and psychological torture and pioneering techniques of interrogation – right here on the doorstep, in good old *cor-blimey-guvnor* London.

For the good of the country.

Beatings and threats. Threats and beatings. Sleep deprivation and the promise of 'unnecessary surgery' hanging over the heads of those subdued German soldiers. Cold water and cudgels.

Cold water and cudgels.

Right here on this doorstep. Out there in the darkness of the park over the road on the most expensive street in Britain.

For freedom.

For democracy.

For King and country.

*

Hide and seek in the long grass in the summer time. Peeling scabs from knees and poking the raw flesh beneath them, which is more red than anything you've ever seen. Hurling rocks into the beck. Gulping down a tall glass of concentrated orange juice, helping yourself to another biscuit, then running out the door again. Out down St Tudor's View and onto Gordon Road. Left through the estate and down to Pengam Road or right down to the High Street and, beyond that, the river. Each presents so many possibilities.

So, so many possibilities.

Because life presents options to you in all directions.

Life can be whatever you want it to be, but right now it is a fat lip from a misjudged frisbee in the face. It is a Twix melting into a gooey mess in the back pocket of your shorts. Life is Jason Stoker eating a worm for a dare and Roobarb & Custard. *It is you squashing your balls during a backer on someone's Chopper, or slip-sliding in dog shit down the rec.*

Life is a mixture of the mundane, the mysterious and the magical.

And endless possibilities. Endless options. There is so much fun to be had.

Sledging down the Scrambles in winter. The world's largest snowman – coal for eyes and a carrot for a nose, naturally. Blackwood down the hill in the distance. Numb fingers and numb toes. Red cheeks. Blockbuster. Chitty Chitty Bang Bang *at the pictures. Mum's chintz dressing gown. Gran and Granddad's wood-chip wallpaper. The childish calls of 'Coming ready or not . . .'*

Rhyl.

Newport.

Barry Island.
Home.

*

West goes to Notting Hill and Kensington, east leads to Hyde Park and Marble Arch, then Oxford Street, then beyond the High Street shopper's paradise, Soho, where I spent so many nights in '91, '92 just wandering and gazing and wearing out the soles of my shoes.

I was not so much awestruck then as anonymous. Glad to be anonymous. Glad to see that the city was what I had always suspected it to be: a Petri dish of human amoebae colliding but never connecting. Always bouncing off one another without apology, without true communication. The very 'neon loneliness' we wrote about.

I wish I had retained at least some of that enthusiasm for discovery, but it has all gone now. Never to be replaced. I don't have the energy for enthusiasm any more. I don't have the energy for anything. Books, music, people, sex, money, but most of all – me. I no longer have the energy to be me. I can be what people want me to be, but I cannot be who *I* want me to be.

Because I no longer know. Will probably never know.

It's cold and quiet and cars are slowly passing by, their lights a slow trail of burnt red in the night, and each of them contains a body or bodies, and I wonder who they are, and this view from Room 516 isn't helping.

No sleep and nervous, I want to wake up in a city that always sleeps.

Soon I'll need to make a decision.

Before I leave Room 516 I will know what to do.

*

Everything is cold and hard, as if weighted down by history and an unspoken sense of burden. The wooden benches sit on a wooden floor.

Coughs and creaks. The shuffling of feet.

It's draughty and you're wearing shorts so you shove your hands in your pockets to keep them warm.

You spend hours staring at the pattern in which the floorboards were laid decades earlier by a team of carpenters from another age, a different era.

You wonder if the carpenters were religious men, whether theirs was a Godly mission, or just another paid job.

You drift off, your mind wandering and you stare at that floor, your eyes following the diagonal pattern of wooden boards, the varnish worn away by decades of feet shuffling from the front door to the altar and back again, or restlessly moving beneath the pews as the vicar delivers another long, nonsensical sermon.

It's as much a shack as a glorious stone church; more a corrugated prefab than a cathedral designed to evoke awe. The only thing this place evokes is chilblains.

There's no stained-glass window, no mysterious musks and scents being wafted through the air by sombre altar boys. None of the alluring rituals that the Catholics have.

Just coughs and creaks. The shuffling of feet.

So right here and now, on the cold hard bench on the scuffed floor amongst the coughs and the creaks of a Sunday morning, you vow to be in service to no man but yourself, and to never give up the one asset you were born with: your ability to think and act freely.

*

I have yesterday's newspapers spread out in front of me and I'm scanning the headlines.

CLINTON TO LEND MEXICO TWENTY BILLION DOLLARS.

SIX THOUSAND DEAD IN GREAT HANSHIN EARTHQUAKE: THOUSANDS MORE STILL MISSING.

KUNG FU CANTONA!

I wish I had a map right now. A map of London. A map of Britain. A map of the world.

A map of my mind.

I've had no sleep and I'm nervous, my stomach is in revolt.

Soon I'll need to make a decision. But I can't think. Can't think. Can't think straight. Can't think straight in Room 516.

Room 516 The Embassy Hotel, Bayswater Road, London.

Everything is predictable. I know how the story ends

and it doesn't end happily. It just ends like a big black punctuation mark. It just ends.

Ends.

I can't think straight here in Room 516.

Room 516 with the bedspread, the kettle, the locked minibar. The adjustable mirror and the little packets of soap.

I can't think straight. I'm reaching out into the darkness trying to grasp something tangible.

Something tangible in Room 516.

Room 516 The Embassy Hotel, Bayswater Road, London.

Room 516 with the bedspread, the kettle, the locked minibar. The silent corridors. The window that won't open. The window they've nailed shut.

The TV is on but the sound is turned off as it casts strange formations on the walls. Formations like my thoughts – nebulous and foreboding. Washed out. Just beyond reach. Shape-shifting images that are flat and meaningless; which once had meaning but now are just shapes on the wall. Shapes on the wall of Room 516.

I need to make a decision.

Before I leave this room I will know what to do.

In this sea of uncertainty though one fact remains concrete, steadfast and immovable: there is no way I am going to America today. No way.

Not today. No way.

Not today. Not ever.

No way.

America?
No.

Dawn breaks but I can't see anything beautiful in it. It simply gets lighter, the traffic flow heavier. Another day of repetition lies ahead. Or maybe it won't this time.

Because I'm pacing now. Pacing the room. Pacing and thinking.

Trying to think. Thinking about everything. Thinking about nothing.

Thoughts piling up, none of them clear.

I flop down onto the bed, onto the newspaper.

I need to make a decision.

Repeat after me . . .

I need to make a decision. I'm going out of my mind. My fucking mind. Maybe it's the pills?

It's not the pills. It's anything but the pills.

I'm not going to America.

Repeat after me . . .

Not going to America.

I'm in no fit state.

No fit state for America. No fit state for anything.

No way. No today. Not ever again.

America? No. America can wait. It can wait for ever.

I don't want these pills in me any more.

I don't want to be in me any more.

Repeat after me . . .

No more, no more, no more.

I need to make a decision.

So make it, then.

I can't.

Why not?

Because I'm scared.

You're always scared. That's your problem. Always scared.

Not always.

Yes, always. Pussy faggot cop-out bastard.

Don't.

Yes. Pussy faggot cop-out bastard. Talk about wasted potential. What a fucking let down. Spoilt pussy faggot cop-out bastard.

Please . . .

You need to make a decision.

I know, I know . . .

Time is running out.

I can't.

You can. And you will. Because for the first time in your life you'll stop being a pussy faggot cop-out bastard and you'll take control. Understand?

I . . .

Understand?

I . . .

Here in Room 516 you will make a decision and you will stick to it and you will stand by it and you will see it through. Whatever the circumstances. Whatever the consequences. Because for once in your life you will stop being a spoilt pussy faggot cop-out bastard. Understand?

. . .

Understand, cocksucker?

Yes. I understand.

So do it. Make that decision.

*

*You stay at Gran's a lot. Every Saturday night and some-
times in the week too.*

*Gran's is a bubble. A warm, clean bubble full of
strange curios, like her collection of coloured glass vases,
her crystal decanter and the silverware that she takes out
and religiously polishes once a month. The smell of the
polish tickles your nostrils. Gran cooks you proper chips
in a deep fat-fryer and you eat huge knickerbocker glories
with a crumbled Flake on top.*

*Granny always whistles the same song all day long:
'Zip-a-Dee-Do-Dah'.*

*You play Consequences and Ludo then you sit
watching Saturday night TV together – you at her feet
marvelling at her contorted toes and bunions like golf
balls.*

*You sleep in the spare room on a fold-out bed. You
always pretend that the bed is the car in* Starsky & Hutch.
*The landing light illuminates the glass panel above the
door and in the darkness of the room it looks like a
faraway space ship. You fall asleep thinking about Suzi
Quatro.*

And downstairs you can hear Gran whistling.

— Zip-a-dee-do-dah, zip-a-dee-day . . .

*

Everyone seems to think that you are somehow 'better', as if a rest and nice bowl of fruit for breakfast is the cure-all for any ailment. They must do, otherwise why would they send you off to America to talk up the new album, in advance of the band making their most concerted effort to crack a country that remains completely indifferent to your band.

It is because I've done such a good job of convincing them, that's why. I have worn my mask of recovery well. I have assimilated those twelve steps and my new smile makes my face ache. Sobriety shines in my eyes.

And it's also because the new album is my baby. My ugly baby. My stillborn. But like an ugly stillborn baby I am duty-bound to somehow love it anyway.

I certainly won't be able to better it, lyrically. And it's hard to see how the boys could ever write music that fits as perfectly as it does on *The Holy Bible*.

The Holy Bible.

My last will and testament.

Anyway, who else is going to be able to explain the concept of an album whose basic prevailing themes are – broadly speaking – the Holocaust, child prostitution and anorexia?

It wouldn't be fair to put that responsibility on anyone.

But still.

America.

Interviews. Radio stations. Breakfast brunches and power lunches.

The meet and greet. What Quentin Crisp calls 'the smiling and nodding racket'.

Having to pretend like you care.

About album sales.

About the American market.

About anything.

Two weeks of stale questions from people with ice-hockey hair and white, white teeth.

Having to charm DJs.

Journalists.

Pluggers.

Having to excuse yourself all the time. To puke. To sob uncontrollably. To scream into the nearest pillow.

Two weeks of fakery.

Can't do it. Sorry.

Just can't do it any more.

None of it.

Sorry.

Sorry.

*

Your first week at Oakdale Comprehensive and you make a new friend.

He's not human. He's something far better.

He's just a tiny pup when your parents bring him home – big brown eyes, big brown face. Floppy ears and floppier chops.

You all agree on a name. Snoopy. It's the ears and his comical face.

He spends the first week shitting and yapping. Dad

feigns annoyance at the noise and the stink but you know he loves him just as much as you do.

At first he sleeps curled up in a circle in a basket in the utility room, but soon he's scratching at your door, burrowing under your duvet, nuzzling your leg. You're not meant to let him sleep with you – something about establishing a groundwork of rules – but you like that solid feeling of warmth against your leg, the rise and fall of his ribcage, the occasional sigh or whimper.

You spend hours at a time just stroking the waterfall of fur that runs up from his wet black twitching nose and along his back as he blinks back his gratitude.

He grows in size, quickly.

— Eats like a horse, he does, says Dad. We should enter him in the National.

You're growing too, but not half as quickly as your new best friend. You're one of the smallest in the year. You still have your junior-school looks, while some of the lads, the dunces who the girls predictably swoon over – Joseph Sowerby, Gaz Jones – are already growing wispy moustaches. Dad says you'll fill out in time.

You're not sure you want to fill out. You certainly wouldn't want a 'tache, even if you could grow one.

Then after school there's usually a kickabout down the rec. The teams change daily, a revolving cast that's dependent on who is allowed to play out from this end of the estate.

You enjoy football. You enjoy the simplicity of it; you enjoy being breathless and feeling your muscles ache. The sweat on your brow. It's so much more fun than the dreaded rugby.

Nick Jones is one of the best on the footie pitch. He usually brings the ball and picks the sides. A year younger than you and already his legs practically come up to your shoulders. He's all right. He's not a wanker like some of the rough lads from the villages; for a sporty kid, he's all right. He always makes an effort to pick you, and it's appreciated. He puts you on the right wing and opti- mistically tells you to 'do some damage'. And he brings the trophy for your on-going tournaments. Says it's the old Welsh FA Cup but we know his dad found it in a skip somewhere.

Sometimes you bring Snoopy. You let him off his lead to join in and he gets in the mix to run rings around everyone, desperately attempting to burst the ball that's twice the size of his head.

He won't be able to play for ever, though – in a few months, he'll puncture Jonesy's new Wilson and he'll be forced to watch from the sidelines, barking orders like John Toshack, as frustrated as any boy would be at the inexplicable exclusion.

You joke about getting him a fur-trimmed manager's coat.

Then afterwards you trot home to Woodfieldside, analysing the game.

You eat your tea and get told off for throwing scraps from the table.

— Those chops are too good for a dog, says Mum,

even though you see her saving the bones and strips of fat for his late-night treat.

He's Snoopy and you're Charlie Brown. Life is Peanuts.

You feel ecstatically, joyously happy.

*

There's one thing I need to do first, though. It's only fair.

I open up my notebook and remove the pictures that I have carefully cut out and accumulated over the past week or so – from magazines and papers, mainly. Pictures of girls and movie stars, buildings, landscapes and cartoon characters. Pictures of animals and singers and cities.

Pictures of war zones and bodies, faces and flowers.

I take the glue stick and begin to stick them onto the cardboard box that I got from reception earlier. I paste them on and smooth them into place. The pictures form a decorative collage around the rim of the box, then when the glue is starting to dry I carefully copy out a number of literary quotes from my notebook.

Camus.

Sartre.

Mishima.

My old friends, the old boys, all together for one last time.

When I'm done I put what is left back into the box. My VHS copies of *Naked* and *Equus*, a couple of T-shirts, some photos of me and her – a girl, the one girl I have come closest to falling in love with – and my books. The rest of my books.

I take a pen and a sheet of the hotel's headed note-paper and sit staring at the carpet for a long time. I think about what to write but my mind is as blank as the page. Minutes pass. There is so much to say, but I don't know where to begin. Perhaps there is actually nothing to say.

Then I realise what it is I want to write – something that, fearful of sentimentality, I can rarely say, or perhaps rarely have cause to say, but nevertheless find easy to convey with a pen. I write *I love you* – love that will be forever unrequited – on a note, put it in the box, tape it shut, then put the box on the table.

*

Paul Winters says, Wait here a minute – you've got to see this.

You're round his house and his parents are out. It's the summer holidays and they are letting him stay at home by himself. Actually his big sister is meant to be keeping an eye on you but she spends most of her days down the town with her boyfriend, an older boy with a motorbike and the obligatory leathers.

You're in the Winters' living room, watching the farting scene from Blazing Saddles *again – the one with the beans – munching on biscuits and slurping juice. Paul disappears for a couple of minutes, then you hear him charge back down the stairs.*

Then he's behind you.

— Close your eyes, Eddie.

He's the only person who calls you by your abbreviated surname. Most people call you Richard. Or Teddy.

— I'm watching telly.

— Just close your eyes and hold out your hands.

You reluctantly turn away from the film about the farting cowboys, and you close your eyes.

He places a magazine in your hands.

— OK, you can look now.

You look down and the magazine is opened to the centre pages. You see a naked woman with blonde hair, her legs spread wide open. She is laid back on cushions, invitingly. You see her pink, hairy fanny first. Then her breasts. They're large and weighty. The first pair you have ever seen. Her vagina looks odd, like nothing you've never seen before. It's not how you had imagined it to look. (Had you even imagined it?)

The hair on her head is so blonde it's nearly silver but the hair on her fanny is much darker. She's wearing silk gloves up to her elbows, and nothing else. Her mouth is open ever so slightly and her eyelids look heavy over blank eyes. Your mind reels.

This is alien territory and you feel strange to be inhabiting it.

— Isn't it great? Look at them tits.

You don't answer.

— Turn over – it gets better.

You turn the page and see the same woman turned sideways this time, positioned on all fours. In front of her, a couple of inches from her face, is a long dark penis.

It's not erect and you can't see the man it belongs to, only his legs and part of his torso. It's just dangling there. It is strange. It is huge.

The woman has her head positioned so that she's looking out from the pages with the same blank-eyed look as before. You notice that she's wearing more lipstick in this photo than the last one. A continuity error.

You also notice the wallpaper in the background, the colour of the scatter cushions; a birthmark on her upper thigh. Her hair is impossibly blonde and you're struggling to guess her age. She could be twenty-five, she could be fifty.

Her breasts hang down below her, pendulously. They look different at this angle.

— Isn't it great? Paul says again. My brother keeps them under his bed. He thinks I don't know about them. Look at them tits.

This image – this glimpse into another world, a world you didn't know existed – awakens something inside you. Something that feels strange and cold and inexplicable. Something adult that you want no part of.

— He's got loads of them. Wait a minute and I'll go and get the others.

— Paul, I don't think I . . .

He leaves the room. You know you don't want to see the other magazines. You don't even want to see any more of this one.

Suddenly you feel terrible. Like you're gripped by the horrors, your stomach turning somersaults.

You throw the magazine down, run outside and retch

into the bushes at the side of the Winters' drive. A string of sick comes out of your mouth. It tastes of the Ribena you drank earlier, only it is bitter and it burns at your throat.

You don't bother going back into Paul's house.

You don't want to see any more of those magazines.

You don't want to look at them tits.

*

And then it all happens in a flurry.

I throw the remaining unpacked items into my holdall. My notebooks, passport, road atlas, a bottle of water, a couple of books, my cassette copy of the new songs James has been demo-ing and the new Nirvana album, some clothes, my jacket, sunglasses, cigarettes, lighter. Roll of cash.

I put the pre-packed suitcase – the suitcase that will never see America, the suitcase containing clothes that I will never wear again – on the floor by the bed.

I walk into the bathroom and select the toiletries I might need while I work out what the hell is happening. I choose the bare minimum: toothpaste, toothbrush, deodorant.

Everything else I leave behind: my moisturiser, aspirins, aftershave, razor, dental floss, my hair products (there is no hair left to care for), shaving foam, shampoo, conditioner, tweezers, nail clippers (there are barely any nails to clip), an old stub of an eyeliner pencil, a peel-off mask, a comb, a brush. I leave them all in the bathroom. Don't even bin them.

Just leave them.

My hair still in the brush. My razor blunt.

I scan around the room. The papers and magazines I dump in the bin. I also empty the ashtray then take a minute to light a cigarette. I stand in the centre of the room, smoking it, trying to draw the different strands of thought together, trying to weave them into something solid and tangible. Something of worth.

Deep in the hotel I hear a door slamming shut. I hear cars outside. I hear my own heartbeat.

I grind the cigarette out, empty the ashtray again, go to the bathroom and drink some water from the tap, splash some of it on my face, then in one decisive move I pick up my holdall, scan the room, place the room key on the table, then leave.

The door quietly closes behind me of its own accord.

Swish.

Click.

*

Your Easter-holiday homework assignment is titled 'The Life and Times of William Shakespeare: An Introductory Study'. Who he was. When he lived. What he did.

Why he mattered.

You spend the best part of the week on it because you have bugger-all else to do. While everyone else is out playing or trying to cop a feel of their first teenage tit, you hit the Blackwood library and spend hours in there, nose-deep in the books, cross-referencing the critical theories with the plays themselves. You return, day after day, and occupy the same table in the corner by the radiator. You skim-read Shakespeare's complete works in one thick hardback edition and you even read some of his sonnets. Then you move onto his rival Christopher Marlowe.

The librarian gets to know you. She even asks if everything is OK at home because young boys don't normally spend so much time reading.

By the time you're back at school on Monday you have filled an entire one hundred and twenty-four page notebook on The Life and Times of William Shakespeare. You have provided a critical overview of his oeuvre and interspersed it with an appraisal of the most significant moments in his working and personal life, and some historical and socio-political context too.

You are thirteen years old.

*

The corridor is long and empty and smells of stale cigarettes. The dimmed night lights are still on and cast a strange orange hue and the nicotine-tinted Artex ceiling tiles feel like they are bearing down upon me as I walk and I'm suddenly aware of the peep-holes on each door that stare out like unblinking eyes. I wonder if anyone is watching me at this very second, and if so what do they see?

A man.

A skinny man with a shaved head and a bag over his shoulder.

A skinny man with a shaved head and a bag over his shoulder wearing an anorak with a fur-lined collar and woollen hat pulled low, walking with purpose along the corridor, eyes wide, cheeks sunken, lighting another cigarette as he turns the corner to the elevator and moves out of sight.

Just a man. Any man, off to do anything. Work. Shopping. Travel.

Whatever.

Just some man in the hotel, a nobody, passing through, a ghost, like we all are.

As I walk, Room 516 ceases to exist. It falls away behind me, a black hole in time and space. Just a void to be filled by some other drama, someone else's second-hand smoke.

And I'm gone.

*

Friday afternoon and raindrops hit the prefab window like bullets.

Outside, the school's two punks – two fifth-formers – are caught in the downpour. They dash for cover, their blazers pulled over their heads to stop their hair flopping, their DIY dye jobs running.

Last year they were wearing Led Zeppelin and AC/DC T-shirts, this year it's The Clash and The Ruts.

It's double history. The Fall of the House of Tudor. History is normally your favourite but today you can't concentrate. You're staring out at the rain that falls in grey sheets, layer after layer of it sweeping across the landscape like death shrouds on a giant washing line.

Death seems to be everywhere at the moment.

That guy Sid Vicious is dead from a drugs overdose. Twenty-one years old. Apparently punk is also dead and you've not even heard it yet. You've seen his spotty face squinting insolently from the front pages of the papers, though. And Sex Pistols is a great name for a band. Dirty and dangerous and scary.

The rain keeps falling and the classroom is stuffy. Someone drops a ruler with a clatter.

The sense of pre-weekend distraction is tangible in the room; few people are paying attention.

The rain drums down on the flat roof and the sports fields are collecting puddles that will still be there next Tuesday when you're forced to play rugby sevens. You're looking forward to a night in front of the telly with Snoopy. Shopping for new shoes in town tomorrow. Then tea at Gran's.

It is 1979 and the end of the year is looming. The end of the decade.

Out in the real world, beyond Oakdale Comp, beyond Blackwood, 'I Will Survive' is on the radio all the time; a maxim adopted by people the world over. The drummer from The Who dies from drugs. More victims of the Yorkshire Ripper are found. The Times *closes for months during strike action. Callaghan out. Thatcher in. Disco fever. 'Do Ya Think I'm Sexy?'*

Ten minutes until home time.

*

The elevator doors close and I press the button for the ground floor. The interior is mirrored and my reflection stares back at me. The skinny pale man with the holdall again. The shaven head. The black eyes.

I turn to my left and he's there, and to the right also. The mirrors reflect one another, my image repeated on and on into infinity. Dozens of me in all directions. Dozens of Richards staring back blankly. My stomach flexes nervously and nauseously at the thought of what I am about to do.

What *am* I about to do?

I don't even know. Maybe nothing.

Maybe I'll just suck it up. Maybe I'll walk around the block, look in some shop windows, maybe stroll in the park before going back to my room, realise that I don't have a key and then go back down to reception to find a porter to let me back in, where I'll take a shower, change my clothes, drink some tea and then wait for James to knock on my door so that we can go downstairs together and get in the car that will drive us straight to Heathrow Terminal 4.

But the wheels are already in motion. Different wheels. I've packed my bags, locked the room and I've walked away. I am walking away right now. I'm going to miss the flight to America. I'm going to screw it up again. I'm going to fuck up the itinerary for the next two weeks. Those dozens of interviews, all those hotel bookings – they'll all have to be cancelled. James will be pissed off. Everyone will be pissed off.

I'm going to let everyone down again.

I'm going to let everyone down again and the thing is I know I am going to do this before it has even happened. For once I am in control of things. I have the power to stop it, but I can't bring myself to. So perhaps I don't have that power at all. Maybe I'm even weaker than I think.

Either way, I can't do it.

People who are sound asleep in their beds this very moment in London, New York and Los Angeles are unaware that they are about to have their lives inconvenienced over the coming days. People in Boston and Chicago and Blackwood too. Only I know it because I am that inconvenience. All this fleetingly gives me a strange flicker of excitement – the notion that this mystery, this mess, will unfold as and how I choose.

My mess.

The phone call to Mum last night was the hardest thing I have ever had to do but even now, a few hours later, it already seems an age ago and a dark night like a prison sentence has passed since then.

Trying to tell your parents that something is wrong, that something within you is rotten, is the hardest thing in the world. Parents have such high hopes for their children and it is they who feel the responsibility for their children's happiness, even into adulthood. I've been blessed with parents who care, who taught me, protected me and encouraged me and all I have given them is worry and despair and sleepless nights.

They can't *not* have looked inward at themselves when they've seen me lying in a hospital bed with self-inflicted wounds, or held my hand in a twelve-step meeting; they can't *not* have blamed themselves at some point.

So really what I'm about to do is for them.

I'm doing it for them because I have put them through so much already. I'm doing it so they no longer have to feel guilty. So they can absolve themselves of all responsibility. So that they can finally realise that this mess is my mess.

Yeah, you keep telling yourself that, Edwards.

But it's true.

Whatever.

It'll stop them suffering. It'll stop them worrying.

Bollocks. This will just make this worse and you know it. Selfish bastard.

Don't.

You selfish cunt.

Honestly. I just want to break away from everything. I just know I need to get away for a while.

'For a while?' What will that prove?

I don't know.

I'll tell you what it will prove. Nothing. It'll just get everyone worried again. More worry, more expense. It'll get you in hospital again. The clinic. The health farm. The papers. They'll just think you're bluffing.

I'm not, though.

I don't give a fuck. They'll say you're doing it to promote your shitty new album.

Shut up – that's not true.

Yes it is, and you know it. Just like when you cut yourself for the photographers.

That was heartfelt.

Bullshit.

It's not. It's not bullshit.

Well go on, then, if you're going to do it. Be a man for once in your life.

I will, then.

Go on, then. Stop all this bullshit attention-seeking and prove it to me. Prove it to yourself.

Maybe I will.

You won't.

The lift judders to a halt, the bell rings and the doors swish open. I step away from the infinite version of my ugly self and walk across the lobby.

＊

You're eating your dinner on your lap and watching ITN News At 545. You can still hear the voice now: 'Death in IRA hunger strikes.'

Pictures of Bobby Sands flicker across the screen. Emaciated, translucent, defiant. Bobby Sands as a younger man. Bobby Sands' arrest photo. Bobby Sands on his self-made Maze death-bed.

Dead after sixty-six days without food.

Sixty-six days.

They call it 'suicide'.

Dad shaking his head, Mum sighing. She's seeing the human side of it, as are you.

Even at fourteen you know this is beyond 'The Troubles' you don't yet fully understand, beyond politics. But you know that this is what integrity means. This is conviction. This is control.

This death matters, you think. This death means something. Fourteen years old and you already know. You know. This death spells conviction. This death spells control.

The human body as a weapon. Once witnessed, never forgotten.

May 5th. 1981.

*

As I walk across the empty lobby of this 4-star rated hotel with my head down ('*with the charm of Notting Hill, the elegance of the Royal Kensington Gardens and all the buzz of the vibrant city of London, this is a comfortable, relaxing base, whether you are exploring London as a tourist or visiting the city on business*') I can't help thinking I've unintentionally left something important behind.

I glide like an apparition across the carpet, through the glass doors that part as I approach them and out to the cold London morning. Adjusting the holdall over my shoulder, I pull up my hood and head straight to the hotel's small car park. I go to the car, the band's communally-bought

Cavalier that only I am legally insured to drive, unlock it, throw my bag onto the back seat and in one fluid movement start the engine, rev it, reverse out of my space, look left, look right and pull out onto the Bayswater Road.

Don't look back.

I won't.

I mean it. If you look back you'll change your mind.

I reach for the rear-view mirror and tilt it off to the left so that everything behind me – the hotel and, beyond that, central London – stays there. It stays there as I move away from it, fiddling with the heater to get a bit of warm air circulating.

It's only then that I realise I haven't got a clue as to where I am going.

Not a clue.

*

James and Nick see it first, late one Friday night. A repeat of some regional arts show that Tony Wilson from Factory Records used to host, called So It Goes. *(You recognise the title as being cribbed from the key lines of* Slaughterhouse-Five.*) It's on again on Channel 4 as part of some 'Ten Years of Punk' celebration.*

— Here, watch this. It's amazing.

James has taped it and passed it on to you. It's an hour of footage from 1976 and 1977 of all the key movers of punk, a scene you only saw in the newspaper and in those two lowly punks at Oakdale. You have vague memories of seeing some local news footage of some scary-looking band called the Sex Pistols having their show cancelled, but that's about it. You were too young, and up until now there's been too much new music to get into, so why bother with the old stuff? Especially when the few punks you see around town are glue-sniffing wankers with terrible, terrible hair.

But you watch it and you have an epiphany. Some of it – the bands you're already aware of like Siouxsie and the Banshees or The Jam – leave you a little cold, but some of it (most of it) makes the hairs on your neck stand on end. Sex Pistols, The Clash, Buzzcocks, Joy Division, Iggy Pop. It's both ugly and beautiful. Inept and dazzling. Basic but visionary. Within each performance there are bum notes, broken strings and furious, almost violent, intent. And each band looks amazing. Cheap, but amazing.

Watching it, it is as if your television is breaking out into a sweat and it has taken this insight into the past to show you the future. After this moment you become enamoured with punk: what it was, what went wrong with it, and why it could still have value now.

When you return the VHS to James he and Nicky have already been into Cardiff and bought Never Mind The Bollocks and the first two Clash albums. Nicky has cut his hair and James has ripped the sleeves of his old T-shirts.

Your lives have been changed.

It's as easy and as sudden as that.

*

At a little after seven the traffic isn't too heavy. I turn on the heater and the radio for the warmth and distraction.

Noise bursts forth from the speakers: a gaggle of cartoon voices, comedy effects and sycophantic giggles. The jingles tells me that it is that twat with the 'tache, *Steve Wright In The Morning* on Radio 1. The nation's favourite station.

People are actually able to listen to this mindless crap in the morning?

I turn the dial to Radio 4 and crank the heater up a notch.

*

The bus station in the rain; slate sheets tumble noisily. Nick is off playing football and James is late. There are three lists in your pocket: one for you, one for James and the NME Writers 100 Best Albums of All Time *list, torn from last week's paper.*

You sink into your coat, check your watch then look up to see James running around the corner, guitar case in his hand, then, seconds behind him, from the other direction, the bus turning into the road. The reliable Red & White *service of South Wales. You turn to him, smile and wave. He doesn't wave back, merely digs in deep and runs faster, his hard case clattering off his legs. Trench coat and combat boots. He's always late. James, always running. He'll be the new Ovett, that one.*

The bus pulls into its stand. The doors hiss open and the queue nudges forward. Then he's at your side, gasping but trying not to appear breathless.

— Late again, Bradders?

— On time, I'd say, he shrugs, cracking that sideways smile.

He smoothes his hair back, rifles in his pockets for change.

— So are we going to fucking stand here all day or what, Edwards?

Funny fucker.

Cool fucker.

— Come on then, Strummer . . .

You edge forward, pay the man, then move down the aisle to the back seat, the windows steaming up with the hot breath of Saturday-morning shoppers. The doors close with a sigh, then you're reversing through a three-point turn and out the station, first taking a right, then the next left for the first exit to Cardiff. All packed in like sardines in the hourly Red & White.

— No Sean, then?

— Still in bed.

James writes his name in the condensation on the window with a finger.

— Do much last night?

— Brandy and a wank, he says.

You both settle in for the long slow crawl to the city by the bay. It's a little too early for heavy conversation, especially with this hunger growling in your bellies. Beyond your record-buying budget you only have enough for a pasty each, maybe more if James gets lucky with his busking. Gets lucky? You mean gets good. Learns how to sing.

— Got any new tunes?

— A couple. I've only got five strings, though. I snapped the D.

— How much do you need?

— I'll pay you back.

Standing in Spillers, the rain drops glistening on your shoulders, your hair matted. Even in here you can hear James barking his way through The Clash's 'Stay Free'.

Bless him. He acts like he doesn't care but deep down he's fragile, a misfit too. You know you could never do what he does: you don't have the time, the skills or the gumption.

You'd give him ten out of ten for effort. A high three for finesse.

The lists then. You unfold the NME writers' piece. There is lots of the usual stuff listed. Beach Boys, The Beatles. No – you've already heard them. Dylan's Highway 61 – maybe. The key punk stuff you've already all devoured too. Elvis' Sun Sessions. James has it already. Dexy's is more Nick's bag and you still can't 'get into' Kevin Rowland.

Ditto Weller and The Jam's All Mod Cons. The modernist who only looks backwards.

And The Band? Smokey Robinson? The Temptations' Anthology? Too risky.

Instead you select two albums you think you'll like and have been meaning to buy for months: Unknown Pleasures and Marquee Moon. Then you take a risk on the third. Swordfishtrombones. You pick it up, flip it, look

*at the sleeve. Tom Waits looking campy and vaudevillian.
The* Whistle Test *stuff you saw was cool, but what if he's
a one-trick pony?*

*You stand and you deliberate and you wish the Bunny-
men had a new record out. Your eyes scour the wall
and stop on the latest Hanoi album.* Two Steps From The
Move. *Mike Monroe looking devastating. Simultaneously
stupid and hilarious, but fuckable too. His namesake
Marilyn meets Candy Darling in a Soho backstreet. No – a
Cardiff backstreet. Blank eyes and blow-job lips. Hips
skinnier than any goth girl.*

— Could I see that one, please? The Hanoi Rocks one.

*The guy with the Crass hair passes it to you. The
sleeve is amazing, but they open with a cover of a Creedence Clearwater song. Hmm. Suspect, highly suspect.
Creedence are a bit too much like the boyos back home's
band of choice for your liking. But still. Five camp Finns
tackling a sacred cow. Yeah, why not? It may be worth
buying for the cover alone. You can always ditch the vinyl
and frame the picture.*

*So: Joy Division, Television and Hanoi Rocks it is
then.*

*You check Nick's list. It is comprised entirely of seven-
inch singles.*

*The Woodentops. McCarthy. New Order's 'The Perfect
Kiss'. 'Barbarism Begins At Home' by Moz and co. Simple
Minds' 'Don't You Forget About Me'. A joke? A joke
slipped in at your expense? It's hard to tell with him sometimes. He's the one paying anyway, so maybe you'll have
the last laugh.*

Darkness on the Edge of Town by 'The Boss' for James, as requested. On cassette.

Outside he's still barking and thrashing away.

The inflection is wrong, but you have to hand it to him – he sounds a lot like Strummer. Shame Mick Jones sang that one . . .

Still he's got balls as he barks and thrashes and jerks and scares the Saturday shoppers.

You give the list to the Crass guy and he wanders off to get them.

He returns, slides them all into a carrier bag, then tots up the total. You hand him the money, then watching you watching James he says:

— Fucking shit, inne? The silly twat is here every Saturday, giving me a fucking migraine. Going nowhere, he is.

Barking and thrashing.

And in that moment you know that you love him because he's everything that you know you can never be: he's fearless and you're fearful. That's why you get on so well.

Yin and yang.

You take your change and leave.

2

'And then it started like a guilty thing
Upon a fearful summons.'

(*Hamlet*, 1. 1)

CLASSIFIED MACHINE

The people in Holland Park and Chiswick look healthier, wealthier and more beautiful than in other parts of the capital. That's the way it is in London; being born and raised in the wrong postcode can take years off your life. Driving through the city this morning is like passing through the ranks of the British class system within the space of minutes.

At this time of the day it's mainly morning joggers and early commuters who are out and about. The only people pushing pushchairs are paid to do it; glamorous big-titted nannies from South America and skinny exploited things from the Far East.

I drive past the multimillion-pound town houses, past the delicatessen and gastro-pubs towards the Chiswick roundabout, where the traffic slows down to converge and circulate then converge again.

I check my mirror, then signal, manoeuvre, and pull out and around to take the turn-off to the M4, the road that has always taken me home.

The escape route from Sodom.

I drive on, passing rows and rows of suburban houses, a golf club, Osterley Park and Heston Service Station –

the scene of many a late-night stop-off in the early days of the band – and nudge the car up to fifty. Fifty turns to sixty and the engine begins to hum.

The early morning sky is seven shades of grey as the road unfolds before me, a blacktop asphalt shadow pointing westwards.

I leave London behind, yet for a quick, painful moment what remains of my conscience wrestles with itself as I consider pulling over into the nearest suburb or petrol station, picking up the phone and calling James, who I know will now be awake and agitated as he waits for me in the lobby. Or maybe he's still eating his breakfast, sipping coffee, smoking and chewing nervously in anticipation of the flight and wondering whether I've slept in; both latecomers to international travel, neither of us are good flyers.

Across London and elsewhere – New York, Los Angeles, Boston, Chicago and, yes, Blackwood too – there stretches a loosely linked line of people whose lives, or certainly their day and probably their week, will be affected by my selfish and unplanned defection.

The irony of it all is that my absence will have far greater impact than my presence (though, for once, impact is not something that I am seeking).

There's a second irony too: I'm actually approaching Heathrow and could easily make my flight if I wanted. I could find the number of the hotel and get a message to James to tell him that I have set off early and that I will meet him there, where I could leave the car in one of the long-stay car parks, or call management and have someone come and pick it up, then we'll check in and fly to the States to spend two weeks talking about ourselves, and this solitary journey will go unmentioned or maybe dismissed with a vague excuse like 'I couldn't sleep and fancied a drive.'

That's all it takes: one ten-pence phone call and a few words to right the procession of wrongs that I have set in motion; a quick-fix solution to the house of cards that is about to fall.

But I know I won't. I won't find a phone and make that call.

I won't because I don't want to. That's the crux of it: I don't want to.

Because you're a selfish bastard.

Because I'm a selfish bastard. Because I don't want to engage in any of that any more – the sense of duty, the familiar, soul-sapping formalities of life, the responsibility for other people's feelings.

I've already let too many people down and I'm tired of it. I'm tired of making excuses and tired of the sympathetic silences.

So I shall ask nothing and I shall give nothing.

If a parasitic creeping vine is strangulating all life around it, you cut it out at the root. That's just common sense. And so it is I have decided to simply remove myself from the equation.

Common sense.

Some might say such an act is more selfish than self-less, and they'd be right, but isn't that one of the many reasons why I no longer wish to be in people's lives –

because ultimately my selfishness bleeds them dry like a revenant who moves from one host to another to another, until they all fall, eyes blank, their skin-like paper drained of all life?

It's time to stop being a disappointment.

*

You can't sleep, of course, so you're up at the crack of dawn. Tea and toast and the sun rising over the houses, Snoopy by your side, restless for his walk. He sits up on his hind legs, begging, head cocked to one side, just like he used to when he was a pup.

On Good Morning Britain, *on the beige couch, they're still talking about Prince Andrew and Fergie Horseface's wedding and you think: no one you know cares. Not here anyway, not in Wales. No one who would admit it. Not now. Not in this 'climate'.*

Cut to the main news at eight.

They say that that London estate agent Suzy Lamplugh is still missing. Vanished into thin air after arranging a lunchtime viewing of a property with someone called 'Mr Kipper'.

You can't imagine what that must be like for her family. Her friends. They say that all the police have to go on is the log-book record of the viewing and an eyewitness who saw her arguing with someone outside the property. Then nothing, just gone from the Fulham streets. Maybe she'll turn up, they say, but who can really know. It must be hard to just disappear, though, unless someone really wants you gone.

Then it's on to the weather: fine. A clear mid-August day.

And back to Anne and Nick on the beige couch and the world carries on as normal.

You turn off the telly and take Snoops out for a run around the fields.

It's quiet and in the shade the grass is still wet. It soaks through the bottom of your jeans. You'll have to change them before you head off to pick up your results.

You run until you're out of breath, playing fetch with a stick, Snoopy retrieving it with boundless energy, his ears flapping, his eyes wide open as he runs five metres for every one of yours.

Back home you put the kettle on. Mum kisses you before she leaves. A peck on the cheek.

— Good luck, Richard. We know you'll do us proud. Call me as soon as you get a chance.

— Yes, good luck, son. We're proud already.

Dad.

— We know you put the work in. We know you gave it your all.

And then they're off to the salon and the house is quiet.

You change your trousers, say bye to Snoopy by giving him a big scrag behind the ears, and walk to college, finally allowing yourself to speculate as to how you might have done. You allow yourself these few nervous minutes.

The potential for failure is certainly there – it's always there in anything one chooses to do – but you don't think it can be that bad. Can it? No.

You don't think so.

Like Dad says, you put the work in. It's not like you froze in the exams either. It all came easy. They asked the questions you had revised for. No surprises.

You have put the work in.

You are one of the first to arrive. Oddly, there's a TV film crew from BBC Wales milling about outside. A cameraman, sound guy and a reporter who you think you recognise.

You walk through the entrance hall, say hi to a couple of people, exchange pleasantries about what you've been up to this summer, say hello to Mr Rogers, Miss Pearson – hello, Miss, hi, Sir, are you well? – then over to the trestle table where there are piles of envelopes with your names on, all neatly piled alphabetically.

— Hi, Richard.

— Hi, Mr Wareham.

He flicks through the envelopes and pulls out yours.

— Good luck.

— Thanks, Sir.

You can't open it in here, so you go through the front entrance and into the teachers' car park. You find a quiet corner and open the envelopes.

English – A.

History – A.

Sociology – A.

It's a clean sweep, the proverbial whitewash. You have nailed it right across the board.

Your chest swells with pride and you beam to yourself.

You look around to see if anyone is watching – they're not – so you carry on grinning. Nice one. Three As.

You leave the car park, walk into college again.

Mr Rogers and Miss Pearson are still there. Rogers raises his eyebrows expectantly but he can already see it in your coy smile.

— Well?

— Three As.

He nods and smiles.

— Well done, Richard. Well done! You deserve it.

— That's just brilliant, says Miss Pearson. This gives you so many options and opportunities.

She gives you a hug and a kiss and you feel her big tits pressed up against you, smell the milky coffee on her breath. It feels slightly weird being kissed by your teacher but you don't mind. Not today. Today anything goes.

So many options and opportunities.

You hang around for a bit to see how some of your classmates did. It feels odd, this time of change and finality sitting the cusp of adulthood, even though you feel like you've been an adult since the age of ten, eleven.

Maybe it's because you know that you may never see some of them again, kids you've grown up with through school and watched as they developed from children into young men and women. Friendships forged by geography and circumstance. Men and women whose lives, like it or not, you've been a part of, and they yours. That's the strangest part: after twelve years of sharing desks and classrooms it can just end so suddenly; that everything just sort of splinters as you go off out into the world, like chicks leaving the nest.

So many options and opportunities.

You swap a couple of numbers and addresses, promise to keep in touch then say your goodbyes. As you walk out the entrance to find a phone box so you can call Mum, the cameraman and the reporter are there, vox-popping pupils for a lunchtime news report. There's a microphone in your face and the reporter is talking to you. You pause on the front step, feeling presidential. Regal, even.

— How did you do? she asks.

— Three As.

— Well done. Sorry – what's your name?

— Richard. Richard Edwards.

— And what were you expecting, Richard?

— Three As.

Options.

Opportunities.

*

The sprawling Heathrow complex is behind me as I slip my copy of the new Nirvana album into the stereo and turn up the volume.

Morning has very much broken and most of the traffic is thankfully heading in the other direction, drawn to the busy hive of the capital like moths to a flame. The motorway is a hollow hum, an artery alive with metallic bubbles.

My speed peaks at a steady sixty and it feels good to

be in this state of motion, as if I am somehow one step ahead of the demons. And there are so many to run from: the demons of the Whitchurch, the demons of the Priory, the tour bus, the rehearsal room; the demons of the dockside flat, the demons of Room 516.

I can never out-run them, of course. That's the one thing I have learnt: you cannot out-run them. You can only shake them off from time to time.

But know this: they are always there. They are always waiting, salivating. They will not let me live in peace; they will never allow me silence.

As such, silence is now an impossible ideal to me. It is an unachievable goal and I cannot remember the last time I enjoyed silence or, more importantly, peace.

Because it may not even exist. Even perceived silence is shot through with other noises – an amplified breeze, a rustle of clothing as loud as thunder and my ears flush and roar like the wax and wane of the sea.

Then the stereo crashes in: the jagged howl of the underweight dirty-blond waif from Seattle who set the world alight. The cold, stabbing riffs of 'Serve The Servants'.

It's not his best song, but it's still better than anything I have ever written.

Bastard. He made all of it seem so effortless: living, creating, dying, all of it.

An ascending Heathrow plane crosses my path. It is so low that I can just make out the forms of faces at the windows looking down at the grey ribbon of the M4, and I wonder if it is the plane I was meant to be on.

No – it can't be. It is still too early.

There's still time.

I pass signposts to Datchett now and drive on towards Eton and Windsor, where the real rock stars live in solitude in country houses with their trout lakes and landscaped gardens dotted with rusting, neglected Henry Moores.

Meanwhile poor dead doomed Kurt sings on the stereo.

*

It's only a journey of fifty miles south to Cardiff then west to Swansea, but it feels like five thousand.

When you leave St Tudor's View it feels like you'll never be back, like you'll never see the clean lines of the uniform houses and the neatly trimmed edges of the green, green lawns again, like you are the reluctant boy on the cusp of adulthood being prodded and cajoled out into the real world that he wants no part of.

Only he does. He wants to see what's out there.

He wants to taste the flavours and feel the feelings, but he is scared too. He is scared because this is all he knows and what if he can never return unscathed? What if all that is familiar and fixed in his cul-de-sac life to date somehow becomes tainted by what he sees and experiences out elsewhere?

For now though he's still here, looking out you see the clean lines of the houses and neatly trimmed edges of green, green lawns.

Neighbours who nod and smile.

Hear the hum of hedge-trimmers and the laughter of children playing. The barking of distant dogs.

Snoopy.

Poor Snoopy.

Saying goodbye to him is difficult. You hug and you kiss him, and you scratch behind his ears because you feel like you are abandoning him. And he knows it. It's in his hooded eyes and balefully tilted head.

But you leave anyway. You fill the car with your new pots and pans, your posters, your books. Mum and Dad get in the front seats, you climb in the back and then Dad reverses out and drives through the estate and away from the town and you go through the undulating hills of the only land you know. Mum and Dad are chatting but you're concentrating on recording the mental map of all that constitutes your home surroundings; one foot in an already nostalgic past, one foot in an unknown future of possibility.

It is only fifty miles from Blackwood to Swansea but it feels like five thousand miles. Five thousand light years.

Five thousand generations of young curious men striding out into the world.

*

I've missed my alarm call. I've missed my pickup.

James will be anxious now. He's probably gone to reception to call up my room after futilely banging on my door. He probably thinks I've gone for a walk, but now he'll be beginning to wonder. He'll be eyeing the clock and checking his watch. *Bloody Richey.*

He'll be pacing the lobby and smoking his second cigarette of the morning, still subconsciously stocking up on nicotine in advance of the seven-hour smokeless flight that he optimistically thinks we can still make.

His bags are by his side, his hair gelled. Clean clothes pressed.

And now he's calling management. He's telling them he can't find me and that if we leave now we might – might – still make check-in, but only if we run through the terminal and only if security doesn't decide to shake us down and turn us inside out.

He's cursing me. He's calling me a useless fucker.

Every bloody time.

He's lighting another cigarette to replace the one he had intended on leisurely smoking outside Terminal 4; the nicotine is making him feel nauseous but he knows he needs to load up now.

The girl on reception is glancing at him and wondering what he does for a living to make him so agitated so early in the morning.

Management aren't sure what to do. It's early and everyone is sleepy. No one in music does business before 10 a.m. It's kind of an unwritten rule.

More calls are made, no doubt. To my room. To our publicist. To Nick at home to see if he has heard from me during the night. To the airport, to find out the latest time we can check in. To the car company to ask the driver to wait for as long as it takes, even though he is just outside and James can see him waiting patiently behind the wheel, blank-faced in the shadows of the hotel forecourt.

And twenty-five miles away my hands grip the Cavalier's wheel as distance becomes my goal, my reward. I drive on past Chalvey.

Eton Wick.

Bray.

Holyport.

I've travelled this M4 corridor so often that the signposted names are as familiar as old friends, yet it occurs to me that I have been to none of the places themselves. They are merely acquaintances who litter the route from home to work and back again. They are words chosen to encapsulate the living experience of people I will never know, nor care to know. Just names of places I'll never see.

And then the motorway seems to open up as fields glide by on either side, still crisp and grey from the winter. Beneath their surfaces and in their hedgerows life is preparing to unfold itself from hibernation. Plants and animals alike are mere weeks away from the first flush of spring; proof that they have endured another sub-zero season and that their species has survived another year for the perpetuation of the cycle to begin all over again.

Hermitage.

Snelsmore.

Welford.

Having long since established that spring follows winter, that nothing really changes, and that, in fact, existence is merely a series of freezing and defrosting of feelings, it is this predictable cycle from which I intend to remove myself. I'm opting out of nature's way in the only way I know how: by trying to out-run it. By removing myself from all that is fixed in life: the people I know, the places I go, the possessions I own.

My life is condensed to rubble now, a widely scattered moraine left by the cold glacial crush of life – flattened worthless by the silent squeeze of it all.

Swindon.

Hook.

Grittleton.

Then following the motorway at Bristol, I turn northwards towards the unseen sea.

*

This could be problematic.

The problem is they're all so bloody noisy. *Like shrieking kids in a playground. Like braying animals on a farm, rolling in their own excrement and humping in the bushes.*

It's not that you hate noise or are a prude as such – in fact when you cashed your first grant cheque the first things you bought were a Big Black album and a couple of Henry Miller novels, so you know you're not – it's just that here the corridors resound with the endless echo of screams and drunken nonsense. Which is fine, except you can't sleep and it all seems so banal and formulaic. Obvious. So awfully, predictably studenty.

Slamming doors, drunken yelling, ghetto-blasters

bursting into life at antisocial times – and always with the worst music. Arguments, singalongs, footsteps, more slamming, more braying, giggles outside your door, then the sound of knocking, quietly at first, then more insistent, determined to mess with what little sleep you can get.

You find yourself craving silence and solitude, perhaps truly for the first time. But here in the halls of residence in Swansea, during this pre-Christmas term, with autumn burning the leaves in the trees fiery oranges and reds, the dark nights creeping in and a constant breeze blowing from the sea across the campus, such things are clearly unobtainable. You're just going to have to get used to it. You're going to have to learn to integrate.

Or at the very least, tolerate.

*

Even though it is still morning my stomach is growling and I desperately need a piss so I pull over at Aust services, the last stop before crossing the river. My bowels also feel somewhat troubled, like a washing machine on a spin cycle.

The car park is busy. I park up and head into the main building. I find the toilets, enter the cubicle furthest from the door, wipe the seat clean and sit down and do a pathetically runny shit – the product of three days living off little but fruit, coffee and cigarettes.

A small acrid explosion, it splatters off the white porcelain bowl.

As I sit on the toilet my right leg starts to involuntarily spasm, as if tapping out a song on the floor. Strange. I have to use my hands to hold it still, and even then I feel a surge of energy coursing through it.

I clean off, wash my hands and head back into the services. I wander past the bleeping and flashing arcade of slot machines and a lone man in a baseball cap playing them with a bored look of resignation on his face. In the shop I pause by the magazines and newspapers to scan the headlines.

CAR BOMB EXPLODES IN ALGIERS,
42 DEAD.

EXILED BURMESE LEADER CONDEMNS
WASHINGTON OVER ATTACK.

BOYZ II MEN, ACE OF BASE WIN BIG
AT AMERICAN MUSIC AWARDS.

The same old numbing landslide of man-made detritus, then. Death, mayhem, murder, exploitation and endless reams of distracting banalities disguised as culture.

I'm done with it.

I carry on walking to the food section.

Pausing in front of the opened-fronted fridge I stop to buy an egg sandwich, a big bottle of water, a Mars bar, two apples, toilet paper, mouthwash. At the counter I also buy cigarettes and lighter, gum, and a new Stephen King novel entitled *Insomnia*, which I will almost certainly never read.

Just as I'm about to leave, I grab a half-price pair of

binoculars for no reason other than they are strategically placed and I am nothing if not a willing participant in the endless cycle of useless overpriced consumerist products. I'm a sucker for it; an impulse buyer. A marketing man's dream.

Then I take a look around me at the Severn View Service Station that was built in the year before I was born. Back then it was much heralded for housing the largest public cafeteria of all British service stations. Top Rank owned the building then and the fashionable use of concrete and glass in its construction was considered cutting edge – the future of travel in Britain.

It doesn't feel like it now, though.

Now it just feels like a crossroads of the lost, the bored and the transient. A place to fill up in, then move on.

Or maybe I am just romanticising the past again.

I cross over to the cafe where I queue to buy a large black coffee and a double espresso, which I add sugar to, then knock back in one throat-scorching hit.

With my carrier bag of food and my binoculars in hand I take the other coffee outside into the car park where I light a cigarette and start to sip the drink. It's too hot and I scorch my throat again. I need to let it cool.

I walk to the edge of the car park that sits alongside the English side of the bridge, from where you can see out across the full stretch of the Severn.

Looking out along the line of the bridge and the choppy bistre-brown waters speckled with flashes of sun-silver below, I can't help but think of the poet Harri Webb's words written upon the bridge's opening in the Sixties:

'*Two lands at last connected / Across the waters wide / And all the tolls collected / On the English side.*'

We're still bitter for what they did to us, the Welsh. Some of us, anyway.

Me, I couldn't care less.

From here, against the washed-out and foreboding sky and waving slightly in the exposed space above the water, the bridge seems inordinately fragile, as if it could come down at any point. There's something beautiful about the way the structure just hangs there, confounding expectation, defying the odds, defying the elements, cocking a snook at its detractors. As I stand sipping hot coffee and looking out at it, it is as if the bridge is at the centre of a drama just waiting to happen.

I need to leave.

*

'Fuck A Fresher' week has been and gone and you have resolutely failed to fuck or, indeed, get fucked. Fresher or otherwise.

Not that you were trying, of course, though it would be nice to try it once, with the right person, but you're really in no hurry. You're just too sober and square for all that, anyway. It is a known fact that no one at uni has sex sober. In fact, pretty much everything of consequence is experienced or undertaken under the influence – hence Swansea's appalling drop-out rate.

And while your virginity is not particularly treasured

you don't feel any major pressure or urgency to relinquish it. Most people you know who have had sex admit to feeling disappointment. For you, that kind of intimacy can only be shared with someone you can fully trust.

And that, perhaps, is the problem: you don't trust anyone enough with your body.

You don't trust anybody enough, period. You sometimes think it would easier to be gay. To be able to go out cruising and pick someone up for a simple bit of sex. A quick exchange – a quick fuck and then, bye-bye. But then that surely comes with a whole other set of problems too.

You've tried. You really have. You've made friends with a few people on your course and you get on with most people in halls. You suspect some of them think you're boring for always retreating to your room and consistently politely declining their invites to go clubbing ('But it's student night – free entry and trebles for a pound!').

Like attracts like and you find yourself mingling with the withdrawn book-reader/geek-pop types: a really cool guy called Nigel, an Irish boy called David who is as into the Wolfhounds and the Jasmine Minks as you are. Daniel from the Valleys. Becca and Sally, who you know from back home. Their friend Jill. A French girl who looks alarmingly like Morrissey.

You even got involved in rag week, dressing up as a spermatozoon – complete with cumbersome, three-foot-long tail – and going round the pubs collecting money in a bucket. You joined the Indie & Alternative society, only to discover that all it entailed was crawling around the same clubs, but on different nights. You even did the communal-cooking thing for the first week or so, before you tired of the same vast plates of half-cooked pasta sprinkled with a meagre helping of Netto's cheapest grated Cheddar.

You do join the library though and it soon becomes your sanctuary, the one place where you're guaranteed respite from the whooping and hollering of your contemporaries. You go there in your spare hours – and as a student there are plenty of those – and your reading rate increases exponentially.

It's the enforced wackiness and ironic stance of your fellow students that bothers you the most. Not all of them – but certainly those for whom the concept of freedom has arrived late: 'Oh, I got so pissed last night – there's no way I'm going to make my lectures today.'

The ones who go on about Hob-Nobs and Block-busters all the time, who insist on viewing everything from behind a screen of irony or a detached and highly juvenile sense of post-modernism.

These are the people who cannot quite appreciate the opportunities being offered to them: free education, free accommodation, offensively long holidays, free access to books and some great teachers. All they have to do is turn up, show their faces and hand in a half-baked essay from time to time, yet some of them can't even seem to manage that.

Maybe it's a class thing. Maybe the middle classes aren't called the working classes for a reason.

And some of them actually do steal traffic cones, completely unaware of what clichéd student existences they are leading.

They fill your communal kitchen with them – cones and a stolen shopping trolley.

— Oh yeah last night me and Si thought it'd be a total laugh to nick some cones.

Eventually, sometime in early November, you drop your guard, cut yourself some slack and partially admit defeat: you start to drink. Not binge drinking down the Union, but carefully regulated drinks in your room at night, on your bed with your books, your bedside lamp and some incense burning. Vodka is your preference because when mixed right it's tasteless. Vodka and a good fresh orange for the vitamin C and none of the sugar overload you get from carbonated drinks. It's tactical drinking to avoid killer hangovers, putting on weight or turning your good teeth to blackened stumps.

So you regularly get a little bit drunk, for the first time. Not falling-down, cone-stealing pissed, but warm-fuzzy, smiling-in-the-mirror drunk.

Red-cheeked drunk. Have-a-little-dance drunk.

You play some light music while you dwell on the depth of your own brilliant thoughts and maybe write a letter. You feel a bit better. Scribble a bad poem. Forget your worries. Overindulge on crisps. Sleep soundly for the first time since you moved here.

Despite attempts to resist it – and despite your pro-longed denial, and without even realising it – you become a student.

A proper student.

*

I pull out of the car park and take the bridge road. I throw the £3.70 into the coin bin, take my ticket, the barrier lifts and suddenly I'm out there, over the water, Wales ahead of me behind the lazy dappled haze of the mist and framed by the boundaries of the windscreen like a Turner painting on the eggshell white wall of a London gallery.

My ticket is clamped between my teeth.

Wisps of mist stroke the car as I look first to the right, inland to England, then to the left, out to where the channel opens up, past the unseen outcrops of Portis-head, Clevedon and Weston-Super-Mare and then, beyond them, the long finger of Cornwall that points to the Atlantic Sea.

But I can't see any of this. I can't see that far; I just know it's out there.

All I can see is the water below me, and the space around me, and for a few brief seconds I can breathe easily, and I feel free. There's nothing but sky and water and the barely audible crackle of warm rubber gripping tarmac. It feels like flight.

It feels like freedom.

And then just as quickly, the bridge is gone and the land has closed in around me again, and I'm staring at the white line ahead of me again and thinking, well, you've crossed the border, there's no going back now. That bird has flown.

*

You need to miss something to appreciate it.

Christmas term comes and goes and all the while you still miss Blackwood; the streets you could walk blindfolded, the familiar faces of the town's freaks; the oppressive familiarity of it all; your family and friends.

Especially your family and friends, even though you've barely been away. Sometimes in Swansea you can go without doing any laundry, so frequent are your trips back home.

You start to see Blackwood in a way that only comes when you leave a place behind to later return with new eyes.

They say familiarity breeds contempt, but you're not so sure. There's something satisfying about having people who are pleased to see you, who are pleased for you. Pleased you got out there to 'better' yourself.

You know you couldn't live here forever and that the world is too big to be ignored, but for now Blackwood provides respite.

So your life splits into two halves that exist in tandem. Not symbiotically, but tangentially. Term-time weekdays are spent in lectures, up in your room reading and drinking or – very gradually – engaging with your small circle of friends.

This being Morrissey's mid-80s, you are surprised to find you are not alone in your tastes and interests. It turns out there are other people who find sport, drinking games and fighting equally as repulsive as you. It turns out that you are capable of making friends after all, and that there are some people who actually find you interesting or enigmatic. The quiet guy with the Bunnymen haircut and the bag full of books.

And so university progresses from being tolerable to being enjoyable but you never allow yourself to forget that to be here is nothing but a privilege and that Dad had to give ten thousand haircuts in order to help pay your way.

Meanwhile back home in your other life the boys have been busy: Nicky revising for his A-levels and writing off to UCCA, Sean doing filing down at the Civil Service and playing trumpet at the weekend, James pulling pints and going out running four mornings a week. But it's all for a greater cause: they've formed a band. Specifically, James has formed a band. He and Sean have pooled resources to get themselves kitted out and now even Nicky is mastering the basics of rhythm guitar. Miles the blue-haired punk is on bass.

You feel a twinge of jealously knowing that life is carrying on back there without you, that things are happening in your absence, but you're smart enough to recognise it as solipsism and know you could never be in a band anyway. Nick isn't the most talented of musicians but he has something that you don't: confidence and presence. He's had it since day one on the football pitch.

*He could turn his hand to anything – him and his brother
Patrick. They just have it, both of them.*

*But they at least involve you, ask your opinion on song
ideas, band names, tell you they're going to be 'bigger
than Birdland'.*

— *It's time to put Blackwood on the map, says James.*

— *Why would you want to do that? you laugh.*

— *Hmmm . . . good question, he grins back, flashing
his baby teeth. Someone has to, I suppose.*

*

I turn the stereo on again and it kicks back into life at full
volume. It's still *In Utero*.

'Pennyroyal Tea'.

'Tourette's'.

'All Apologies'.

I follow the road westwards, past Newport towards
Cardiff.

The road signs are in both Welsh and English and the
egg sandwich is tasteless in my mouth. Stale and tasteless.
I only manage two bites of one triangular half. The rest
goes out of the window.

I sip some water and light a cigarette from the electric
lighter in the dashboard whose tight coil burns orange
just centimetres from my face. For a flickering, fleeting
second I think about sticking it on my forearm, branding
myself once more, but knowing my luck I'll crash the car
and kill some innocent traveller and wind up in prison.

(Imagining what they'd do to someone like me in

prison does not bear thinking about. Imagining what *I* would do to me is just as bad. I'd make sure I was dead before they shut the cell door – that much is certain.)

*

— *I can play that.*

You're back in James's bedroom and it's like you never left. Back from college for an endless holiday. Back to being teenagers again. The debating hall, you call it. The house of rancour. The arena of arguments.

— *Fuck off, can you.*

— *Yeah, I can. It ain't that hard.*

James and Nick are arguing. You've noticed James dropping American-isms into his speech patterns recently. Too much of The Boss, probably. Too many daytime Mickey Rourke films.

Nick is revelling in the new nickname we've given him. Nicky Wire. He reckons it's much more rock 'n' roll than Jones. Wales is full of fucking Joneses, he says, but I've never met a Wire.

It's the meaning he likes though, really. Mr Gangly Limbs. The Bag of Bones. The Conductor.

James and 'Wire' are arguing over the stereo, arguing over James's latest discovery, Guns N' Roses' debut album.

— *I can play that.*

James again.

— *Fucking go on, then!*

Wire again.

James plugs into his amp, turns it on. Sean sits on the

68

bed, bemused. Sean knows. He knows his cousin inside out. Knows him better than anyone.

— Stick it on again, will you, Rich? Back to the beginning. And turn it down a bit.

You lift the stylus and drop the needle back down to the wide groove before 'Mr. Brownstone'.

The opening descending chords crackle out and you turn it up slightly.

James slides his pick down the strings, then – whoosh. The riff kicks in and he's on it all the way, riding it, his knees bent slightly, face contorted in lip-chewing concentration, his fingers fluttering up and down the neck of the guitar.

Axl Rose's vocals come in and you and Wire and Sean look at each other, then back to James. You can't quite believe it: he's good. Really good.

Then the solo comes and he slides into it with ease. Cocky fucker.

Cool fucker.

You look at Sean on the upper bunk and he's grinning quietly like a cat and shrugging, twirling drumsticks. Drumsticks in search of a kit. He's the human shrug, Sean. Another reason to love him. Nothing surprises him, nothing fazes him. But then, sharing a bedroom with James he has heard this already. Ten times a day, every day, probably.

James goes back into the main riff again and he's in full flow now, his eyes closed tight, his mouth silently mimicking the words, his fingers running riot.

In less than four minutes it's over.

Then silence.

James slowly opens his eyes, almost surprised to find himself back in his bedroom.

— Told you, he sniffs. It's not that hard.

There's a banging on the floor from the ceiling below. Wire grins that big shark-face grin of his.

— Bleeding hell, James. You've been a busy boy, haven't you?

James feigns nonchalance.

— You've been getting your education – we've been getting ours. Eh, Mooro?

Sean shrugs and grins again.

Just twirls his sticks again.

*

Do you know what your problem is?

See? Voices.

Persistent. Torturous. Inescapable.

Voices.

Do you know what your problem is?

It's like a nail being hammered into my skull, only without the euphoric release that trepanning brings. It's like the breath of another on the back of your neck, but every time you turn around it is gone. It is like being prodded every five seconds for every waking hour. It is like a car alarm that can never be switched off.

This bloody voice. Always niggling. Always prodding. Always accusing.

It is dismantling me slowly and there's not a thing I can do about it.

Do you know what your problem is?

I don't know. Insecurity, lack of confidence, narcissism, addiction, selfishness, hypersensitivity?

I said, do you know what your problem is?

I sigh and say nothing, but cannot stop my mind from speaking.

No. No, I don't know what my problem is.

Your problem is you don't have a girlfriend.

Like a prisoner under interrogation I opt for silence. Torturous silence.

Your problem is you don't have a girlfriend. Normal people have girlfriends. You see, normal people can love other people. Normal people aren't self-obsessed and selfish like you are. Normal people do normal things, like go to restaurants and hold hands and share beds. Normal people. People who aren't fucked in the head. People who aren't self-obsessed narcissists whinging weak-willed cocksucker imbeciles.

I grit my teeth. Stay silent.

I know you're listening.

A pause.

I know you're listening.

And another.

You really are a stupid little prick, aren't you. You think that by ignoring me I'm going to stop? That I'm going to go away? Only it doesn't work like that, does it? You seem to have forgotten that I am you. I am you. Mr

University. My smart-arse literary man. Your own worst enemy.

I can't seem to get a girlfriend . . .

'I can't seem to get a girlfriend.' Have you heard yourself? Normal people seem able to tear themselves away from the mirror for a second to get a girlfriend. Any ugly cunt can do it. Except you. 'Richey Manic'. What a joke. 'Manic'. I've seen more life in an open casket. You're a joke, son. A cruel joke. You might as well chop your cock off and become a eunuch.

I turn over the Nirvana cassette that has played itself dead and insert it again.

To drown out the noise.

To drown out myself.

※

Friday night in Blackwood and it feels like you're off to war.

Four young soldiers.

Four beautiful, young naive stupid soldiers waging a war on mediocrity; waging a war on this cul-de-sac town.

Your town.

Because you've all spent too long arguing in Blackwood bedrooms; too long breathing James's second-hand cigarette smoke and Nick's farts. And you – you feel like you've spent too long learning historical facts by rote in the lecture halls, and endured too many strained attempts at conversation with equally awkward strangers brought together through circumstance.

It's time for you to step out now, time to take advantage of a town with more pubs per head than anywhere else in Wales. It is time to announce yourselves: the prettiest debutantes in town.

Try telling that to some of the boys, though. When you walk through the pub door even some of the girls are antagonised.

— *Oi, oi! It's Shirley. Get your cock out, darling.*

Shirley is the nickname some of the boys have bestowed upon the Wire. No one knows why. Something to do with Shirley Temple, maybe.

— *That doesn't have a cock, Terry.*

— *Halloween was months ago, ladies.*

You can feel James stiffening by your side. He's less at ease with them than you or Nicky are, less at ease with this; this display of vanity and provocation. Sean meanwhile – Sean who arguably is the most accidentally androgynous of us all – is ambivalent. So long as he's involved at all, he doesn't care.

Wire, though. Wire was born to do this. He was born big and toughened himself up on the footie pitch. Six foot tall at fifteen had its advantages. No one messes with Jonesy. There's that smile, for starters. No one can resist that nuclear smile. As wide as the Severn it is. Ten O-levels and two As at A-level got him in with the smart kids and a biting sarcasm took care of the rest.

That he's actually as soft as shite has never really been an issue.

And now he's revelling in this new role as 'Nicky Wire'. Wire the rock star. Wire the agitator. My best friend. With him and James flanking me I begin to feel fearless, perhaps for the first time in my life.

Nick leads the charge to the bar in his mother's fur coat, dusted off and brought down from the attic last week, Green Flash on his feet as he leaves a trail of glitter across the carpet. You're wearing a similar coat, bought for a mere fiver from the British Heart Foundation in town.

White blouse.

White jeans.

James is in white jeans too and his ever-present Docs and bomber jacket. Shades on his head even though it's pitch black out and two below. Sean joins in with the white jeans but draws the line at blouses. No one tries to persuade him otherwise because Sean cannot be persuaded to do anything he doesn't want to be involved in. Ever.

They look great, though, these three. They're starting to look like a band. They've got a new name too. They've ditched Baby Blue and gone for Manic Street Preachers. It's as good a name as any.

Better than Ride.

Better than Whirlpool. Better than the monosyllabic necrophiliac groups digging up the corpses of the past.

Plus it references one of your favourite groups, the Jasmine Minks' One Two Three Four Five Six Seven, All Good Preachers Go To Heaven.

It almost makes you want to learn guitar and join them yourself.

Nicky cuts to the bar with a sharpened shoulder.

— *Babycham, please. What you having, lads?*

No one within earshot attempts to stifle their guffaws.

— Yeah, just four Babychams then, please, love, says Nick turning back to the bar. With straws.

No. He doesn't give a fuck, that one. And in that moment it seems like the mood is set. A mood of defiance. All for one and all that.

We clink bottles and take a seat in the corner to suck on our straws with pursed lips.

*

The M4 passes by the familiar streets of Newport and though I'm tempted to turn off and park up, something propels me forward.

I keep going. I pass signs to Bassaleg.

Duffryn.

Coedkernew.

I take the A48, then drift down Eastern Avenue towards the city centre where the traffic gets thicker, the streets narrower and my breathing sharper.

I'm back in Cardiff again.

Did I plan to come here when I woke this morning?

No – because I didn't wake this morning. I didn't wake because I haven't slept and I've barely eaten. Not properly, anyway. Not for weeks. Maybe months.

Christ, I'm tired. I'm suddenly so very, very tired.

Missing my turn-off I end up going the long way round past the university, along the side of Bute Park, then taking a swift left before the castle and on towards Adamsdown, then finally to Atlantic Wharf and my flat.

Compared to London, everything is new and pristine down at the old docks now spruced up by the benevolent sweep of pre-millennial, red-brick regeneration. It's the pride of Cardiff down here in what they call a 'leisure village'. Though I've never quite been able to figure out why exactly. I've certainly never been able to explain why I bought a flat here of all places; here where everything is a characterless new build and where the smell of plastic and uPVC fills the air; here where the yuppies live behind tinted windows and pantiled roofs, their fake Doric columns standing at the water's edge like pretend fortifications against a lapping, laughing sea.

And now I'm one of them with my two double bedrooms. My fully fitted kitchen. Lounge / diner. Bathroom with shower.

Sea views.

No pets. No smokers. No children. No character.

I park up.

*

Your twenty-first birthday. Three days before Christmas. Another Friday night. Newport, this time. It's not exactly Cardiff, but then it's not exactly Blackwood either.

You're all going further out there these days with your aesthetic, especially you and Nicky. You're really pushing the reworked punk look as far as you can. Eyeliner, cheap hair dye and half a can of hair spray. Each.

A dash of Anaïs Anaïs behind the ears, on the pulse of a wrist.

76

Only Nick's not here yet. He'll be down later, he says, with Sean and some of the others. Miles, Jenny, Sarah, Sam, Pete. For now it's just you and James, starting in on the drinking early.

James is still conflicted about his look. He's been experimenting with peroxide and army fatigues, study-ing pictures of Paul Simonon and The Specials, John Cassavetes, Alain Delon and – of course, his favourite – Bruce The Boss, back when he was lean and hungry, back before he was co-opted into Reagan's view of 'America'.

You hit McDonald's in the High Street to load up on ballast before heading on to TJ's where you have tickets to see Talulah Gosh.

You've just got your cheeseburger dinner and are walking to the table when a load of lads pile in. Swansea fans. It's only 7 p.m. and though they don't even look that pissed they're obviously in search of something more than French fries and lukewarm, floppy Filet-O-Fishes.

You see it happen before it actually does. It's as if you have leapt forward into the future by about thirty seconds. Or maybe you're used to the predictable patterns of the feral Welsh man. You see one of them looking over, then nudging his mates.

— 'Kin hell. Get a load of these faggot cunts, boys.

And then there's a leering, ugly face up close in yours. You see the lips moving and the flecks of spittle flying, but you don't hear the words. It's like you have gone deaf. You see your burger coming at you, then being rubbed in your face. Cheese, relish and meat in your eyes and up your nose. The stench is that of instant humiliation. Degradation. Degradation and salt.

Then comes the shriek of the war cry as you see a slow-motion karate chop to your neck. You feel it too. A bell rings in your head and you can't breathe. Then you're on the floor, gasping for air and rolling under a table as three or four of them lay into James.

Poor Bradders. He could probably take any one of them on his own – but a gang, a frothing hyped-up gang feeding off each other's testosterone, egging each other on, pathetic male archetypes. No chance.

It's over before it has started and then you're in a taxi to Casualty and James's face looks all crooked and he can't speak. He doesn't need to speak because his eyes say it all: We've got to get out of this place, Richard.

Then comes five hours folded up in a plastic chair sipping tea under a blinking strip light while they wire Bradders' broken jaw. Poor James.

Phone calls home.

Police statements.

Thumping headaches.

A twenty-first to remember and all because some men are scared of their own penises. Scared of each other's penises. Scared of themselves.

Happy birthday to me. Happy birthday to me.

Happy birthday, dear Richard.

Happy birthday to me.

*

It takes another hastily smoked cigarette before I can peel myself away from behind the wheel and make a quick dash through the front door and up to my flat before anyone can see me. Not that I know my neighbours, mind.

Once inside I put my keys down and ignore the mail.

Then I go blank again.

Why am I here? Why am I here when I should be halfway across the Atlantic?

Because you're a lazy cop-out bastard who only thinks of himself.

I see James's face. I think of that night in Casualty, and the attendant weeks he spent wired up and drooling, and I wonder where he is now.

We had to check out of the hotel by midday, so it is doubtful that he's still there now.

I wonder if he went without me.

There you go again: always placing yourself at the centre of any scenario.

The flat is cold as I walk through the rooms feeling like a burglar, an intruder who shouldn't be here. I recognise the postcards on the wall, the clothes in the wardrobe and the pile of videos and CDs in the living room, and the box filled with gig posters, laminates, tickets, flyers and magazines, but they all seem unfamiliar, as if they are relics from another age, from someone else's life.

A thought strikes me: I could walk away from these material possessions now and none of it would be missed. It's just useless ephemera that I've accumulated on my travels, each little thing a reminder of some sad event. A panic attack in France. An awful gig in Germany. Crap sex in Cambridge. Our dwindling record sales.

I lie down on the bed in my coat and my shoes and I close my eyes. Behind my eyelids colours swirl and my ears ring and roar with the silence and the feedback and the tinnitus and the abject emptiness of being 'home', yet never feeling more alone.

*

Terminal darkness. Months in your room with your books, taking notes on your second-year electives: a lot of Third Reich stuff, but also reading Marx, Engels, Mishima, Burroughs, etc.

Appetite For Destruction *and* Some Candy Talking *reside on the stereo for weeks at a time.*

Your exams are approaching and sickness sits dormant in your stomach and your bowels flex at the very thought of them. You're vomiting regularly and in a semi-permanent state of mild anxiety.

Each night the corridors continue to echo with the noises of academic life: the screams of your drunken contemporaries and the pulse-like throb of a muted dance beat five doors down. Closer by, in your kitchen, a Wonder Stuff album on endless loop. Their music makes you want to burn their fucking violin, immolate their tartan trousers. It's all so bouncy and 'nice'. So painfully innocuous.

(Note to self: never wear shorts in public.)

A door slams. Another shriek.

You keep returning to see the boys at the weekends.

Both you and Nicky coordinate your visits home. He's still wearing a disturbing amount of Pringle – a hangover from his golfing days – but is now juxtaposing it with dashes of eyeliner and extremely tight jeans that he is unable to take off by himself.

— It confuses the Sport Science studes, Teddy, he says of his recent flirtation with a 'glam golfer' look.

Teddy. He still calls you that, even after all these years. Teddy Edwards. He's the only one. The only one who is allowed.

And the boys have been busy.

They have ditched Miles the bassist, Blackwood's sole old-school punk, and pared down to a three-piece. They have also penned some new songs (sample titles: 'Behave Yourself Baby', 'Sunglass Aesthetic', 'Suicide Alley') that are pitched between the turbo-urban charge of early Clash and the last vestiges of '80s jangle pop.

And you.

You are given the combined multitasking role of driver and photographer and the nebulous-sounding Minister of Information.

— Like Public Enemy have, says James of his new discovery.

Soon you're playing PE continuously as you drive them to shows and it's not long before you're all enamoured, even Sean, and he never gets enamoured with anything except hitting drums and collecting gadgets.

You reach a consensus: Public Enemy's post-Panther/ quasi-Nation of Islam rhetoric is unerring, unambiguous and exactly the kind of militancy that you think is lacking in contemporary white-boy dead-end rockism of today's indie charts.

You reach another: there's no way your band could ever be as cool or as threatening as PE. Not with your skin colour and upbringings.

But still. If only a guitar band could harness that power or suggest that level of threat, they could be on to something.

You begin to write the first of many letters to Chuck D, letters you know you will never send.

Meanwhile the local gigs come in earnest: the Little Theatre in Blackwood, an inch-high stage in a rugby club in Ponty on a wet Tuesday, the Square Club in Cardiff the following Tuesday.

At each the band play to minimal audiences who can barely disguise their a) disgust or b) complete indifference. You stand at the back sipping blackcurrant throughout, clapping at the appropriate moment and watching the patchouli-drenched crusty-goths and the students get slowly sozzled before collapsing into each other's arms, then each other's beds, like puppets with their strings cut.

Then up in your room in Swansea you post poems to James with notes scribbled in the margins and key phrases underlined – 'for possible use in next Bradders/ demi-God/Welsh Slash masterpiece?'

And he starts using them. He starts twisting your words into songs in ways you never knew possible and he and Sean pool their dole cheques to buy themselves forty minutes' down-time in some cheap studio. They come out with 'Suicide Alley' and as a B-side, your indictment of US post-colonialism, 'Tennessee (I Get Low)', inspired by last term's reading of Cat On A Hot Tin Roof.

They press them up as singles and you suggest – by letter, of course – they use a picture of Paul Newman as Brick on the cover, but James wants something 'classic' so while the rest of the world is celebrating the sexless loose fit of baggy clobber, you instead take a picture of the three of them looking stiff and moody in black leather and white jeans.

The three of them. One – two – three.

A power trio.

Like Rush. Like The Jam. Like the Police.

Something doesn't seem right; aesthetically the symmetry is lacking.

You tell James this and he responds by offering to give you guitar lessons in exchange for all your driving. That's how he pitches it anyway, but really he has other plans.

So just as your finals approach you find yourself configuring awkward fingers into shapes on a Telecaster that even James deems too awful to contemplate playing in public and somehow, without any official decision being verbalised, and without any real desire, skill or propensity towards working in the world of entertainment, and going entirely against your better judgement, you find yourself doing something quite ridiculous.

You join a rock 'n' roll band.

*

I'm placing my hand palm-up on a desk.

It is a brand-new expensive mahogany writing desk with a decorative gold-leaf trim around the edges and ornate hand-carved legs.

I'm sitting at the desk and I'm placing my hand palm-up on it.

Also on the desk is a box of brand-new six-inch nails and a hammer.

It is more a mallet than a hammer, with a large, rubber-coated head that makes it easier to hit the target.

I look around me and I am in an empty room with a sandstone floor in a building I don't recognise. The room is round. Cylindrical.

With my other hand I select one of these nails and position it in the middle of my palm. Dead centre. I take great care over this.

Once I am satisfied that I have found the centre of my hand, I look at the mallet, then I pause.

I haven't thought this through.

One hand is laid out like a sacrificial lamb, the other is holding the nail in place.

There is no third hand to complete the task.

You haven't thought this through. Idiot.

I put down the nail, pick up the mallet and briefly contemplate holding the nail in place with my teeth only to dismiss the idea as absurd and highly unworkable.

Idiot. Stupid idiot twat.

This is just a problem to be solved.

A test.

Like Mensa. Like the *Krypton Factor.*

I think about asking for someone's help, but there is nobody to ask.

The room feels as though it might be a turret. It has an air of elevation to it. A feeling of height.

It is warm. Feverishly warm.

Dry heat.

There is a breeze blowing through the one window. The window has no glass in it; it is just a square hole in the wall. The thick stone wall.

The room feels ancient and although everything is silent my ears are screaming.

I am instinctively aware that this is another time, a different age and I know that there is nobody I can ask to help me do this.

I place the mallet to one side, then turn to the door.

Only there is no door.

The cylindrical room has no door.

There is only the one small window built into the infinite wall. The only way out.

The room is warm and dry and dusty and the ornate desk is completely at odds with it.

I stand and walk to the window, then put my head through the gap.

I am so high up that I gasp at what I see. The ground is

many hundreds of metres below me. I am almost incomprehensibly high above a landscape that is utterly alien.

No building is this tall.

It can't be.

Vertigo hits and I pull my head back into the room, gasping for air.

Then once I have collected myself, I put my head out again, slowly this time. I can see nothing but sand below me. Sand windswept into dunes that are barely perceptible from this height.

Below, in all directions there is nothing but desert sand. Pale yellow sand.

No roads, no building, no signs of life. Just sand.

I want to scream. Then I want to cry.

I want to do both at the same time.

I pull my head back again and sit at the desk, looking at the nails and the mallet, then the window. I start to sob.

Oh, there's a surprise. You're even a pussy in past lives and alternative landscapes.

Don't, I tell myself. Don't sob. Hold it together.

This, I think, is just a problem to be solved.

A test.

A dream.

No – a very vivid nightmare.

*

It is a bad week.

A bad, bad week.

You've not felt anxiety like this before. Three years of

work and all it comes down to is three exams. The thought of them has rendered you barely able to sleep or think straight. You don't want to drink but you find yourself taking sporadic, measured nips of Kirov vodka to stop the ticking of an internal clock.

Yes. A bad week of no sleep.

All you seem to eat is carbs and starch. You have been living off nothing but carbs since February's mid-semester break. Jacket spuds, bowls of rice, corn on the cob. A diet you have affectionately dubbed as 'white noise'.

Carbs and starch; the opposite of brain food.

Rich Tea for a treat.

You've not dared to weigh yourself as the last time you did you were six and a half stone and you were scared.

A bad week, then.

A bad week of carbs and starch and worry, and always this nagging sense of losing control; of not being able to mediate your feelings.

Instead you force yourself to focus by cramming your revision. When you emerge from the library blinking into the sunlight for the long walk back to your room, you're amazed by everyone else's relaxed attitude. You can't work out whether it's all a pose or a genuine disregard for what's at stake: three years of work and the outcome of their lives.

A bad week. A bad week where thoughts tumble over one another.

Triggers. One bad thought triggers another. Then

another. And another. All of them based upon fear, insecurity, anxiety.

But mainly fear.

A fear of failure.

A fear of time wasted.

A fear of disappointment and obscurity.

A fear of wasted potential.

Triggers. Your mind cocked and loaded.

It's only one week, then it's over. This is what you tell yourself: it's only a week. If you can just get through it, it will all be worthwhile. You won't waste what you have. You'll take it, nurture it, and do something of value with your life. Your education. Your potential.

Nick came to visit last week. He remarked on your weight loss then took you down the union where you held his Babycham and lemonade in a plastic pint glass while he fed 10ps into the fruit machine.

He put in a tenner – your weekly food budget – and was ecstatic with the five pounds he got back.

— That's not winning, you said.

— It is to me. Most people get nothing. Anyway, what about the band. What do you reckon?

— What do you mean?

— We want you in. Properly in. Onstage and that.

— But why? I'll never be able to play that bloody guitar.

— Who cares about that? I can barely play my bass but the girls don't seem to mind. They're the only critics that matter. It's not about ability, anyway – it's about

looks, ideas and attitude. Presence, you know that. Look at Lou Reed or Iggy – they can barely hold a note. Look at John Lydon, look at Flavor Flav. Elvis barely even wrote a song in his life. Bez is the coolest member of the Mondays.

— I'd be terrible onstage, though.

— You'd be amazing *onstage. You're prettier than any of us and you'd just have to keep doing what you do. Reading books. Writing lyrics. Coming up with more ideas. You're practically in the bloody band, anyway. Anyway, you have to. Whoever heard of an exciting bloody three-piece?*

You can't help but smile at this. You smile because Nicky's telling you what you need to hear. He knows you too well. He's feeding your lines back to you. Yet still you falter.

— I don't know, Nick. All I can think about is these exams. If I don't get a first I might as well have not bothered.

— Bloody hell, I'd kill for a first. I'll be lucky if I even scrape a Desmond. But in two years' time it's not going to matter, is it? Because in two years' time we'll be on our way to being rock stars.

— All rock stars are wankers, though.

— Exactly! We're perfectly qualified.

*

When I wake the darkness has me in its grip. It is night and I lie still for a moment, unsure as to where I am, waiting for something familiar to emerge from the blue-black. I check my watch and it's just after eight.

I've been out for a long time.

The heating has not been on for days and the flat is cold as a tomb.

I lie for a moment as the darkness slips away to reveal the shapes of the room: my shelves, a pile of books on the floor in the corner, the wardrobe. The inanimate shapes of silence. I still have my shoes on and outside Cardiff is twinkling.

I think about the dream (the nightmare): the nails and the sand and the tower, and I shiver.

Half-formed sentences run through my mind; nonsense words and the endless chatter of shrill voices that remind me of the chorus of mice in *Bagpuss*, that show I loved so much as a child. All thoughts trail off only half realised, to be immediately replaced by others. An alarm call of echoes and strange incantations. This must be what it is like to feel the rapture. To speak in tongues.

They'll probably be wondering where I am now. In fact, they'll definitely be wondering.

Casual concern will by now have evolved into something else and management will be ringing around trying to find me. They'll have rung Nick and Sean, Mum and Dad. Friends. The airport, maybe. A girl or two. That's when it hits me.

Stupid idiot.

You can't stay here.

If you stay here they'll come and get you and they'll bring you back and put you on that plane to America.

Or even worse, they'll send you back to the Whitchurch again. Or the Priory.

No, I cannot stay here. Because I cannot face another night in an institutional bed, nor another second of group confession. I'd rather find my own way out of this eternal bloody darkness.

So I must keep moving. I must keep one step ahead of those who will want to bring me back. The baying pack of wolves who want my blood.

I must be swift and keep to the shadows. I must keep running and running until my head clears, the mist lifts, the voices stop and I know what the right decision is.

Movement and anonymity.

These shall be my mantras now.

Keep moving. Stay anonymous.

And never go back.

*

So you find yourself in a band.

Reasoning, as the communists did before you, that all members should play to their strengths – 'to each their own ability' and all that – you are delegated the task of using your eloquence and your three years of learning to bombard the members of the British music press with rhetoric. Your guitar-playing is, of course, secondary. Or after your lyric-writing, maybe even tertiary.

Two days of letter-writing swiftly follow, then.

Letters to Swells at the NME. To Bob Stanley, Steve Lamacq. The Stud Brothers. Kevin Pearce. Anyone of influence. Anyone who'll listen. Even some of the smaller, worthier fanzines receive a Richard missive.

The rhetoric flows as you decimate your facile contemporaries. You talk of a NEW ART RIOT and REVOLUTION NOW. Carefully written out in your spidery handwriting, the slogans may be contrived, but the intent is at least genuine.

Besides, all you are doing is giving them what you know they want to hear. Flash and swagger and intrigue.

Your letters reject the useless '80s. You reject dance music too. And indie music. And ecstasy culture. Alcohol. Sex. Money. Thatcher. Cultural hegemony. Wales, England, America, yourselves.

You declare rock 'n' roll to be dead and useless and you tell them you intend to dance on its corpse. Because this is it.

You talk of FUEL-INJECTED FUCKS.

Of being THE SUICIDE BEAT OF THE NON-GENERATION.

Of representing the BURNING YOUTH.

You invite them to come and watch you and maybe write a review.

Thanks.

Love,

Manic Street Preachers.

Kiss, kiss, kiss.

*

Camus said, 'What is called a reason for living is also a reason for dying,' and while I can't imagine a situation in which I could find the strength to take my own life, right now I certainly can't find any justifiable reason for carrying on living either.

What once fuelled me – what drove this band of ours forwards – is now that which cripples me and renders me impotent in all ways: creatively, socially, sexually.

Intelligence, boredom, sensitivity and despair are a deadly combination and it took weeks in an expensive rehab to tell me that all the drinking and the cutting were merely ways to stave off the deadly strain of boredom that arises when a creative mind is not put to use.

Now that the drinking and the cutting have mostly stopped things are infinitely, noticeably, painfully worse; there is simply nothing left to stave off the boredom now. There's no brief drunken giddiness to fill the void and no hangover to drape my day over. No boozy, carefree nights out to romanticise later and get nostalgic about.

And there is no dripping blood that screams: look – you are alive after all. Look – your black heart is still pumping. No scars whose healing you track with the curiosity of a green-fingered gardener tending to his perennials.

I've tried it all and none of it works. I've seen the world and feel no different. Maybe even feel worse.

I might as well never have left my Blackwood bedroom.

Might as well never have bothered at all.

My greatest fear is having to stop and think for more than a minute at a time. For in that void lies the potential for great harm, great destruction. Pain is what I fear and right now I am in great pain. Pain that stabs to my very core. Not physical pain; something far worse. The pain of constant agitation, fear, doubt, shame, self-loathing, confusion, emptiness, intellect, boredom and despair.

Fortunately, though, my mind is shattering, so as soon as one thought comes, it is quickly replaced by another. And another.

And another.

Few of them make sense.

*

We're on the B4251.

On the A4048.

The A467.

The B4591.

Then on to the M4, the yellow brick road to the Emerald City.

It is your first band foray to London and James has commandeered the stereo, his head buried in Sounds. *Sean is reading maps and eating a Curly-Wurly, while in the back Wire is adding some accessories to your stage gear: white jeans and BHS school shirts spray-painted with slogans fresh from the Manics' lexicon of discontent.*

CLASSIFIED MACHINE.

SUICIDE BEAT.

— Open the fucking window, will you, pleads James, choking on the fumes coming from the can that Wire wields with a flourish.

Wire laughs from the back of the hired mini-van: what bloody window?

A hundred quid we paid to hire this tin can and it has to be back by 9 a.m. tomorrow.

Your fingers grip the wheel as you nudge it up to fifty, all the stacked gear wobbling ominously in the back.

A hundred quid. Daylight bloody robbery. We could have hired a taxi for that.

As usual you're doing all the driving. Two and a half hours to London, then the slow crawl eastwards through the city. Then the same on the way back, post-gig.

It's been a 9 a.m. start for a 9 p.m. show.

— Here, this one's for you, Mooro.

Nicky tosses Sean a shirt with the epithet THE DRUMMER *crudely sprayed across it. Sean glances at it, sneers and in one deft move it's out the window.*

You pass Heston services.

Hounslow, Hammersmith.

Then you're in London – proper London. Earl's Court. Across Fulham Palace Road. Down through Chelsea.

Down to the river.

James is pointing out the sights to you all: that's Gunter Grove, where Lydon formed PiL and Wobble chased off one Sidney Vicious with an axe. That's where they filmed some of the 'London Calling' video. The one where they're wearing suits in the rain? And that street there is where Jagger ponced about in Performance . . . *probably.*

James slips a reggae tape into the deck. A Big Youth and Dillinger compilation.

Sean opens the Maltesers.

Two days ago you opened the envelope with shaking hands and were horrified to find you had missed a First by two marks. Two marks.

A high 2:1 in Political History.

A high 2:1. It is your worst academic performance ever.

By two marks.

You'd like to blame it on the band – but you can't. You can only blame yourself. Your stupid pathetic useless scared scarred self. Your nerves and your anxiety, your distraction, your diet and your lack of discipline.

A 2:1. Missed a first by two marks.

Two days later you're still smarting. Mum and Dad are aglow – 'Well done, the first in the family, son' – but you are far from it. You're quietly crushed.

They buy you some HMV vouchers and plan a celebratory family meal and it somehow makes you feel worse, even more of a letdown. To them. To yourself. And being in a band is little compensation when it is costing you money just to play a twenty-minute set for people who can't even be bothered to hate you.

Wire was over the moon with his 2:2, though.

— A bloody miracle, really, he beamed, the result slip in his hand.

You envy him. You envy his 'that'll do nicely' reaction. You envy his confidence in the success of the band

*too. Because right now you're still unsure. Unsure about
everything. Especially yourself. Your abilities. Or lack of.*

*But Wire is Wire and you're not. He went out and
made friends, lived in a proper house. Cooked communal
meals and played golf at the weekend. He engaged with
academia in the way that you were meant to. He did it
properly. Not like you.*

Not like you, up in your room, alone.

Drunk and bitter.

Hungry and shaking.

Compass points across your skin.

By two bloody marks, though.

Two bloody marks.

*You pass Battersea Power Station over on the other side
of the river. You head towards Victoria and Vauxhall.*

Westminster and the Houses of Parliament.

By two marks.

*Whitehall. The Strand. Left into Covent Garden. A
wrong turn into a dead-end street.*

Two marks.

You don't want to be in Covent Garden.

*— Excuse me, do you know how to get to Great Port-
land Street?*

— No idea, pal.

A sigh from the back of this van. Sean.

— I fucking 'ate this place already.

*

I remember when I first read Camus and filled my notebook with quotes, stockpiling them for some unknown future use. One particular line from *The Outsider* has been with me ever since, carried on a scrap of paper in my wallet. Because I knew the quote was written for me. And even if I didn't fully comprehend the import of it all those years, I instinctively knew that it would at some point come to hold particular new meaning for me.

I've written it down, typed it or read it out on so many occasions that I don't even need to reach into my wallet now to remember it: 'From the dark horizon of my future a sort of slow, persistent breeze has been blowing towards me, all my life long, from the years that were yet to come. And on its way that breeze levelled out all the ideas that people had tried to foist on me in the equally unreal years I then was living through.'

That persistent breeze has become impossible to ignore. The unreal years have come to an end.

Reality is here and I have chosen to reject it the only way I know how: by fleeing from it.

*

Upstairs at a pub called the Horse & Groom it's not exactly the bright lights, big city glamour you had hoped for.

It's just a pub like every other shitty pub back home, maybe worse, and the drinks are twice the price, the haircuts more ersatz and the voices louder, as if pleading to be heard.

But you're all secretly excited anyway.

You're secretly excited because you're in London and London is where Things Happen.

So after you have arrived early and unpacked your gear, you take a wander down to Oxford Street. Hallowed Oxford Street, the home of British consumerism, the shopping Mecca for the tourists. You stroll past shop fronts selling pizza slices and something called falafels, you see miniature Union Jacks and replica red London buses, T-shirts with images of the Pope smoking cannabis and smiley acid faces on them.

The Megastore is massive.

Dwarfed on the corner of Oxford Street and Tottenham Court Road you take it all in, none of you saying much as the evening crowds swirl around you. You're the subject of plenty of sideways glances from people taking in your matching clothes or hearing your twisted accents. But that is all they are – sideways glances.

No 'fuck off, fucking poofters' or 'What have you come dressed as?' here.

Just detached glances, brief flickers of air-sniffing interest. And it is then that you realise that London might be the place to be seen but it also a great place to be anonymous; a place where everyone is a freak of one variety or another. That's kind of the whole point of it. It is a place for reinvention.

You buy chips and Fanta and eat them walking back up Tottenham Court Road, passing pubs you think you may have heard of and pavements worn smooth by everyone from Dickens to Marx to Jagger. Homeless forms fill the doorways. One dirty, sockless tanned foot protrudes from beneath a piece of cardboard. Sleeping bags rise and fall with sleeping breaths. The dogs are homeless too.

There are so many bodies with so many stories.

You feel anxious, nervous, nauseous, excited and completely out of your element with the thought you are here to entertain London – a city of entertainment.

You know you could never be a solo performer, of that much you are certain. You make a mental note: never go solo. As if.

You shouldn't even be in a band in the first place. James covers all your mistakes and shortcomings. You just do the driving, some of the lyrics and Nicky's hair when his roots are coming through.

Back at the venue you meet Kevin, the promoter and editor of Hungry Beat *fanzine, the guy you've been firing missives to. He seems decent and unpretentious, but it feels awkward finally meeting someone you have been corresponding with. You think maybe the world would be a much easier place if you only had to deal with people by writing to them. Real conversation is so much harder, so much more awkward and you know you must be twice as much of a disappointment to him as you stand there mumbling into your cola.*

You soundcheck and it is brief, perfunctory. There is a moment of embarrassment when James tunes the guitar that is hanging around your neck. You pretend not to care.

Actually, you really, genuinely don't care. This band stuff is never going to last, anyway.

Then it is back into the van to hit the hairspray and kill what few minutes there are before you go on. It's a good job you're already dressed: there's no dressing room and you're too shy to share your space with anyone. In this case, some preppy mod throwback band called The Claim who are headlining.

Time freezes as James smokes four cigarettes in succession, Nick complains of stomach pains and Sean eats some crisps.

And you. You chew your nails down to their nubs.

You chew and you watch people wandering into the pub in dribs and drabs.

— Look at those two, Nick says, nodding towards two young men in expensive-looking suits.

— Trendy twats, says James. They look like something out of a Martin Amis novel.

— And look at that duffer in the anorak! Christ, he could have made a bloody effort. You have permission to shoot me if you ever see me with a beard.

— I just want to offend them all, says James, rolling his neck until the bones make a cracking noise. I think it's the least we can do.

9 p.m. on the dot and you troop out of the van in a line with butterflies in your stomachs and snakes in your arms. Eight skinny legs are squeezed into the tightest, whitest jeans in Wales.

The guy on the door, a thick-set Cockney, stops you.

— Two pound.

— We're the band.

He looks you up and down.

— Oh yeah. In you go, then. Try not to get killed.

Then it's through the crowd – about twenty, maybe twenty-five, people – and up onto the stage, your backs to the punters sipping their pints. Pick up the guitars. Turn on the amps. One last look at the nine-song set list. Fag smoke hanging in the air – ribbons of it. You clear your throats, shuffle your feet, try not to look at each other.

James repositions his mic, then meekly says:

— Hello, London scum. This one's called 'New Art Riot'.

Wait for the click of the count in . . . wait for it:

A-one, a-two, a-one, two, three four . . .

And off you go.

*

They've got me under the chemical cosh.

I've replaced drinking and cutting with cigarettes and coffee and a regime of tablets that has my stomach rattling like I'm a human bubblegum machine.

The pills have stripped away whatever was left of me after rehabilitation; whatever was not worth repairing. They leave me languid and bereft.

Sitting on the edge of the bed in darkness I make a decision here and now: no more medicine. This cannot go on.

This cannot go on because it is not working. So: no more pills to compress the anxiety, no more pills to stabilise my moods. No more false euphoria, no more lucid dreaming. No more dry mouth, no more thick words sitting on my tongue or sticking in my throat like hairballs.

No more pills to plug the holes in my personality.

I'm going it alone now. I'm going it alone because it's the only option left to me and it's time to confront my feelings and face the reality of who I am, whatever the outcome.

It's the coward's way.

Yeah, because you're a coward.

I know, but at least I'm trying.

So: no more pills, no more prescriptions.

It's time to face whatever it is that lurks within me.

I stand on unsteady legs and walk through to the living room, reach into my bag and remove the tablets so neat and beautiful in their silver-sealed packets like precious stones in a tray in a jeweller's window. And, along with my passport, an old notebook, my toiletries and some CDs, leave them on the kitchen table.

I roll up some blankets and put them under my arm then I pick up the disposable camera from the coffee table and put it in my coat pocket. I don't know why. There are images captured forever on that camera and undeveloped they sit in limbo. Like me. I remove it, place it on the table, then pick it up again.

Then I light a cigarette and smoke it staring out past the darkened flats of my neighbours, past the wharf and out to the sea cut through silver.

The desire to pour a drink is strong but I resist it. If I drink now I won't leave the flat and if I don't leave the flat they'll come find me and take me back. The cycle will start again and I'll look like a coward who can't face himself; the man who let everyone down.

Again.

No, I cannot drink right now. I refuse to.

Besides, there is nothing to drink here in the flat; they poured it all down the drain weeks ago, the day before I came back here from the last place they sent me. They didn't say so but I could smell it in the air. I have a nose for it.

*

Applause is polite at best, but you surprise even yourselves. London brings something out in you as you deliver the songs with more venom than you knew you had, a blur of limbs and jumps and star-shapes. James sounds good tonight, Nick kicks over his mic stand and you manage not to trip over any leads or unplug yourself like you did at the last two shows. You even stay in tune.

The people of London clap and smile and don't try and kill you. It's the most applause you've ever had.

The only *applause you've ever had.*

Afterwards some guy with a haircut comes over and offers his congratulations. It's Bob Stanley. Bob Stanley from the Maker *and Saint Etienne. Another recipient of your hyped-up missives.*

— You reminded me of The Clash, he says. Early Clash. Before they learnt to play.

— Aw, thanks, Bob, says Wire, beaming. You remind me of Lester Bangs. Before he learnt to write.

A pause, and then he's laughing, thankfully.

— Cheeky twat. If only I were that good . . .

A couple more pats on the back or silent nods of approval from passing strangers and you're thinking: you know, I might just be able to do this.

Perhaps I can actually do this.

The next time you play London, Bob Stanley will offer to let you stay in his flat. It's big and it's packed with tonnes of great records and loads of retro furniture and, most importantly of all, it is warm, but after some late-night drinks you will decide to sleep in the van instead because you're still all too shy to contemplate sleeping on a mattress on a relative stranger's floor. And perhaps you always will be. Writing to people is one thing, but interacting with them is another.

It will be freezing in the van.

Ice fractals will form on the glass and Sean will fart all night.

*

Hours pass. I drive and I smoke and play music to keep the voices at bay.

It's not working.

It's night and the roads are clear. I leave Cardiff by the back streets, twisting and turning through them, then head east again, sticking as closely to the banks of the

105

Severn as I can. Knowing it is out there in the darkness somehow comforts me.

None of this is working.

The road takes me inland again towards Newport, but I just want to drive without thinking, without having to worry about road signs and pedestrians and other cars; without having to see the young and the drunk spilling out of the pubs and clubs I used to inhabit. In order to avoid that world I take the most obscure nowhere-roads passing through Monmouthshire hamlets trapped between the M4 and the Severn Estuary. Nowhere places with names like Nash.

Whitson.

Summerleaze.

Places you wouldn't visit.

Street signs spring from the darkness like rabbits trapped in the glare of my full beam, and then they have passed and I'm on to the next place, the next rows of houses flashing by, the lights of their living rooms a brief phosphorescent streak in the darkness.

I switch stations to listen to a late-night phone-in on local radio on the subject of ghostly apparitions and poltergeists.

I can only drive like this for so long before the back roads deliver me up to the motorway again, and I soon find myself on it heading towards the southbound river again then crossing at the Beachley peninsula that sits proudly on an outcrop between the Wye and the Severn.

Then I'm on the bridge again, only this time it is dark and I can see nothing, no sky, no water, no concept of distance and it unnerves me so much that I pull off at the next turn off and I'm back at Aust services. Back at the old Severn View.

It's late and the car park is much emptier now. The front of the building is illuminated in such a way that it bathes the near-side of the car park in falsified, man-made light but leaves the rest in darkness.

I park away in the far corner, away from the light, in the shadows.

In the darkness.

I lock the car and enter the service station.

*

Walthamstow seems like miles away from the West End streets, where the sex, violence and the false allure of showbiz somehow flavour the air in a decidedly exotic way.

Walthamstow is a dreary nowhere hole and it is here that you find yourself in a suburban side street in the house of the guy who runs Damaged Goods.

Damaged Goods have released records by bands with names like Pork Dukes and the Snivelling Shits but as they – or, rather he, for it is very much a one-man opera-tion – is the only label who is actually interested in your band, you don't hold it against him. He has also reissued some Adam & The Ants records, so the label can't be completely terrible.

It is at least a rung on the ladder.

So here you sit in the living room of this guy who runs

the label – another unshaven, slightly awkward music fan – drinking milky tea and playing EA Hockey on the Megadrive, casually interviewing each other. It is not clear who is auditioning who, but after two hours of this it is decided that you will release an EP on his record label.

There is no contract, no legalese. Just a quick hand-shake, before you say your farewells and fold yourselves back into the van to begin the long drive back home.

*

Maybe I'm oversensitive to the strip-lighting or the bank of garish colours of the magazine racks before me, or maybe it is the muzak that is being piped into the build-ing at all angles, the same music they were playing twelve hours ago, in fact, but whatever the reason, standing in the foyer I'm suddenly gripped by an absurd sense of euphoria. The phrase 'like a kid in a candy store' pops into my head and stays there for a few moments, where it goes around and around while I just stand there doing nothing, like a parent watching his child on a carousel horse.

I get giddy with the sounds and colours. The service station gives me a head-rush and I feel filled with an over-whelming sense of joy. I smile at the absurdity of this change in mood and it occurs to me that I am famished for the first time in many, many days. Maybe weeks. It is as if my appetite, suppressed for so long by nicotine, caffeine and medication, is now defiantly staging a loud and aggressive comeback.

I'm utterly ravenous – for salt, sugar, grease; anything. I also have the beginnings of a headache deep in my temples.

I need to eat. No – I actually *want* to eat.

Suddenly it's all I can think about. Suddenly I'm excited.

The cafeteria contains three people: a couple in their early twenties deep in conversation and an older man in his fifties, who looks like he could be a lorry driver.

They sit in a large empty space.

I make myself comfortable, survey the menu and decide to push the boat out by ordering the Full English Breakfast.

A waitress takes my order. She is of a mature age and looks like she should be working anywhere but here. She is wearing a hairnet and reminds me a little of my grandma, the way her shoulders are rounded and her movements measured.

Thinking of Gran makes me feel sorry for the waitress and I can't help but wonder what brought her to here, waiting tables in a cafeteria perched above a black, black river in the small hours of the morning. I wonder whether there is anyone at home warming her bed and missing her.

Your problem is you don't have a girlfriend.

I smile at her as warmly as I can and she responds with a question.

'Are you going anywhere nice?'

'Yes.'

'That's good.'

Then as an afterthought:

'It's one of the best things about working here, getting to hear about all the places that people are travelling to. It's a real crossroads here, you know.'

I smile and nod and say nothing.

The moment for conversation passes.

'Right. What can I get you, love?'

I remember coming here back in 1989, 1990 on our drives home from shows and meetings in London. This was where we would stop for cups of tea and post-gig analysis, defrosting our feet after the drive in a van with broken air-conditioning, further plotting our futures. And always in the early hours, always in the dark. We never once collectively questioned whether we would actually make it or not. It was an unspoken given. To express doubt would have broken the impenetrable circle of hope that we had constructed around us like a forcefield.

Normal people have girlfriends.

It was here that we would breathe a sigh of relief knowing that we would soon be back in Wales, back to the stability and warmth of our parents' homes. Back to the domesticity that kept us all soft inside.

The bridge was symbolic of our return and began to take on increasingly mythical qualities to us. The bridge was the beginning and the end of the journey. Here we would joke about being marauding Taffs returning victorious from our blitzkrieg missions in enemy territory, though really we never saw it that way; even when we talked one day about bombing the bridge to seal Wales off from England we could never decide which side we would want to be on as we were far too long-sighted to fall for things like patriotism and national identity. Both too close to xenophobia for our liking. We weren't 'proud' to be 'Welsh'. We were much more modern and forward-thinking than all that.

We prided ourselves on being 'European'.

*

You check the levels for your showcase then quickly and nervously tidy up the place.

While the three of you do this, Sean pops out to the shop in case this potential manager guy who is driving up from London to see you fancies a drink. He is the one person who received a promo copy of your new 'New Art Riot' EP on Walthamstow's finest punk-rock record label Damaged Goods who has actually bothered to respond positively.

Sean returns with four cans of Skol lager and a tube of Pringles, half of them already gone.

— Sorry, I couldn't get beluga for the Londoner, he says. The offy was all out.

You've been practising in this old school hall a mile down the road from Mum and Dad's for the past few weeks and, save for the odd quizzical head of someone who has arrived a day early for the WI evening popping around the door, you have written and rehearsed here in complete isolation.

Just how you like it.

Left to your own devices in this way you are actually getting better. You can feel it happening. Something instinctive is developing in the way the songs are tightening like the skins of Sean's snare that he keeps having to replace. Repetition is the key. Repetition. Learn by repetition, then repeat it again.

The same half-hour set over and over, for four nights a week.

Repetition. For you it's the only way you can hope to achieve a passable level of competence.

And because of the volume restrictions imposed upon you by the caretaker who always wants to talk to you about Max Boyce, you're aware of the flaws within your songs. There is less margin for error when there is no wall of feedback to cower behind. Instead you're forced to strip it to the bare bones, to constantly refine and edit your words, James valiantly making sure yours and Nick's awkward, soundbite-strewn lyrics scan. He does an amazing job. You marvel as your friend turns into a stout colossus in front of your eyes. It's when he's arranging and orchestrating that James is at his best: total commitment, an immovable boulder when he wants to be, steadfast in his beliefs and abilities.

He and Sean are always first to arrive and last to leave, as if they know that they have to put in the extra hours in order to take up the musical slack if this band is to proceed.

You turn the electric heater on and rub your cold hands together to get the blood circulating in them. Your fingers are soft. They are not the fingers of a guitarist.

You sit on your amp and wait for the Londoner to show.

*

The waitress brings me coffee and I light a cigarette.

Before I can smoke it though she returns with my food, a huge deep plate containing bacon, sausages, black pudding, two fried eggs, beans, mushrooms and one solitary cold wet tinned plum tomato.

Beside it she places a side plate of fried bread glistening with oil.

'There you go, love. I've given you extra beans.'

I smile back, then stub out my cigarette and start eating very slowly. From the first mouthful I am overfaced.

Across the cafeteria the lorry driver folds his newspaper, coughs loudly, then spits into a handkerchief as I scoop up some eggs and beans.

Well, I think, here I am, eating a Full English Breakfast at – what? – one in the morning in an empty cafeteria when I should be in America.

I nibble awkwardly on a sausage end, belch, then push the circle of black pudding to one side.

Heartburn from the beans stabs at my sternum and I suddenly feel very sick.

*

So now you have a manager called Philip. And with this manager comes hope. Hope that someone outside the four-cornered square that is this band believes in your collective vision too.

No professional manages a band for the fun of it, you tell the others. They do it to get rich and successful. This bodes well. He must think we can make some money.

Plus, he doesn't seem too bothered about contracts or any of that stuff.

In fact, it is you, the band, who insist on having it down in writing.

He has plans too. Plans for repeat visits to London to play showcases. He wants to arrange meetings. He wants you to meet people. He is out there spreading the word.

And sure enough, a few weeks later Philip stays true to that when he introduces you to the guys from Heavenly Records, one of the hippest indie labels around, one of the few labels you genuinely respect and admire, even if their roster is completely at odds with much of your own taste.

And the big surprise is, despite sounding nothing like any of their current bands, they like you right back.

So you drive up to London to meet the label owner Jeff Barrett, who has the traces of a Midlands accent, a big genuine smile and a mane of hair like Robert Plant.

After regaling you with talk of his time looking after Happy Mondays and discussing the current state of the Nottingham Forest first team with James, he casually offers to put a record out and invites you to play one of his label nights.

London has welcomed you into the fold.
And you? You are in business.

*

Half-chewed bacon rind and barely digested, sweet-tasting beans float in the toilet bowl as I stand and lean against the cubicle wall, wiping my mouth with the back of my hand.

The shock of all that food was too much. My system cannot cope.

I flush the toilet and rinse my mouth out at the sink, take a sip of water and feel even weaker than I did before. Before I made the mistake of attempting to eat a meal made from salt and sugar and meat.

The straining from the vomiting has also worsened my headache.

I survey myself in the mirror under too bright lights: hollow cheeks, wide red eyes, hat pulled low, a shadow of stubble around my protruding jaw.

You look like shit.

I know.

Pathetic.

I know.

A grown man and you can't even look after yourself.

It's not my fault.

Puking like a teenage girl. You need to sort yourself out.

I know. But how?

Don't ask me.

But I *am* asking you.

I don't have the answers.

You act like you do.

Maybe there aren't answers. Life isn't a question, you know.

I know. But I'm asking you: what should I do?

No one would miss you.

What does that mean?

It means what it means. Work it out.

*

After the show you're all a bit pissed and on a high and even Wire is drunk after necking a bottle of cheap red wine during your set, opening up this, the Heavenly Records showcase.

And now it's afterwards and there are people milling around, pretending not to look at you; pretending that they aren't going to approach you within the next sixty seconds.

— Great show, mate.

— Nice shit-stoppers. Where did you get them, the Spastics shop?

— Fancy a cheeky line?

Everyone is here, all the minor indie stars and Camden ace faces of the day. It's like you've been allowed into the club. The London music biz club. Their club. Your new managers Philip and his brother Martin have stayed true to their word. They are making things happen. They are opening doors, even if you do only find other doors behind them.

They are likeable too – young and funny, wildly ambitious but wilfully unpretentious. And they bloody love *the* Manic Street Preachers.

While you all hold court in this underground corner feeling like four exotic foreigners, the hand of a woman – and she is a woman not a girl – closes around yours while the other brushes across your crotch. Dizzy and sloppy and drunk and floppy you allow yourself to be led like a dog through the tatty curtain by the side bar that leads to a dark storage space tucked behind the dressing room.

And then she's kissing your neck and falling to her knees on the floor, deftly dropping your zip on the way, and then it's out and she's nuzzling on it, and you're getting hard and thinking, Just pretend you're in a porno, and you can hear one of the other bands, some druggie types called Flowered Up, lording it up in the dressing room next door and you're looking down at the crown of her bobbing head and her roots are showing and you're thinking: I genuinely *can't remember what she looks like, and this strikes you as funny so you start giggling and she's back on her feet lasciviously going, What are you* laughing at?

And then she's kissing you again and close up you realise that she's at least ten years older than you, and you're being taken advantage of, and though this isn't quite how you imagined it would happen, you begin to enjoy yourself, and you let go, squeezing tits that may or may not be augmented while she determinedly tugs you off, then takes your hand in hers again and slides it into her knickers, where you feel she is wet with a fluid that is viscous and oily on your finger.

Then her trousers are coming down, and you're glad it's dark in there, and you can hear the boom-boom of the music, then voices close by in the corridor – Let's 'ave it then! – and the roar of the crowd as another band goes on, Flowered Up maybe or Saint Etienne, and you reach round and feel her arse, and your tongues are intertwined and you can taste the stale cigarettes and wine on her, her – this veteran of the London music scene that you sneered at from afar – but now are a part of, in every way – and she turns and bends and tries to guide you in, but you freeze and falter awkwardly mumbling something about condoms.

But she's already one step ahead of you, already ripping one open with her teeth and unrolling it onto your cock, then you're in with surprising ease, and she's bent over what appears to be a speaker cab, and you're going at it, and your white jeans are around your ankles and you're thinking, 'It's a porn film, it's a porn film, and you're a rock star. She's a groupie slut and you're a rock star,' and the spontaneity and sleaziness of it all just turn you on even more – and you're writhing around in the dark and the music is loud, loud, loud and it's night and she's moaning and all you can see is her white arse and it's like the moon so you grab it and push yourself in as deep as you can go, and you're thrusting and gasping for air and thinking, 'So this is it . . . so this is it,' and it's all so

*brilliantly base and animalistic and ridiculous and devoid
of any meaning other than the physical sensation of the
moment, and then the music stops and the crowd cheers
and you can hear your heartbeat pulsing in your ears and
you arrive in more ways than one.*

*

It's cold here in the car. Painfully, painfully cold.

But I don't need to sleep, so instead I sit and stare into
the night, taking an almost perverse pleasure from the
shivers that violently ring through my body as I alternate
between drinking water, chewing gum, smoking, changing
stations on the radio and attempting to read a crappy
Stephen King by the beige glow of the light overhead. I
can't concentrate, though.

Because I won't let you.

Instead I sit and think and try to ignore the headache
by watching frost fractals form across the windscreen.
The only sound is that of the syncopated *whooshes* of
rubber on tarmac from the cars passing on the main road.

Motorway traffic at night is perhaps the loneliest
sound.

Finally dawn breaks over a tilting world and at the
very first sign of light I climb out of the car.

Everything is askew. It is as if my sense of balance has
been disturbed. It feels as if one leg is made from an old
spring and another from a steel pole. My head hums and
my vision is jarred.

It is still freezing and the day steals my breath from my

chest. I do a strange little dance to get my circulation going. I stamp my feet and rub my hands but can only manage a few seconds before I feel dizzy and have to lean against the car for support, coughing and wheezing. It takes a few moments for me to regain my composure and recalibrate my senses.

Then I walk across the car park and into the service station.

It is dead: a lone cleaner drags a mop and bucket across the tiles. I can't see any other customers around.

I have a long noisy piss, then go into the cafeteria and am relieved to see that the old lady of last night has been replaced by an unsmiling man around about my age. I couldn't face a conversation right now. I couldn't face having to create an explanation as to why I am back in here again so early, so soon.

I order coffee from him and take it outside where a thick Hammer Horror fog is rolling in from the river and beginning to settle. Its off-white, narcotic fug cushions everything, compressing sound and muting the dawn chorus.

Within minutes the earth is flattened by its beautiful muffled stillness and everything seems to slow in pace, including my heartbeat. I stand there for a few more moments and let it envelop me too.

I follow the fog around to the front of the service station to where a paved promontory overlooks the bridge and the river. It is the last stop before the water, the final outcrop of land but the bridge itself is obscured by the swells of fog now, and only the very top of it protrudes from the mass of white, like the crow's nest of a silent galleon.

I walk to the walled edge and three fixed viewfinders that have seen better days. Here, tourists can insert a 10p coin to enjoy sixty seconds of views of the mouth of the Severn in both directions. All I can see is the thickening fog.

Visibility is down to a matter of metres now.

3

'A violet in the youth of primy nature,
Forward, not permanent, sweet, not lasting,
The perfume and suppliance of a minute.'

(*Hamlet*, 1. 3)

LONDON – DEATH SENTENCE HERITAGE

With the fog closed in so tight the bridge is tantalisingly close, but just out of sight. Just out of reach, although I feel its presence.

The first cigarette of the morning gives me another head rush and fills my mouth with an acrid sharpness. I draw on it, then pull the hood of my coat up.

A strange light alters the colour of the fog, shifting from off-white cream, to cream, oatmeal, beige and on to an almost purplish hue; as soon as I grasp a new shade, it subtly changes again, or perhaps my tired eyes are just deceiving me.

Perhaps I am feeling the first signs of withdrawal from my medication; I certainly feel decidedly off-kilter.

An old sign at the edge of the promontory points in the direction of a public footpath. I follow it and find myself tramping through wet grass on something that is less a footpath and more a faint trail at the bottom end of a sloping field.

The path takes me away from the service station and follows the river inland, into the unknown billows of this late winter mist. Thick brambles conspire with the fog to obscure any view of the river that I might have, visibility is down to a matter of metres.

After a couple of minutes the service building and the car park are gone from sight too as bushes and brambles close in on either side and the trail leads me into a wood.

It's more a copse than a wood. A *Crimewatch* copse.

A place to bury the mutilated bodies.

The ground is thick with a carpet of green ivy. It covers the trunks of trees too, smothering sound and space.

Bury them in a lime pit.

It is like stepping into a petrified forest. A Grimm fairy-tale forest.

He did unspeakable things to their still-warm corpses.

The wood has an atmosphere of death, but I feel no fear or apprehension. Quite the opposite, in fact.

This is what Britain would look like were mankind to be wiped out – an island of creeping vines asphyxiating everything in sight. It wouldn't take long to return to this state either. A decade or two would do it.

A few years and nature would reclaim the cities and the streets. The concrete would crack as roots and shoots pushed through, houses and tower blocks would be dismantled by the elements, churches would sacrifice themselves, pylons would rust and topple, signposts would drown in seas of grasses and weeds, and soon the land would be consumed once again.

In time, all traces of civilisation would be gone and forgotten.

*

1990 ends with the vague promise of new possibilities.

You all go out on Christmas Eve – the four of you, plus a few friends – on a pub crawl around Blackwood to celebrate and you spend the next day silent and green-gilled as you poke at your turkey and do your very best not to think of the numerous martinis you drank from a pint glass and the crabsticks you bought from the fish man who does the rounds every weekend.

And then you do what you all said you would never do, but always secretly knew you would: you 'relocate' to London. You move in with Philip and his wife Terri in Askew Road, Shepherd's Bush. All four of you.

You share a bed with Nicky, top to tail. James and Sean squeeze in the box room.

In some ways it isn't quite how you imagined it to be, life in the city. But then in others when you step outside it's exactly how you imagined. Rude, overpriced, noisy, violent, dirty, sexy, exciting, restless, corrupted. Everything seems tailored towards selfishness here, and it turns out there are two Londons: one city for the upwardly mobile and the wealthy, a place where one can flit from gym to restaurant to theatre without ever having to cross the path of a beggar or a junkie; and another for the rest of us.

Philip is only recently married and you appreciate that a bunch of daft Taffies up in London for the first time wasn't part of the dowry, so you collectively agree not to take the piss. In fact you do everything you can to make it easy for everyone: the washing up, the shopping if you have any money (Fray Bentos pies, home-made oven chips, frozen peas, Turkish delight, Lambrini), the clean-ing.

Philip's generosity knows no bounds, but things still feel awkward. Especially for you. You're not used to living in such close quarters to other people. Not since Swansea years have you cohabited so closely, and back then it was different. Here in Askew Road, you are on top of each other, under each other's smelly feet. Six people – five of them young men, at least two or three of whom are known to regularly dye their hair and wear make-up – sharing one shower, one toilet, one sink. One fridge.

Then there is the communal-eating thing. You've never been able to eat in front of others. Not properly, not without anxiety. At uni you were able to bake your potato and carry it buttered and steaming into your room where you would prop yourself up on a pillow and eat it from your lap while reading. No one would watch you and no one could enquire as to why you had abandoned it after three mouthfuls. But now you find yourself eating together, in front of the TV of an evening. Sometimes James or Nick cooks up a pot of Bolognese for you all to share, or for Philip and Terri to dip into if they're on the way out to gigs, which they are many nights of the week. Their management and publicity company is thriv-ing so you usually only see them in passing, except when discussing Manics business.

James, Nick and Sean all like their food, but you have to maintain a pretence for fear of causing offence to whoever has cooked. You spoon it into your mouth and you chew it. You toy with it a while, until you're finally

*forced to meekly swallow, making sure to wash it down
with many mouthfuls of water.*

*Because each forkful feels like one step closer to vom-
iting; eating makes you nauseous and food has long been
perfunctory for you – a practical necessity.*

*You put it in your mouth and you hope that everyone
is watching the telly instead of watching you.*

*

I can smell the unmistakably bitter scent of a fox trail
and I come across a tree that has been toppled by the
wind, most likely during the storms of a couple of months
earlier. Its roots are showing and I notice how symmet-
rical trees are once you see them at full length, their
reaching roots much like their tangled branches. I sit on
the trunk and drink my coffee, watching as the fog rolls
on through the copse.

I could stay here, I think. I could stay here amongst
the foxes and the ivy and the uprooted trees and never
leave. I could become part of nature's cycle, rather than
attempting to resist it.

Birth, life, death, decay, then rebirth. There's not much
else to it. Beyond that, not much else matters.

This sudden epiphany sends a shudder through my
body.

Nothing else matters.

Least of all my own selfish obsessions.

I finger a bulge deep in my anorak pocket then remember the disposable camera. I pull it out. There's one shot

left, so I decide to take a photo of the copse to mark this moment. I look deep into the green cathedral, squeeze the button and the camera's weak in-built flash momentarily illuminates the near vicinity.

I lean back against the tree trunk and close my eyes.

It is still early.

*

Everything is up in the air and you don't feel right here in London.

While Heavenly work on the single Philip and Martin continue to tout the band around to anyone who will listen.

And while you're writing new songs – your best yet – on a practical level, you have no privacy and no control. Sometimes when you're a bit drunk after you've been to the pub for a few drinks or shared a bottle of something cheap, it's all you can do to stop yourself from going to the bathroom and cutting your arm up. You crave the short-term release and relief that the shock of pain and sight of blood gives you, but you have to restrain yourself. You need solitude for this, but you don't get it. You are rarely alone.

As a house guest you are now part of a team. You owe it to everyone not to become a fuck-up, at least not publicly. So you focus your energies on the coming months. You work on new lyrics and scour the shops and stalls of Camden and Portobello Road for new clothes for everyone. You tear out pictures from books and magazines and make large gluey collages to help steer the overall aesthetic direction of the band. You even make imaginary record covers for twelve-inch singles. Seeing them like that makes them seem somehow more achievable. 1991 is here and the common goal amongst band and management alike is: a) sign a major-label record deal and b) achieve world stardom.

Or: c) die trying.

Because although you miss your family home and Snoopy in some deep-rooted way, and you're more at odds with yourself than ever, you're a stubborn bastard and there's no way you're going back to Wales until something big has happened. Something of worth and value. Something that extends beyond the small, tightly controlled, hermetically sealed world that you have occupied for these twenty-three years.

You put aside your self-centred concerns and you get busy attempting to become famous.

You are, on the surface at least, focused and happy.

*

Rustling.

The sound of rustling stirs me. I open my eyes and not more than ten feet away is a fox, his hide a burnt umber in colour.

He's not like the mangy city foxes I used to see around Shepherd's Bush after dark rifling through bins for a discarded chicken bone or the chewed remains of a Big Mac. Those city foxes were fearless and quite used to the presence of humans at all times, unlike this rural fox whose senses are so refined that the mere opening of my eyes or the lightest of exhalations is enough to alert him to my presence.

We have a stand-off – the fox poised to flee in a half-step as I lean back against the tree. Ten seconds pass as he assesses the situation. He is wondering who I am and why I am here on his territory. I too am wondering who I am and why I am here.

Then in a second he is gone, a pointed red dart through the green thicket.

I like it here. I want to stay here for ever.

*

January 1991 and the oil fields of Iraq are burning. They'd rather set fire to the refineries and let them burn like roman candles than relinquish power to the allied forces.

You sit watching it together in the living room of the house, marvelling at the new lexicon of war: 'smart bombs' that can fire around corners, 'antimissile missiles', General 'Stormin' Norman' Schwarzkopf, the caricature general and his 'Operation Desert Storm'. Everything is reductive but even so The Six O'Clock News *becomes your anchor for each day – it becomes a focal point. You meet each evening on the sofa to watch the events unfold.*

January 1991 and you should be out on what is your first proper UK tour, but everything has been delayed while Nick is in hospital having a cyst removed from his throat. It actually stops him talking.

— For the first time in his life, remarks Sean, reaching for the remote. This is boring, he adds. And depressing. I'm putting T-Bag and T-Shirt on.

Something good happens, though. 'Motown Junk', your first single for Heavenly, is released in the midst of the war. Though it is by far your best recorded song, the release has been fraught with difficulties and has provided a glimpse into the mechanics of this industry. And what you have seen is conservative ugliness, a fear of controversy – a fear of free thought. You might as well be working for the civil service.

Heavenly do their best, though. In a greasy-spoon cafe off the Uxbridge Road, you meet with Jeff and the Heavenly lot to agree on a series of compromises, the first being the change of song title of a B-side track 'Ceremonial Hate Machine' to 'We Her Majesty's Prisoners'. Apparently the pressing plant had complained about the song title. James is initially adamant that the original title stays, but is persuaded otherwise.

— It's only a B-side, says Sean.

— It's only our fucking integrity, James fires back.

The artwork is changed too, from a shot of John and Yoko with a gun to their heads to an image that you yourself sourced from a Soho picture archive: a burnt and battered Hiroshima clock that stopped at the exact time of detonation. 8.15 a.m.

You don't see how the new cover is any less disturbing

than the original, but by now you all just want the record out there. The window at the pressing plant is rapidly closing, tour dates have been rescheduled and a TV appearance – your first, for a youth show called Snub *('We just want to mix politics and sex and look brilliant and say brilliant things,' you announced) – already recorded.*

So the record is pressed up over Christmas and is in your hands one cold January morning.

When it arrives you put it on the turntable and sit around listening to it and drinking cups of tea, pleased to hear that it sounds so much better than the first EP. It sounds like an important song – urgent, riled, acerbic.

— It sounds great, beams James when it ends. Stick it on again, Sean.

You have to agree. It sounds powerful and a million miles away from the numb cute nothingness of the Deee-Lite and Betty Boo singles, or the mindless nonsense of The Farm and The Charlatans singles that the NME critics chose as the best of 1990. And even though you don't actually play a single note on it, you're still proud of it, primarily because the most powerful line of the song – your line, a riposte to the current trend for Sixties revisionism: 'I laughed when Lennon got shot' – stays, if only because no one knows what the hell James is barking about anywhere. But you all know, and that's what counts.

It's a pyrrhic victory, possibly, but a victory nonetheless.

And you think perhaps it's time to seize the moment, that people might finally be ready for this.

The single stalls at No. 94. It stays there the following week.

And the week after that.

And the week after that. It spends a total of three weeks wallowing in the sedimentary layer of the pop charts, before disappearing completely.

— At least it sustained its relative failure, Sean notes.

You don't know whether to laugh or cry so you do neither and go on tour instead.

There's no easier way to escape your problems than by running away from them.

*

It is cold and still early so I stand and slowly walk out of the wood, across the field, around the rear of the service station by the wheelie bins and to the corner of the car park, where I retrieve the rest of my cigarettes, an apple, my water and the blankets from the car.

Then I walk back through the fog into the wood, to the fallen tree.

There's just enough room to slide beneath the trunk so I wrap myself in the blankets then squeeze myself under there. The ground is thick with so many dead leaves that the top layer is dry and crunches beneath me as I pull my hat down low, zip up my anorak, then light another cigarette.

And here I lie alone, smoking beneath a dead tree in a

copse at the end of field that sits high above a river that flows all the way to the sea. No one knows I am here.

No one but a fox.

I lie back in my bivouac and close my eyes and all I can see is wood and vines and leaves and beyond them tiny fragments of the white sky, shapes that change as the tops of the trees sway in the morning breeze, a mosaic of light reinventing itself over and over.

*

As sole designated driver, you're at the helm again. It feels good to be with your friends, the road unfurling before you like a dirt carpet into the unknown. You feel like Marlow in Heart of Darkness, *going upriver to find Kurtz, only the river has been filled in and tarmaced over, the trees replaced with Little Chefs and there is no Kurtz.*

You've decorated the inside of the dull blue mini-van for the occasion with one of your collages – a hastily glued visual explosion of torn-out pictures of Elvis, Wilde, Titian, Farrakhan, Dahmer, Axl, Kylie, Twiggy, Trotsky, Kinnock, Ozzy, Flavor Flav, Van Gogh, Dylan Thomas, Aneurin Bevan, Lydon, Lemmy, Lennon and McCartney, Lenin and McCarthy, Morrissey and Marr, Ronald McDonald and Adolf Hitler, photos stockpiled from six months of glossies and snaking their way around the interior of what is to be your home for the next three weeks.

All icons; no obscurities.

— Fucking hell, you use a Pritt Stick like Michelangelo used a brush, Edwards, smiles Nick as he folds himself into the van for that first drive of the tour. Bloody masterful.

Suffice to say, after some delay, you're in fine spirits. Nick has had his stitches out and is back at his best and James has been training again. He has put in many road miles of running in advance of this tour.

And suddenly the distractions and setbacks of the previous weeks are forgotten and all that lies ahead is gig after gig after gig. You soon slip into the new routine of long drives and load-ins, crap food and soundchecks, booze and gigs and more booze. Stupid conversations with strangers and cold mornings in crappy motels or B&Bs, all punctuated by random acts of abuse or threats of violence against you coupled with added attention from girls wherever you go.

Because for the first time there are discernible crowds to see you. With the single gaining favourable press review – piss-taking and with vaguely racist, anti-Welsh undertones, but largely favourable nonetheless – you hit all the glam spots on what is your first proper tour.

Reading and Southampton.

Leicester and Warwick.

Stoke.

And there are people there to see you. Thirty, forty, fifty, depending upon the day of the week.

This is the true heartland of Britain – the hateland: the smaller towns, where people are crying out for a bit of flash and sparkle, some mid-week escapism. These are the people you want – the people like you.

The crowds increase, week by week.

Forty.

Fifty.

Sixty.

And somewhere out there, for the first time, you begin to become someone else.

The hair becomes a little longer, a little bigger.

The eyeliner becomes thicker. The face powder whiter.

The trousers tighter.

The moves sharper.

The eyes blanker.

Somewhere out there 'Richey Manic' is gestating.

Somewhere in the rooms of the Ramada, the Radisson, the Ibis and the Travelodge, the butterfly prepares to crawl forth from his cocoon.

It is a process of metamorphosis that you feel at ease with. Each night you assume your mask; you hide behind your foundation and a steady flow of vodka.

In tandem with Nick, who has embraced his new Wire persona with equal brio, you adopt your role with ease. James however remains slightly schizophrenic, still undecided between his Strummer/Springsteen/Slash ultra-man mode, or whether he should – or could – embrace the androgynous Keef/Thunders/Liz Taylor vibe that you and Nick are going for, but his musicianship compensates for any identity confusion.

Sean meanwhile is growing his hair out completely, his cherub face framed by dark shiny bangs that seem to make him even more ageless, androgynous and sexless than any of you.

What begins as a thirty-minute nightly performance soon grows into something else.

Richey Manic begins to encroach upon your day. And you realise that you actually like his company more than you like your own.

You embrace him.

*

A whistle then the tiny tinkle of metal wakes me. The whistle belongs to a human and the tinkle is of a dog collar.

I can't see it but I know the dog is nearby because I can hear its hot panting breath. Then I hear a cough and footsteps down at the bottom of the copse on the path that I came in on, a path that looked as if it has not seen human footsteps for years.

The path leads to another field. There are signposts. It is a public right of way.

I hold my breath. I can't stay here during the day. I'll be found. Unearthed like a relic.

*

You enjoy the tour because you become him. Because you become him, and he is striking and outspoken and beautiful. He can't play guitar any better than you, but he sure looks a whole lot cooler, more at ease and confident. People want to approach him. They want to hear his opinion. They want to know where he bought his pearls or who did his hair. They want to ask him about something he said in that Sounds *interview they read. They want to stand next to him and have their photograph taken. He is outside of the outsiders and all he needs are his friends in the band and a mirror to tell him that everything is OK.*

Richey Manic is the new thing. Richey Manic is everything that you are not.

Hull, Sheffield, Dudley.

Coventry, Taunton, Aldershot – watch out.

*

Time has fallen away.

I don't know how long has passed when I crawl out from beneath the tree and stand. I feel dizzy and see stars. They spin around the axis of my head but before I can focus on them they are gone. They are not stars anyway; they are more like silver flashes, like tiny faraway explosions.

The copse is clear of fog. It must have lifted while I have been sleeping.

Sleeping in the woods like a fugitive.

Like a nonce.

I can't decide whether to leave my blankets or not, so I roll them up and put them under my arm. Overhead the sun is straining to shine through a white sky and looking around I can see that the copse is even smaller than I thought.

To my right I can see a long curved field, ploughed, and then left for the winter, its furrows now frozen rigid. To my left I can just make out the distant form of the service station. In front of me, at the bottom end of the copse is the footpath, then beyond that a tangle of hedgerows. Then beyond that, unseen, the river.

Slipping in the wet earth, I walk down to the path, and then follow it away from the service station. There is a fence separating the path from the unseen river. More symbolic than functional, it is just a slackened, rusted wire. I follow it until it drops to the ground and there is a gap in the hedgerow.

I step through it, pick my way through the long damp grass and weeds, and take a few paces before the ground suddenly slopes away dramatically. It is so steep I cannot see where it goes, it simply disappears.

I realise I am at the very edge of a cliff.

I push the branches aside and there before me is the full sweep of the River Severn.

*

On a rare day off you take your design to an inner-city tattoo parlour: a single tilting rose, with the words USELESS GENERATION written below it in a scroll.

You know it is rockist and cliché, but the fact you know this somehow makes it OK.

It hurts like hell, and not in a good way.

You bleed everywhere but everyone agrees: your new tattoo looks great.

*

I have to cling to a tree trunk and push more branches aside with my free hand to get a proper view of the river.

It is vast and silent and I see it as if for the first time.

Over to the left is the bridge, now free of fog. An amazing structure, it is supported by two huge white H shapes held fast in massive concrete blocks the size of houses. Between the supports, thick cables keep the suspension taut and steady.

It, too, is vast and silent, save for the whisper of the cars that cross it.

*

— *Well, no reaction is the worst reaction, eh, ladies?*

It's a typical mangled Wire quote, but you all know what he means.

You're squeezed into the backstage room at some shitty Glasgow venue that is unequipped to handle the rabble that turned up to see you tonight. You're sweaty, drenched and all catching your breath, the set still ringing in your ears. You were loud tonight. Fucking loud. James is bent double, his fingers to his head. He looks at them and sees blood.

— *No danger of indifference tonight, you say, taking a swig from a warm can of Stella.*

Right at the start of tonight's set, two guys in the front row had pulled out syringes, dipped them into their pints and begun to spray you with lager. Then came the taunts from further back in the crowd, back beyond the glare of the stage lights, deep from the darkness of the pit.

— Fucking shite . . .

— Doss fucking English poofters.

— Ah'll tack ya fucking heeds aff.

This last one just a split-second before a can connected with James's head and sent him staggering back into the kit.

And this was all before some of the crowd decided to join you on the stage, half of them jostling you, half hugging you. Some made an attempt to sing Celtic songs down the mic before security pushed them back into the melee, then advised you to cut short your set. You didn't, though. You didn't give an inch. The more abuse they shouted, the more you decided to play.

Out of spite.

Out of sheer fucking spite.

— Any Rangers fans in tonight? James asked, prompting some cheers of approval and even more cans. I heard the Celtic lot stuffed you last week.

Even more cheers as the tide turned and the crowd came on side.

Identifying the mood of the majority of the crowd and then saying something to endear you to them was a nifty move on James's part. Of course, Nicky waded in with his own opinion on matters.

— Football is for idiots, he bellowed. We'd rather be

backstage getting our dicks sucked. You're all welcome to join us. This song is about Glasgow – it's called 'Faceless Sense Of Void' . . .

And now, afterwards, you are exhilarated by the violence of it all; overjoyed that you could provoke such a reaction.

— Did you see those maniacs with the needles? you say.

— Let's hope it was Buckfast and not Aids juice, says James forlornly feeling his scalp and looking at his bloody fingers once more.

He needs stitches. You need a drink. Nick needs a lie down. You all need an escort from security to your van afterwards.

Yes, says Nicky, mock-dramatically throwing a long floppy arm around James's shoulders. There's only one thing worse than being talked about, dear boy – and that's not being talked about.

The tide has definitely turned: people are really starting to hate you now. It's amazing what a few choice quotes in the inkies can do. There are those who like you too though, of course. More and more each night. You can spot them from their make-up and their furs. Male and female. It's them that you feel sorry for, having to deal with the beer-boy rabble out there in the crowd, or on the way home. You however are safe in your van or tucked up in anonymous B&Bs with their fry-up breakfasts and quiet disapproval from the landladies.

You hire a soundman.

A driver.

A tour manager called Colin.

And the road trip rolls on: Newcastle, Lancaster, Derby.

Cambridge, Aldershot, Buckley . . .

The next time you check it is nearly April and you've just lost two months and half a stone.

*

I take a step back and sit down in the grass to smoke another cigarette to try and collect my confetti-like thoughts.

If only it wasn't on a dog-walking route I could go back to my space beneath the fallen tree and stay there for a very long, long time. I could eat and drink just enough to stay alive and when it got cold I could just get up and walk around a bit. I could stay there so long that everyone would forget all about me. I could grow old beneath that tree. I could grow a very long beard. I could go feral.

Dogs would piss on me, rain would penetrate my makeshift home and foxes would amble on past in the night, but no person would ever know I was there. Just the animals. They'd know but they can't speak so it wouldn't matter.

And then finally, when I was sure that all traces of my memory had been erased from the minds of everyone who ever knew me, I could roll out from beneath the fallen moss-covered tree and re-enter the world. A young man with no history; no past, only a future.

A mystery man.

I could start again.

I *could* start again if indecision didn't reign and cripple my every choice with doubt and corrupt all possibilities with confusion. I'm coming and I'm going, yet I'm not getting anywhere.

*

— *Wire.*

No response.

— *Wire.*

You're fumbling around in the darkness of your shared hotel room.

— *Wire. Are you asleep?*

— *Hurgh.*

You have a great idea that you absolutely must share with your best friend this very second.

— *WIRE!*

— *Oh,* fucking hell.

The bedside light comes on and a squinting Wire emerges from beneath the duvet, his matted copper-coloured hair springing in all directions.

— *What is it? What's wrong?*

— *I have a great idea.*

He offers no response, but you continue anyway.

— *Yeah, I was thinking we should do a free show on the Falls Road in Belfast. We could make a stage from burned-out joyrider cars. It'd be* amazing.

— *You're pissed.*

— *That's no barrier to clarity.*

— *You should get some sleep.*

— *I want to go to Belfast. We could unite the two sides.*

— *Oh, they'd love that. A bunch of mincing Welsh boys. Who are you – Bob Marley?*

— *Do you think Sony will pay?*

— *No.*

— *Do you think we'd get shot?*

— *Probably just kneecapped.*

You pause to think for a moment.

— *It's a terrible idea, isn't it?*

— *Yes.*

— *Maybe I should get some sleep.*

— *Yes. Yes, that's a good idea.*

You fall onto the bed with your boots on. Nick turns off his bedside light.

— *Nick.*

— *Yes?*

— *The room is spinning.*

— *Put one foot on the floor and you'll be all right.*

— *You might want to pass me the bin. Just in case.*

You hear him shuffling about in the dark. He stubs his toe and curses. Then you hear the bin being placed on the floor next to your heavy pillow.

The pillow smells of other people's hair.

— *Nick?*

— *Yes, Rich?*

— *Night.*

— *Night, Rich.*

*

There's a girl. There's always a girl, but this one is special. She asks for nothing.

You don't deserve her.

I think I like her because she doesn't treat me like Richey Manic. In fact she doesn't even like the band very much. I don't think she owns a single record of ours.

A girl of good taste, then.

Also, she doesn't lower herself to acting like a groupie, carries herself with dignity at all times and has read more books than I have.

She'll not stick around – she's obviously too good for you.

I don't think people understand our relationship. *I* don't understand our relationship. We only see each other sporadically and we've certainly never fucked. Since I got sober, sex has been out of the question anyway. In fact, I can't ever remember having sex sober.

She's young too.

Paedo.

But not that young.

She probably needs a real man. Someone who doesn't burst into tears all the time. Someone who can keep her satisfied in all ways.

The problem is I don't know what she sees in me.

Me neither; that's how I know it won't last. You might as well end it before it goes anywhere. End it now before you subject the poor girl to the full 'Richey experience'.

But I've never felt this way about a girl before. I think that's why I'm so scared.

You're always scared. So what else is new?

I'm scared that if our involvement deepens one of us will get hurt. I'm not in the right place in my life to embark on a proper relationship. The others seem to be able to do it, but not me.

You're too self-centred for that.

You're probably right.

I'm always right.

But then again I won't know until I try.

You already know: it won't work. You'll reject her. Or your self-obsession and vanity will drive her away. No girl wants a boyfriend who's skinnier and more frail and feminine than she is.

I don't want to be a burden.

You already are *a burden. Don't you see that? Just by existing you are a burden to your family, your friends, your band. Every time you cancel a show or have to go to hospital you are a burden to everyone who works for the organisation. People rely on your band for a living and you are taking that away from them. You're also a burden to the doctors and nurses who have real people with real problems to deal with. People with* actual *illnesses and diseases, rather than made-up, psychosomatic afflictions like yours. The young, the elderly, the disabled. And you're a burden to this girl, whoever she is. The one noble thing you can do is let her go before things get too involved.*

I could have done things so, so differently.

It's too late. You wanted to be the tortured, detached artist and now you are. Deal with it.

I'm not sure I can.

Yes you can. You can because you have to. You'll deal with this situation by any means necessary. You'll do whatever it takes to set the ones you love free. You're nothing but a millstone around their necks and have been for years. So now you need to break those chains and let the millstone drop.

How?

The first links have already been broken. You'll work it out one way or another.

I don't have the strength.

Then you'd better hurry up and resolve this situation once and for all. You owe it to them. You owe it to the people who have had to tolerate you.

Remove yourself.

*

The tour doesn't so much end as pause for breath from time to time.

It's exhausting, debilitating and the ringing in your ears rarely ceases.

You exist on a fiver each per diem, *but when there's free booze and sandwiches, what do you need money for?*

You take to squandering yours on silly things – some crappy Boots perfume one day, a bag of avocados the next. A silk scarf, travel Scrabble, a horrible cocktail in a tacky nightclub, a second-hand book or two. A cheesecake. Some days Wire puts his money straight into the service-station fruit machines while Sean buys practical things like batteries, umbrellas and maps of each town.

Hangovers follow drinks follow hangovers and the mascara is never completely washed off. You just keep applying more.

Everything merges.

Sleep is snatched here and there and clothes are hand-washed in tiny sinks in cold bathrooms on anonymous side streets. It's easier to put your jeans into a bucket of bleach than it is to wash them. There's always time for your hair though because the one rule is you never – never – go onstage looking like shit. Any of you. You might sound it, you might feel it, but you never look it. That type of complacency doesn't feature in your group. You're not a sweaty American rock band; you're not meant to look like you've just walked in from the car plant or the factory. You're meant to look like you've been beamed in from another era, another planet. 'Speed queens from Planet Homo', is how one review puts it.

Your breakfasts on the road vary, from a fry-up for Sean to grapes or a banana for you. Lunch is a sandwich or a Ginsters, or nothing. Tea is some crappy buy-out pizza and Babycham, if you're lucky. A green salad if the venue is decent.

And there are girls. Girls who follow you everywhere. Girls called Leonie and Amber and Jackie and Christy. Girls called Anna and Sarah and Lucy.

Girls called Anais and Kendra.

They bring you books and make-up and stand in the front row, not moving. Some of them intimidate or insult you, by way of flirtation. Others want to cosy up to you in the dressing room and whisper poetry in your ear.

You take them back to your room. You all do. For fumbles and sucking and poking and sometimes fucking.

With the lights off and a head full of the drink it becomes harder to remember their faces and names. Sometimes it takes a minute or two to remember which town you're in.

In Blackpool you're awoken by Wire clattering around in the dark and the stifled giggles of a girl. Lamps get knocked over, zips get unzipped, sweet nothings are swapped and bed-springs creak.

You laugh out loud when you hear a moan, a sigh – Oh Christ, sorry love – swiftly followed by snoring.

You leave Coventry with teeth marks on your shoulder, Blackburn the beginnings of a black eye.

Buckley makes your knob sore.

You're going up in the world, though.

At least you have your own beds now.

*

The light is beginning to fade.

I think perhaps the sudden withdrawal from the Prozac is having some adverse effects. My vision keeps going in and out of focus and I feel an overwhelming pull to one side, as if a great magnetic force is exerting itself upon me. My thoughts seem more scattered than ever and as I try to grasp them they seem to blow away, always just beyond reach. Every so often I forget where I am and it takes a few seconds to calmly remind myself that I am here, in some woods, near a bridge by a river that divides two countries. That I am here because I don't know where else to go. I am here because I am breaking the chains. I am letting the millstone descend.

I pull my blankets out from beneath the fallen tree. I no longer want to stay here tonight.

Later: the cheeseburger sits half chewed before me on its wrapper as I pick at the over-salted French fries, my blankets folded on the bolted-down plastic chair beside me. The service station is busy again; too busy to hang around much longer. I must make a decision and move on elsewhere.

The old lady in the coffee shop has clocked on for her night shift again so I'm forced to come here to the greasy McChain burger bar to avoid her questions or – worse – sympathetic glances.

The lukewarm beef patty and pickle sits uneasily in my queasy stomach, but the coffee is warm and complements the three cigarettes that I have chain-smoked.

An hour passes. More coffee. Then another hour. When the Bristol kid at the counter keeps looking at me, I turn away, ashamed of my gaunt face and the stubble that gathers on it like theatrical soot.

Then I stand and leave.

*

You planned this. You did this. It's your fault.

Afterwards he's there again, backstage, the journo. Self-consciously chain-smoking and hovering sheepishly.

He's just doing his job, you remind yourself. Just doing his job.

It could be you. It could be you getting paid to write for a living.

It could be you hovering in cold, dark dressing rooms with your cigarettes and your Dictaphone, one eye on the deadline.

No. It couldn't be you.

Because you have no interest in the opinions of young drunk gobshites like yourselves.

The room is nothing but murmurs, an airless post-gig void that has just seen forty paying punters throwing plastic cups and spitting at you like it's 1977.

Surly and shirtless, James smokes in the corner. He's been curt to Steve Lamacq all night, in no mood for justification. Not when he has just been spat on and abused by yokels. Nick is cornered by some familiar faces. Jackie and Carrie, the fanzine girls, another girl we secretly nicknamed Suicide Allie and some chubby teen in a Nine Inch Nails top. Sean is staring blankly at his new Game Boy, perfectly still except for his thumbs.

— Can I get a few more minutes?

Him again. Lamacq. Your gateway to the impression-able NME *readership. So far they've been less committed than their weekly rivals so deep down you know you need them now more than ever. You need* him. *You resent it, but you can't deny it.*

Forty paying punters.

Senseless Things pull twenty times that on a rainy night.

So of course he can get a few more minutes.

— Of course you can.

You're in Norwich Arts Centre, a gothic ex-church with tombstones for a floor.

Fucking Norwich.

Forty paying punters.

Mega City Four pull twenty times that on a rainy night.

The dance floor fills up now that you've finished. Naturally. The DJ plays Nirvana, Wonder Stuff, Birdland, 'Head Like A Hole', 'Step On'. Everyone is dressed like Clint Poppie or Wayne Hussey; everyone's dancing like they're on drugs. There's not a decent haircut amongst these Pernod-and-black-swigging, patchouli-oil-doused tractor drivers.

You congregate by the flight cases for the usual round of accusations disguised as questions and for a while you respond with all the eloquence you can muster. All four of you.

But Lamacq has his agenda and you have yours. Yet still you want to convince him so you take him aside, this pallid man from London with the Dictaphone and the concrete ideas of what constitutes 'punk', and you look him in the eye and you go to work on your arm with a blade.

Fifteen slices to your flesh and you feel nothing. Nothing approaching pain anyway. You feel calm. You feel good confirming your commitment in cuts that spell out '4 REAL'.

You planned this. You did this. You're doing it. Doing it now.

You feel the warm flow and see the downwards flicker of his eyes.

— Jesus . . .

Now you've got his attention. You have let him know that the Manic Street Preachers are do or die. The last gang. All of that stuff that you know he secretly wants to hear.

Because you give good copy. Because you give good photographs.

Because you planned this.

(Because you're a pussy for wimping out on the full 'FOR'.)

And then you calmly walk away to the toilets dripping blood across the stone floor of an ex-church down a side street in Norwich. Fucking Norwich with its forty paying punters.

Ned's Atomic Dustbin pull twenty times that on a rainy night.

You stem the blood flow. You watch it turn pink as it mixes with the water and swirls away. Swirls away into the drains of Norwich. Keeps swirling away. You keep bleeding.

The artificial light glistens in the pools of blood like stars.

You look in the mirror. You smile. You feel no pain.

Because you planned this.

You keep bleeding. You did this.

You made a dull night new.

Painted the town red.

Then bandages are stemming the blood flow and someone is driving you to hospital in the van.

There's no sense of urgency. You stop on the way so Sean can get honey barbecue chicken wings and chips at KFC.

In Casualty the lights are too bright, and you're glad you're sober. You wish you'd brought a book, though. It's going to be a long night.

You sit amongst the drunks with the broken noses talking with thick East Anglian accents through blocked sinuses and you sip water from the cooler in the corner. You keep your head down, wondering if maybe you went too far. You forget that what is normal in private isn't always normal in public.

Now you're waiting to be swabbed and sutured.

Smiling.

You're just a bloody show-off, you. A sick fuck.

It didn't even hurt.

*

It's morning when I find myself out on the bridge.

I've left the car park and walked across the footbridge that runs over the top of the toll booths, followed a narrow road above the motorway, then dropped down onto a service road that has brought me out here, onto the middle of the bridge amongst the morning mist.

I don't remember getting here.

I brought you here while you were sleeping.

Cars pass by on their way to work.

Commuters.

I can feel their eyes on me, but I'm paying them no attention because I am looking back the way I came, back to the cliffs that swoop down to the water.

The cliff face is a spectrum of colours, from its grass-covered tops down through the clay-grey lines and the compacted red dirt that moves through burnt carmine and crimson, down to the dark weeds of the lower slopes that drop off and meet the slate beach at nearly ninety degrees. The cliffs stretch westwards as far as my eyes can track them, far downstream towards the sea.

According to a sign up on the promontory, these cliffs are a place of special geological interest due to the abundance of fossil beds. Even from here, viewed in cross-section, I can see that the cliffs are a map of the earth's evolution as layer upon layer of different-coloured rocks chart the different time periods, stretching back way before man ever walked the planet. Apparently they still find bone fragments now on the thin grey strip of beach that sits below the cliffs.

Apparently this land is built on bones.

*

You didn't think people would be so upset by a few cuts.

But it's a quiet time, the NME *need something to write about and this fits in neatly with their whole Van Gogh/*

Iggy/Sid self-destruction-as-art lineage. You can't pretend you didn't think it would go unnoticed.

Of course you can't. That would be stupid and naive. And a lie. And you're not a liar. You are many things, but a liar is not one of them. You are for real.

Yeah, we know, Richard. You said.

But still. What you didn't expect was the level of hatred aimed at you. After all it's your bloody arm, isn't it?

There's no sympathy – not that you seek it – only disgust. And outrage. The thing is, you'd feel fine about it, if you hadn't upset some people at the venue and wasted the nurses' time.

It's really no big thing.

*

My hand is cold on the white rail and my hood keeps blowing down. Below me the waters of the Severn seem lighter in colour than they did from up on the cliff top. They look perilously shallow, as if there is no depth to them at all.

Further downstream a solitary pylon stands on a jetty that juts out into the water as if there is nowhere else in the world that the pylon could be. Against the cliff and the sky it seems strangely at odds with its natural surroundings. If I squint I can also see the steaming chimneys of industry and small clusters of factories beyond it. And more pylons too. Pylons leading off into the distance, getting progressively smaller and fainter. Like me.

Smaller and fainter each time I look in the mirror.

*

You have a band meeting in the morning with Philip and Martin. Despite everything the mood is upbeat.

— *Can you still play guitar, Rich?*

— *Of course he can't play guitar. He never bloody could!*

Ha-ha-ha.

— *Let me rephrase: can you still jump about looking sexy without bleeding everywhere?*

You roll up your sleeve and inspect the tightly wound bandages that go from wrist to elbow on your right arm.

— *Urgh – seepage, says Sean. That's minging.*

A tutting James flicks through the tabloids, a fag dangling from his tip as he drops ash into his tea.

— *You should have cut your cock off, Edwards. We're only on page eleven of the* Star. *You really must try harder.*

Ha-ha, bloody ha.

— *Look, he's still bleeding. We'll have to cancel tonight.*

You sit in silence and let the decisions get made for you.

— *Where is tonight? Wire asks.*

— *The Barrel Organ in Birmingham.*

— *Birmingham's a shit-hole.*

— Everywhere is a shit-hole – that's not the point. The point is he's had seventeen stitches and it's probably best that we let them heal.

You sit in silence and you smile through it all. The cuts are actually starting to sting now. Your entire arm feels cold. Numb. It aches down to the bone, but you can't admit that. You can't complain.

Don't you dare complain, you think.

Don't you dare.

Just keep laughing. Make light of it. Join in the piss-taking.

— Daft twat.

Ha-ha-ha.

Yeah.

Don't you dare complain.

Just keep laughing, otherwise you might just find yourself asking: why?

— Drunk berk.

Yeah.

Ha-ha-ha.

Oh shit that hurts.

*

I feel like a cliché, like Munch's *Scream*, the way I'm standing here on a bridge, above the water, in the morning, the world swirling around me, hunger and chemical withdrawal pulling at me.

So I walk back across the bridge, back the way I just wandered, and when I reach the other side – the England side – I stop to light a cigarette and take in the view of the river. One final look. East to west and back again.

I'm wondering what to do and where to go but the only decision I can make is: don't make a decision.

Because you're not capable.

And as I smoke there's the beep of a horn behind me. A work vehicle has pulled up on the service road. The driver is wearing a luminous yellow flak jacket and has a cigarette hanging from his mouth. He's about my dad's age. He winds down his window.

'Don't do it!' he grins.

'Sorry?'

'I'm only kidding, son,' he says in a soft Valleys accent. 'I thought you was going to jump for a minute back there. I saw you from up top at the depot. We get quite a few up here, you know. A few a year.'

'Oh no,' I smile back, reassuringly. 'I was just taking a look at the rock formations on the cliff. Taking a few photos and that.'

'Ah, a student. Well, it pays to check anyway. We don't get many people on foot, see, and it'd be me who'd get the blame no doubt. Parked up top, are you?'

I pause for a beat.

'No. No, such luck.'

'Need a lift, then? I'm only going into town.'

Another pause. Which town?

Who cares.

Fuck it.

Fuck it. There's a decision right there. It has been made for you.

'Yes, that would be great, actually. I was just about to go up to the services to call for a cab.'

'Needn't bother. It'll cost you an arm and a leg to call a cab to come out here. Best save your money for the beer and hop in, lad.'

*

Giddy and laughing in a cab to Soho Square, your arm still swathed in bandages, London looks different today.

The sun is shining, the sky is blue and the pavements are thick with tourists. Tourists sporting bumbags. Tourists clutching guidebooks.

The city looks somehow less threatening, less daunting today than it did when you first arrived here. It looks like it is yours for the taking.

The mood is good. The mood is giddy and light-headed – like kids on Christmas Eve.

You're all in one car; Philip, the lawyers and his accountant in another.

For some reason that you have not yet fathomed the biggest record label in the world – the most unashamed, proudly corporate structure in the marketplace – has offered you a £200,000, ten-album record deal and you're on your way to the belly of the beast to dot the Is, cross the Ts and happily sign your worthless little lives away. You can't get there quick enough.

Independent kudos and credibility were never part of the band's credo. You agreed on that early on: why go to university and get degrees only to live a life of poverty and relative obscurity? Why press five hundred records when you can do five hundred thousand?

It's not entirely about the money, but it certainly plays a major part in the deal. That and the fact that the guy who is signing you is embedded in the marketing department, so you'll have the weight of a ruthless team of shrewd salesmen behind you; the same people who sell Michael Jackson and George Michael to the masses. People who can sell anything to anyone, so long as the packaging looks good and the concept is 'desirable' to the target demographic.

You certainly aren't doing this to be credible. You aren't doing this so you can maintain careers in the Pot Noodle factory back home. You're doing this to impact on culture.

One fact is certain: there is no way you'll be able to make ten albums. No way. Only a fool would sign you for that. This thing has a shelf life of two years at best. Three, tops.

As you turn onto Shaftesbury Avenue the traffic grinds to a halt. Swerving past at speed, a cycle courier clips the wing mirror and your driver pounds on his horn. The car edges forward a few inches. The driver sighs, James lights a cigarette and puts his sunglasses on. In the front seat, his knees up to his chin, Nicky opens the window.

You pass a magazine stand with a Times *news board out front: RECESSION LATEST: 80,000 PREDICTED REPOSSESSIONS IN '91.*

— It looks like we timed it right. James nods towards the board.

Nicky smiles.

*— I'm going to spend my money on a new carpet –
and one of those new Dysons to clean it with. Maybe I'll
get one for each room.*

*— I bet you do as well, says James. What about you,
Richey?*

*You don't know how to answer because you gen-
uinely haven't considered it. What with budgeting for
the studio, new gear for everyone, management's cut,
lawyers, accountants, it's not like you're all suddenly
going to be rich anyway. Yet for a few fleeting moments
you allow yourself this indulgence, this pretence.*

*— I'm going to get a pool – and fill it with champagne,
you smile. I'll be the ultimate champagne socialist. You'll
find my head a week later outside Blackwood Club –
mounted on a stick.*

*— Champagne's horrible, though, Nicky sniffs. Get some
Babycham in there and I'll be round in my Speedos . . .*

You laugh.

You all do.

*

'At the university, then, are you?'

I don't know what I'm doing here, early in the morning, sitting in the passenger seat of an open-backed truck
full of traffic cones on the way to Newport, talking to a
motorway maintenance man called Rhodri when I should
be eating breakfast in Manhattan.

Perhaps I am more in need of human contact than I

realised. Perhaps I want someone – anyone – to acknowledge my existence, if only to prove that I am still here, that I am actually alive, because right now I can't otherwise be certain.

'Yes.'

'And you study rocks and cliffs and that, do you?'

'Yes, palaeontology.'

'And they teach degrees in rocks, do they?'

'Yes. Well, it's more about the history of the earth, really. Prehistoric life.'

Even I am almost convinced by these lies that I appear to be spinning with surprising ease.

'Great. I like a bit of history myself, actually. War stuff, though. First and Second, mainly. Do you live in those halls of residence, then?'

'Yes.'

My mind scrambles to find a detail brought up from the recesses of my past, back when I was applying for college places a decade ago.

'Up in Caerleon.'

'Ah, nice part of the world, Caerleon. I bet you could teach me a thing or two about the Roman fortress up there. I'm afraid I can't take you that far up though as my missus will be expecting me for a bit of breakfast. I can drop you in the town centre though. That do you?'

'That would be great, thanks.'

That would be great, thanks. What the hell are you doing? You'll be sucking him off next.

*

You give up on arriving in style and ditch the cab on Berwick Street to go it on foot. You cut across Wardour Street, down a piss-puddled alley that reeks of the sex trade, and out onto Soho Square where the office workers of the capital are out in force, sprawled on the central patch of grass eating their sandwiches, noose-ties loosened for a few stolen moments of relaxation and informality.

These are the people who control which films get made, which TV shows get commissioned and which records are destined to be hits. What will they make of you lot, overdressed and road-ragged, cowering too-coolly behind out-sized shades?

A combination of confidence and arrogance has got you this far, but now self-belief has been traded for dis-belief – disbelief that they're actually buying the idea.

Into the reception: marble floors like an ice rink tell of gross annual turnovers beyond your comprehension. Opulent fixtures and polished fittings. The air temperature just so.

The receptionist asks you to take a seat. Someone will be down in a minute.

She doesn't know who you are or why you're here. She doesn't care. She probably sees a new you every day.

The air con is on and large TV screens flicker with the faces of the latest signings, the sound turned down low. You'll be on there soon.

You'd better be. Because that's what you're here for: to sell yourselves to the widescreen dream.

To be used and abused. To be rinsed out and wrung out for all you're worth, then discarded.

You know this. You fully expect it.

You just hope you all come out of it unscathed and wealthy.

— Hi, guys. I'm Claire, Rob's assistant. You can come up now. Shall we do this?

And then you're all in a lift, no one saying anything as you silently ascend into the future.

*

We drive on this way for a while and I can see him glancing at me sideways.

'You're up a bit early for a student, though, aren't you?'

He pauses, waiting for me to offer a name. An explanation. A morsel of info. Anything.

'Simon.'

'Up a bit early, Simon? I thought all you students stayed up all night on the beer, getting your end away.'

'Yeah,' I laugh. 'I've got this project to get done for tomorrow though so I thought I better get down here.'

'Essay, is it?'

'More of a presentation really. About the rocks.'

'You sound like you're a local lad, Simon.'

'Yes.'

'I tell you what, are you any good at rolling cigarettes? There's a baccy pouch in that glove compartment – you can help yourself if you'll do me one while you're at it.'

'Thanks, Rhodri. Thanks a lot.'

I roll us each a crooked little cigarette and we smoke in silence. Two blokes. Simon and Rhodri.

Smoking in silence.

*

Still slightly giddy, you take the first of many Sony expense-account cabs over to the Marquee on Charing Cross Road, a distance of about four hundred yards. It takes fifteen minutes in rush-hour traffic.

The Marquee.

Home of Hendrix. Home of The Floyd.

Only they moved it since then, so it was actually home to none of them (you only know this because the girl from the accounts department told you this 'flirtatiously' an hour earlier as you sipped warm champagne in the cold open-plan office).

The driver drops you off at the back door. You pile out. The band and your new friends, the paymasters. Slave-owners. Whatever.

— Richey! Richey!

There are two kids in the piss-drenched alleyway down the side of the venue. A boy and a girl. They have jet-black hair like you. They have white jeans like you. The boy is wearing a red blouse almost exactly like the one you wore in the 'You Love Us' video. The girl is in a fur coat. They approach you, two wide-eyed balls of excitement.

— Look.

The boy rolls up his sleeve. You know what is coming next.

— I did it because I feel the same way that you do.

— You've met Lamacq as well then, have you? dead-pans James, as he turns to get his guitar case from the cab.

The humour wrong-foots them but they keep on smiling anyway.

— No. The NME are scumbags.

— I quite like the NME actually, you say. I've read it for years. It was pretty much our bible in Blackwood – if we could get copies, anyway. The music press was like samizdat material round our way in the mid-80s . . .

— Will you cut yourself tonight, Richey?

— What?

— Will you do it again – during the show?

James barges past them, clattering his guitar case into their meatless shins as he enters the venue.

— If you come and see us after the show, he adds, I'll cut you up if you like.

Awkward, nervous laughter all round.

— It was great to meet you, you say, your voice sounding hollow, condescending. I've got to go soundcheck. Enjoy the show.

*

And then I'm back in Newport, *bloody Newport*, miles away from my car, miles away from the fallen tree and the ivy and the fox, and all I've got on me is my fags, lighter, a disposable camera and a roll of money, and I'm watching Rhodri driving away, stacks of cones wobbling in the back of his truck, a vague wisp of smoke coming from his window as the back of the truck – CAUTION: MOTORWAY MAINTENANCE – fades from view, leaving me standing there just off Queensway, and it's still only early, and Newport is the last place I want to be, because people know me here, people recognise me here, and so much for just going with the flow, so much for not making any decisions, and then just like in a movie it starts to rain, thick sheets of it, sarcastic and malevolent rain, and I'm getting wet, pissed on by God, and now all I need is for a stray dog to come along and cock its leg on me, and I don't know what the hell I'm doing but all I know is I feel sick and I feel hungry and I feel scared and I feel lonely and I feel cold.

*

Alone on Kensington High Street. The morning after the night before. Slightly tired, slightly wired. A combination of both.

Bloodshot eyes sore from the make-up, sore from the smoke. Throat sore from the shouting over the din.

Your teeth unbrushed, your ears still ringing from the last chords of your first – and last – ever encore.

The new single, of course.

The facts are undeniable: you have become a rock band.

A rock band who play encores. A rock band who patronise their fans at backstage doors. A rock band who are wasteful and decadent.

Last night James smashed his brand-new £800 white

Les Paul to smithereens after a grand total playing time of fifty minutes.

— It felt like killing a baby, he told you afterwards. But I can always get another one.

And now you're in a trendy Kensington shop buying an armful of pre-distressed punk T-shirts that go for fifty notes a pop.

You got up early this morning. You rose before everyone else, skipped breakfast and went for a walk.

You walked for an hour, maybe more, through the busy central London streets, watching as people dashed to work with their heads bent towards newspapers and coffees. You walked until you came to a bank where you checked your balance. You saw that you had many, many more thousands of pounds than yesterday. Than you'd ever had before. You have a lump sum and you also have a weekly wage.

You also have expenses.

You have an accountant.

You have paperwork to file. More contracts to sign. Publishing. Merchandise. Copyright.

You have obligations. You have 'a career'.

You have a lot of new clothes whose price tags you would have sneered at twelve months ago.

Twelve days ago.

*

It's late in the afternoon and I've lost a few hours.

I'm walking down Commercial Street when I see

Richard and Mike from the 60 Ft. Dolls heading towards me, so I duck into a shop. It's a photo-development shop. I pretend to browse for a while but before I can leave the assistant, a girl of sixth-form age with straightened hair and too much make-up, collars me.

'Afternoon. Can I help you?'

Yes. You could have me committed.

Then I remember the camera. The camera I've been carrying around in my pocket, unable to discard or destroy. The camera with all those undeveloped pictures of Mum and Dad on them.

I take it to be a sign. A sign that I was meant to be on the bridge at that moment; a sign that I was meant to take the lift from Rhodri; that I was meant to *nearly* bump into Richard and Mike from the Dolls but instead arrive here, in this shop.

'I just need this developing, thanks.'

My voice cracks as I say this.

'No problem. I'm afraid our last one-hour batch has just been done, but I can have these done for you first thing tomorrow if you like?'

I stare at her for a moment.

'I could really do with them printing today, actually.'

'I'm afraid that's not going to be possible, sir.'

'Is there anywhere else that could do them for me now?'

'I very much doubt it. Actually, we're the only shop in town open on Sundays. Anywhere else and you'd have to come back Monday morning.'

Christ. It must be Sunday tomorrow.

You dumb ass. Of course it's Sunday tomorrow.

I need to do this, though. I need to get these pictures done before . . .

Before what?

Before whatever I do next.

Dickhead. Delaying the inevitable again. You should forget the fucking photos and get some balls about you instead.

'OK, thanks. I'll get them tomorrow, then.'

'We actually have an offer on at the moment: we can do an extra set for half price, if you like?'

'No, thanks. One set is enough. What time do you open?'

'On Sundays we're open from nine.'

'I'll be here.'

'Before you go I just need your name for your pick-up receipt please.'

Pause.

'It's Griffiths. Terry Griffiths.'

'Oh, like the snooker player? Sorry – you must get that all the time.'

'Yes. Quite a bit.'

*

In Thailand a 767 crashes, killing all two hundred and twenty-three of its passengers.

In Japan, near Nagasaki, a volcano erupts and immolates forty-three people with its molten magma.

In Swaziland twenty-six men are trapped underground following the collapse of a mineshaft.

In the Philippines another volcanic eruption occurs, this time killing three hundred people.

In Moscow, following a landslide victory, Boris Yeltsin is sworn in as the first popularly elected President of the Russian Soviet Federative Socialist Republic

In a large tent on the edge of Milton Keynes, hotly tipped, newly signed Welsh quartet Manic Street Preachers play their first festival to a crowd of three.

Their manager, their publicist, and one loyal fan.

*

It feels like madness. Being here. Newport on a Saturday.

I shouldn't be here, even without my hair and my hood pulled up. Maybe you were right.

Yes. Thank you.

I should have just stayed under that tree.

In my blanket.

On the leaves.

With the fox.

I want to be there now, in that calm greenness.

I want to be there now but I can't because I'm miles away and I need to get those photos before I go back to the service station, pick up my car, and just keep driving. Because that's what I have decided to do: keep driving until I come to a remote place with a cliff and then maybe I'll drive off it into it, into the darkness.

Those photos again. What's the obsession with those

175

photos? They're just holding you back. It sounds like the photos are an excuse to me. Another lame excuse to avoid doing what you know you're going to do.

I'll fill the boots with rocks.

And just drive.

I'm done with this shit.

Is that a decision, then?

Yeah. Yes. Maybe.

4

'I am thy father's spirit;
Doomed for a certain term to walk the night,
And for the day confined to fast in fires,
Till the foul crimes done in my days of nature
Are burnt and purged away.'

(*Hamlet*, 1. 5)

NE TRAVAILLE JAMAIS

I walk and I walk.

I walk up Malpas Road and out of town for a couple of miles until I'm sweating and breathless.

I walk and I wheeze.

I walk and I wheeze and I cough and I hack, yet still I keep sucking on the cigs to keep my hands and mouth busy.

My mouth.

My mouth is sore and sick from all the smoking and from where I've chewed away at the cheeks. There is also an ulcer on the inside of my lower lip.

The night is biting. The night has drawn its knives on me.

I'm cold to the core.

To the core.

It's dark now and I just want to be off this road, away from the passing traffic; away from the kids who are hanging around on their BMXs outside the pizza shop eyeing me up and debating whether to give me grief or not, and the small packs of primped and perfumed people heading out early for a night on the beer, dressed in skirts and shirt sleeves, their laughter echoing long after they have passed by in a cloud of cigarette smoke, hairspray and aftershave.

I'm exhausted as I pass through a residential area that I don't recognise. Outside an innocuous-looking town house set back from the road I see a wooden sign for BED & BREAKFAST. Facilities it offers include EN-SUITE, TV and TRAD. WELSH BREAKFAST.

Then hanging beneath it, on a small chain, is another sign that says VACANCIES.

I cough and I wheeze and I spit out something solid and I realise that maybe you're right after all, maybe the photos are just a delaying tactic, an excuse to keep me here overnight, to keep me going when all I want to do is stop and be still and silent, and therefore it feels like punishment, like a twisted form of self-abuse, drawing it all out like this.

I walk up the gravel driveway and ring the doorbell.

*

You're up in your room, drunk in the half-light.

You bury yourself in your books. It's where you feel most comfortable, here, late at night, only you, the lamp, your books, your pens and paper and maybe a little drink or two.

You are internally warm and nothing else is necessary.

You're back in your room, raking through the great-est minds of modern times. You stockpile quotes. You condense each text down to its base elements or extract philosophies that relate to specific songs. You ignore the academic canon and choose only the writers who matter to you.

You approach your lyric writing and art direction as if it were your finals – with diligence and pragmatism.

You feel like an alchemist, turning paper into gold.

You're back in a room, a room in an annex of a studio in Oxfordshire. The country's first residential studio, in fact.

It is the world of Branson. The world of Oldfield. The world of Tubular Bells. 'Situated in 100 acres of lush Oxfordshire countryside, with rooms for wives and girlfriends'. *It couldn't get any more establishment.*

You're interweaving your words with those of others that echo down the centuries: Confucius, Kierkegaard, Nietzsche, Ibsen. Your friends. You pull out quotes to use on the sleeve, while you appropriate others for your songs.

You're working to a deadline; you like it this way. It gives you a sense of purpose. It gives direction to your day. To your night.

It gives direction when you need it. Because although the Manic Street Preachers are laying down demo's for their debut album (working title: Culture, Alienation, Boredom And Despair*) and, more pressingly, recording their first major label single, you will barely feature on any of it. Not musically, anyway. Everything else however – lyrics, art, 'vibe' – is yours.*

It's hard to tell what it sounds like when you wander

in and out of the studio during the day as everything is broken down and recorded in isolation. You barely understand the terminology, let alone the actual process of 'tracking' and 'overdubs' and 'bouncing tracks'.

James is busy to the point of distraction. He treats this album like he used to treat running, with commitment and total dedication. He'll also play all your parts – your job will be to merely replicate the most basic of chord structures live, as accurately as possible.

And Sean.

Sean spends hour upon hour getting his drum sound right. You hear him in there, in that weird soundproofed vacuum, where everything is compressed and muffled and Arctic-sounding; you hear him hitting his snare over and over again until a disembodied voice from the control room clicks in: OK, now try the tom.

It is like being at a month-long soundcheck. Pure hell.

Even Nicky – the self-confessed 'third best musician in the Manic Street Preachers' – is becoming more and more adept on his instrument. You still work on the lyrics together, but it is you who does the final edit.

But now you're back in your room, sipping at your vodka, drunk, working on track lists, working on verse edits, working on what you've all told the world will be the most important album of the 1990s – if not ever.

You have a lot to live up to.

You know you have set yourselves up for failure.

But you also know you'd give your life for this.

*

The room is small but clean. It is a bedroom in someone's house.

I should be in Los Angeles or Chicago or Detroit but instead I am in a bedroom in someone's house somewhere between Newport and – I think – Cwmbran.

There is no sense to any of this.

In order to secure the room I found myself spinning another web of lies. Something convoluted about attending the funeral of a dead relative. A flicker of doubt crossed the landlady's eyes as I told her this but she gave me the room anyway. Death is always a good way to avoid questioning; the great silencer. And I do very much crave silence right now.

No one wants to probe too deeply when death is involved lest they unearth something rotten.

I sign in the guest book as 'Michael Monroe' and pay up front in cash, naturally.

*

The money is too good to refuse. You wish you could be less vulgar about it, but you know how much the Pot Noodle factory pays and to turn it down would be an insult. It's a chance to pay off all of the last tour's debts in one fell swoop.

It's also your only chance to wander the hallowed halls of that hotbed of learning, Cambridge University, which you do before the show.

You're booked as the star turn at Downing College's 'Jive Bunny Lives' May Ball.

You're the working-class freak show for the lawyers and brokers of tomorrow; the volatile oiks invited into the club for one night only.

Three songs in you casually put a foot on the monitor and, fearful that destruction is about to ensue, they cut the sound. Your reputation as a band obviously precedes you.

Frustrated, Wire entertains the crowd by insulting them.

— Inbred wankers. You're not the future of Britain – you're the past!

Drinks come flying.

— Trust-fund cunts!

Some of the rugger boys clamber onstage. Punches are thrown. James gets some good shoves in. Sean kicks over his cymbals and lunges at a prop forward who is so drunk he can't see straight.

The show is over.

You take your money and leave, leave quickly, no messing about, no meets and greets, straight back to London, back by midnight.

Next day you're in the Mirror *and the* Mail: WELSH BAD BOYS START RIOT *and all of that.*

It's the funniest thing you've read in ages.

And the irony is, it could have been you in the crowd if you'd wanted it. It could have been you at Cambridge, you at Oxford. It could have been you mixing it with the Rogers and the Julians, the Camillas and the Persephones.

But you didn't want it. You wanted Swansea.

You wanted Wales.

And besides, Oxbridge wouldn't have got you here: attempting to play guitar in the most talked-about, most misunderstood, most brilliantly ridiculous new band in Britain.

*

At some point I go in search of food but the only shop I can find is an off-licence so I buy peanuts, chocolate and cigarettes, then trudge back to the B&B, coughing something vile.

I have to ring the doorbell to get let in.

In the room my bed has been turned down, so I climb in, clothed, and watch the news: 'Orange Juice' Simpson is on trial for murder. Some new parliament bill has stalled. The football results. The weather: changeable.

Then the local news follows: more of the same, but on a more parochial scale. A stabbing last night in Newport. A farmer in court for neglect. The rugby results.

The weather: changeable.

I scoop peanuts into my mouth. Drink water. Read the B&B's copy of the Bible. Smoke. Wheeze. Cough.

Hack-hack.

Then I sleep a deep blank sleep where everything is grey and pixellated like the static on the TV screen that I awake to pre-dawn, alone, confused and still coughing.

*

You switch one astronomically priced studio for another and the label begins to get nervous. You're already approaching the top end of your budget, but the album is only half done. If that.

Somewhere along the way you have reached the executive decision that it should be a double album, but never counted on it taking twice as long to make.

Your lyrics are done, though.

They were finished in a notepad frenzy weeks ago and now summer is ending and you are stuck in rural commuter-belt Surrey watching James, Nick and Sean gain wrinkles and ulcers over this record.

It's ridiculous, you want to tell them.

It's only an album. It's only a rock record.

Only you know it is more than that. It is your one shot at this and the thought scares you a little.

If the record bombs you will be dropped and you know you can't go back to an indie label. Not after everything you've said in the press – the bold statements and hyperbolic declarations. They'll fucking crucify you. Especially you – the most ham-fisted of the lot. The anti-muso. The godhead. The diva.

So, yes, the thought scares you. Without this band you will be nothing. The lifestyle you could live without, but not the support network. You need these people. You need their love. And you need to give them your love because so far you've never been able to give it to a girl. Only Mum, Dad, Rachel and Snoopy. And the band. You're funny like that, for four young men.

Open.

Open and honest.

And the thought scares you. It taps at your skull: what if?

You know the others are tough enough to survive. James and Sean could still do music. Production or teaching or song-writing. Nick could do anything he wants to do . . . but you, what could you do? Drink vodka and cry for a living?

You realise there is nothing you could do but this, so you throw yourself headlong into the lifestyle.

You take to heading up to London in the record-company car to rinse out the Sony Am-Ex card. You wander the West End and make sure you have a gay old time. You allay your anxieties in the way that half the country does: by spending money on frivolities during the day then drinking yourself to sleep at night.

*

In the morning it's even colder, bitingly cold, and the girl who served me in the photo shop yesterday has been replaced by a man with a crown of wild grey hair.

He looks hungover and pissed off. He carries a large fob jangling with keys and he walks with a shuffle and a slight stoop. He looks like a gaoler from another age.

I'm already outside the shop, smoking and sipping a coffee and hiding in my hood when he opens up a few minutes before 9 a.m. My presence appears to alarm him and he quickly locks the door behind him again.

Commercial Street is quiet. There is a trail of red pickled cabbage like carrion along the middle of it and across the way, in the doorway to Boots, there is a Catherine wheel of vomit that looks like it has spun to a dawn standstill on the pavement.

Beside it sits an empty pint glass.

As he busies himself behind the counter the gaoler keeps glancing my way, as if trying to establish whether or not I am casing the place. I simply turn my back to him and wait until he unlocks the door again.

He relaxes when I hand him my receipt and even tries to make small talk about the rugby, but the best I can do is sigh and grunt at him in response and he soon gets the message.

He gives me my envelope of photographs and I leave.

*

You spend three full days wandering around the capital's art galleries. From the large ones of the West End to the smaller, edgier spaces in the East London wastelands and the many mid-range ones curated by unsmiling ladies in expensive spectacles.

You see Turners, you see Hogarths.

You see Rodins and Gauguins, Whistlers and Dalís.

You view Warhols and Twombleys and Naumans.

You run the gamut from classical to modernist. You see the famed pickled shark and feel nothing. You see bleeping and flashing installations and you pay five pounds to stand in empty white rooms in darkest Shoreditch waiting for something to happen.

You are looking for artwork for the album but have already been met with a series of no's from the label: 'too expensive', 'too blasphemous', 'too abstract'. All your ideas are rejected.

Finally you begin to understand what it means to be on the payroll of a major corporation, and that creativity and commerce exist on two very different planets.

*

'Those who want to live, let them fight, and those who do not want to fight in this world of eternal struggle do not deserve to live.'

Adolf Hitler wrote that in *Mein Kampf* and though I'd disagree about the conceit of anyone 'deserving' to live – because life is not a system based upon privileges – and though I'm loath to appropriate a philosophy from someone who would almost certainly have categorised me as a mental weakling and sent me to the showers, it would seem that I have let myself slide into being one of those who does not wish to fight in this 'world of eternal struggle' any longer.

There is simply no fight left in me because there is nothing worth fighting for. Love, money, fame, relationships, power, sex, hedonism, art – it all seems like too much effort. I've tried them and they've burned me out. It's far more than boredom; this is a sense of hypersensitivity to a world in which I don't – or can't – belong. I can't belong because it's all so hopelessly upsetting. Everything just kills me.

The murders. The floods. The bombs.

The famine. The greed. The cruelty.

The music. The art. The critics.

Wealth. Poverty. Violence.

Love. Hate. Indifference.

Everything.

It's all too much to take and I find myself crying constantly. I want everyone else to feel what I feel – just for a day, and then see if they can cope.

I feel like I am made of the thinnest paper, I feel hollow, like a creature has crawled out of me and I am what is left behind. The husk. The shell.

The useless shuck.

I feel the ill wind cutting through me, and know it carries nothing but bad news.

My bones feel like they can only support me for so long.

Everything is collapsing.

*

August yawns into September. September frowns into October and October curses the arrival of November.

During these long fire-coloured months you become detached from your moorings. The band drifts into dark waters. Uncharted, shark-infested waters.

1991 is nearly over and you are still making your debut album. The record company has taken to sending people down to Surrey, who just happen to casually 'pop in' to 'say hello', but end up scurrying away with their record bags full of various mixes.

You're all alarmed to hear that expenditure on the album has crept up to nearly half a million pounds and that from the week after next there will be no more to spend without reducing the marketing and promotion budget. The in-house catering . . . all those shopping trips up to London . . . the session musicians . . . the producer, the engineer, the multitude of Megadrive games. Everything, it seems, comes at a cost.

You were hoping no one would notice.

The funny thing is, there is absolutely no way the record can match the hype that you have happily helped perpetuate in the British music press – a press who, during your absence, first filled their pages with endless piss-taking snipes and caricature sketches of the band and then, more recently, much speculation as to whether or not the band is in fact one big hoax and you never intended to release an album in the first place. The press haven't turned against you, but they're certainly sharpening their nails and constructing their crucifixes in readiness. Telling them that you are going to sell sixteen million albums, play three nights at Wembley and then commit a collective career suicide possibly didn't help matters.

— You're going to have to get your razor blade out again to convince them, Richey.

That sad fact is, the speculation is more interesting than the reality.

And the reality is, as the year nears its end and you come close to losing your mind, the Manic Street Preachers finally complete their much-feted, long-awaited debut long-player.

And in your heart of hearts, none of you are sure if it is actually any good or not.

*

Images from home. Images in my head.

Images of Christmas gone.

Dad carving the turkey, a too-small paper crown perched askew on his head.

Mum in the kitchen, pinning a new brooch to her blouse.

Snoopy asleep beneath a pile of wrapping paper.

Rachel laughing, eyes closed, face framed by golden hair.

Rachel and Mum.

Rachel and Dad.

Dad with gravy on his chin.

Rachel and Mum and Dad.

Rachel and Mum and Dad and Snoopy.

Bill and Christine from over the road.

Snoopy close up.

Mum shying away from the camera, one hand raised in protest.

My thumb, as large and orange as the sun as it obscures the viewfinder.

The green ivy-covered copse from . . . when? Yesterday. The day before? I can't remember.

Images on waxy paper, twenty-four in all, still warm from the machine, still warm with laughter. These are the last remaining artefacts of my family, my existence, the place from where I came – geographically, physiologically, emotionally. Everything.

I go through them once, twice, then I put the envelope into my left inside pocket, the one by my heart, zip up my coat, and in that moment I know they will all be better off without me.

In that moment I know what I must do.

*

You make it back to Blackwood for one day to film a slot for a BBC2 youth TV show hosted by a Frenchman whose gimmick is to laugh at the British and talk so fast that no one understands him.

You spend an hour in make-up back in James's mum's house in Pontllanfraith making yourselves look pretty. The snow is coming down thick and fast so you don your furs and go for a walk around town with the film crew in tow. You're looking good today. All of you. There's a uniformity, a sense of colour against the whitening landscape.

— Where's the fast-talking Frenchman? you ask them.

— He doesn't do the interviews – just the studio links.

— *Oh.*

It's strange being back home in this way. It's as if the cameras somehow legitimise your band's existence. Where before people used to stare or shout abuse, now they wave at the cameras or try and get in the back of the shot.

— *Oi, Manics!*

Now they know your names.

Familiar faces pass by. Old dinner ladies from school. Neighbours. People who were in your year at school, now looking fat and forty even though they're only in their mid-twenties.

— *All right, boys! 'Ow's it going?*

— *Bought our album then, have you? asks James.*

— *Have I fuck.*

It's freezing. You walk around the streets shivering as they interview you. You walk into the fields and slip on the ice and snow in your Chelsea boots. They film you next to some horses, your heads shrinking down into your coats.

They ask you about your record deal, the escalating costs of the album, about the hype, about your influences, about literature.

They point the cameras at you and they ask about your concepts of love and romance.

— *We're romantic realists, says Nick. We're never blinded by too much flowery aesthetics. Our romance is always based on where we come from anyway and a desire to escape boredom.*

— *Our idea of romance is having total power, you*

add. We have nothing to lose because we're already secure in the knowledge that we lost a long time ago.

*

Newport bus station is quiet and smells of urine, as all bus stations do. Movement is the only thing on my splintered mind right now. Movement and how to achieve finality.

It feels like a thousand Sundays have been distilled down into one archetypal Sunday; lonely, listless and oppressive. No hope for tomorrow. No sun in the sky.

Only the newsagent is open so I go in and buy cigarettes, chewing gum and water. Then as an afterthought I buy an apple. The apple is too hard and it hurts my teeth. I take a few tiny rodent bites, wince, and then throw it in the bin.

A carrier bag blows across the covered forecourt as I light a cigarette and walk over to the bus stands. I stand and count them: there are thirty-one in total.

From here, buses depart for all of South Wales, Monmouthshire, Caerphilly, Torfaen, then beyond them to Cardiff and Bristol. At the far end of the terminus, National Express – National Duress we used to call it – run buses to destinations across Britain. From here you can travel to Birmingham and London or take connections on up to Manchester, Newcastle and Scotland.

This is the escape route, the gateway.

I walk over to the bank of Perspex-screened timetables that have been graffitied, mutilated and burnt with cigarettes, names scrawled across the plastic in thick marker pen.

I look beyond the names at the list of destinations that lurk beneath, trapped.

St Julians.

Rogerstone.

Wattsville.

I look at the times of the buses that go there, then remember that it is Sunday and a different service operates today.

Ringland.

Castle Bingo.

Blackwood.

A noise rises behind me as three girls with their arms linked sweep into the station amid peals of laughter. An old couple follow them behind, also arm in arm, for support. One of the girls kicks a crumpled can of Tango and it rattles through the terminus. I go back to my timetables, back to my cigarette.

I don't know what I am looking for, but I keep looking.

*

Bertrand Russell believed that life is a perpetual compromise between the ideal and the possible. And so it is upon delivery of the finished eighteen songs that the extent of these compromises between your collective vision for the record and the label's cold commercial reality become truly apparent. There are compromises.

Compromises over the artwork. Compromises over the title.

Compromises over the choice of singles. Compromises over the B-sides.

Compromises over videos. Compromises over photo shoots.

Compromises over every damn thing.

John Ruskin said, 'You may either win your peace or buy it: win it, by resistance to evil; buy it, by compromise with evil.'

You choose to buy yours. It just seems easier that way.

*

As I'm trying to make sense of the timetables a shape intrudes upon my peripherals. A shape and a voice coming at me from the diagonal. Even before I see him I can feel the familiar purposeful movements of a fan, of someone who claims some sort of ownership over my existence.

'Richey?'

I turn to the shape, to the voice.

It belongs to a young man. Fairly anonymous-looking. A record-collector type: spectacles and a tatty jumper. Doc Marten boots and a brown leather bag covered in button badges slung over one shoulder.

Hearing my name like that catches me off guard and yanks me back to my self. Back to the old world, the old ways.

My first thought: typical. Just as I've finally come to a decision.

My second thought: deny everything.

My third: I'm tired. Tired of everything, but mainly tired of myself.

My mouth doesn't work so I just stare at him and as I do I see that same flicker of disappointment cross his eyes that I've seen a hundred times before. The sinking realisation you get when you meet someone you have only previously ever seen onstage, on television or in the pages of a magazine.

'Sorry to pounce on you like that,' he says, less sure of himself now. 'I'm a friend of Sally's.'

Sally, Sally, Sally.

My mind slowly clicks through its rolodex of names and faces. Seconds pass before it finally settles on a face I can remember. Sally in New York.

Sally from the fan club.

'Oh, right. How is Sally.'

My voice sounds blank, perfunctory. It offers a statement rather than a question.

'She's great. Still a bit mental.'

The young man blushes and apologises again.

'Sorry. What I meant was, she's still the life and soul of the party . . .'

But I've already clammed up. I have nothing to say. Nothing.

I crave anonymity, peace. I want to be absolved of all responsibility for other people's feelings. I don't want any of this. All I want is to turn and run.

I want to turn and run as hard as I can, out of the station, down the street, and keep running until I can run no more.

'Right.'

'Hey, how's the band? What are you working on?'

'Some new songs. Things like that,' I say vaguely, my gaze slowly wandering everywhere but the young man. The fan.

Then:

'It was great to see you. Say hi to Sally for me, I'm afraid I'm in a bit of a hurry. I've got to . . . return some videotapes.'

I know it's my paranoia, but I imagine I can feel his eyes upon me as I turn and walk away, can feel them at my back like knives. They're stabbing at me and saying: you arrogant bastard.

I imagine that now when he goes and sees his friends in the pub, or tomorrow at college, or at his job, he will be able to tell people that he met Richey from the Manic Street Preachers, and when they ask him what he was like he'll be able to reply with a dismissive shrug: *He was an arrogant bastard.*

Totally up his own arse.

He looked at me like I was shit on his shoe.

Like Newport wasn't good enough for him any more.

I fucking hate rock stars like that, me.

*

Your self-styled Winter of Hate is in full swing.

You are primed and ready. Or as ready as you'll ever be because, as everyone is so quick to remind you, this may be your one chance.

James's skill on the guitar never fails to amaze you and you all know the band would be nothing without him. Nothing. That much is obvious. Every band has at least one person of discernible music talent and James is yours, followed by Sean, then there's a big gap, and at the other side of the gap yawns Nicky Wire, then somewhere behind him holding a guitar and looking at it quizzically, there is you.

Most of the hate directed at us – directed at you – comes not from members of the public, but other bands. Useless low-IQ twattish lad bands who take offence at your band's flirtation with all things feminine, and your unwillingness to join the matey 'all in it together' British music scene clusterfuck. You casually tell an interviewer that the Manic Street Preachers are the most friendless band in Britain and it is only a few weeks later that you realise how true this statement actually is.

They also take your personal lack of ability as an insult to their craftsmanship and say so at every opportunity. It's jealousy, of course. Jealousy that while they're out honing their 'craft', you're getting the money and the magazine covers.

Primarily, though, they are uneasy with the fact that those who look like girls get the girls.

*

'It's OK,' I say, more out of politeness than a genuine sense of courtesy. 'I'm in no hurry.'

The taxi driver at the rank by the big hotel has just lit his cigarette and is leaning against the bonnet of his car when I ask if he's free. He is. I climb in and wait while he smokes.

I will never see Newport again.

Yes, you will.

No, I really won't. This was never my town, not really. Not like Blackwood or Swansea or Cardiff. This was just somewhere I came because, in the words of Mallory when asked why he climbed Everest: 'It was there.'

So why are you even here, then?

I don't know. Maybe, subconsciously, I just needed to be sure.

Be sure of what?

Be sure that I would be fine with never coming back here again. Newport is the past to me. Newport is about coming to see bands at TJ's, before I ever even joined one. Newport is about running from fights and running for the bus. Newport is about the younger, more optimistic, more naive me. It is a me I barely recognise. I suppose I just needed to know that I can move away from all that – that stepping backwards is always a mistake. That from now on I shall only move forward.

You sound very sure of that.

I am sure. I am sure. I know I can't live in the past and I know can no longer live in the present either.

So what are you going to do – build a time machine?

'Right,' says the cabbie, sliding into his seat sideways. 'So where are we off to on this fine freezing morning, then?'

*

The programme is so trashy and pathetic it's brilliant; scum TV for the post-pub masses: your target audience.

You don't debate the pros and cons of appearing on The Word *for once, you just know it will be an excellent excuse for some late-night chaos.*

They book you to play the 'safe' option of your new double A-side, 'Love's Sweet Exile', but at the last minute you switch it for 'Repeat', with its 'fuck queen and country' tag line.

Actually, you don't switch it all – you always knew you were going to play the more vicious and crude cut of the single, you just didn't bother to tell the dizzy dimwit blonde student Ents officer type who booked you. Or your TV plugger.

Damage limitation.

So right on cue, you take to the stage surrounded by camp podium dancers. The sound is terrible. Utterly terrible. Cameras swoop overhead and all you can hear is the out-of-tune klang of Wire's bass. It doesn't really matter though because you look amazing and Wire makes TV history by being the first musician to break not one but two guitars in the space of one three-minute song.

Guitar straps snap, leads become unplugged and the

studio crowd surges forward. Giving up, Wire ditches his second guitar and instead showers you in kisses before it all collapses in on itself, James screaming out the immortal closing words: 'Useless generation / Dumb flag scum.'

A nation of drunk students scratches its head in confusion.

Cut to the presenter and a segment about some desperado eating worms for his five minutes of fame.

Job done.

There's no time for carousing, though: the very next morning you're up at 6 a.m. to play the right song this time on a Saturday kids' TV show. You all behave impeccably, and politely decline when asked if you'd like to feature in the 'gunge tank' section of the show.

Even if they are all under the age of thirteen, it is nevertheless the biggest TV audience you have played to.

*

I am Liz Taylor. I am Gianni Versace.

I'm slouched down low in the back seat as I have the taxi drive me around. My instructions are deliberately vague. I deliver them with a wave of one limp hand.

Take me to Risca.

To Rogerstone.

To anywhere.

All of it is just an alibi of sorts; a decoy or an alibi to convince him that he didn't just have that guy from them

Manic Street Preachers in the back of his cab because that boy in the bus station went and spotted me. Went and spoilt it all.

Yeah, great, climb into a cab to create an alibi. An inspired idea, that one.

No but, see, so long as I stick rigidly to some new story that I spin, delivering it flatly in order to avoid verbalising the non sequiturs that are currently dancing through my mind and therefore to avoid any future weirdness, it'll all be all right. They'll not find me.

Because even though I'm not sure how long it is since I left London – it could be two days, it could be a week – I do know that I don't want to go back there. I cannot be seen. I won't let it happen. Because after today I don't want to go back anywhere. Not to London, not to Cardiff. Not to hospital, not to 'home'.

Not to the band.

Not to 'Richey Manic'.

Not to my old life.

No.

Never again.

*

You wanted Kylie.

You wanted Kylie for the album, for a song, for your song. 'Little Baby Nothing'.

You wanted Kylie in order to fuck off the indie elite and the silly little rockist snobs.

You wanted Kylie but you were told she was 'unavailable', told she was 'contractually tied to PWL', which means she was never even approached, or Sony didn't want to stump up the money to bribe her to sing with a band she'd probably never heard of.

You wanted Kylie but you were told in no uncertain terms to go back to the drawing board. So you do – you go back to the drawing board and you run through some names. Wendy James? Too past it. Patsy Kensit? Too tacky. Scouse Sonia? Too . . . no, basically. Not for us.

Not for the Manics.

Then you remember Traci Lords and it all makes sense. Traci Lords, the girl who nearly brought down the American adult-film industry. The girl who took hundreds of cocks up every hole on celluloid before revealing herself to be fourteen at the time of her first porno roles. Traci Lords, all things to all women: the ultimate modern icon, of both victimhood and empowerment. The girl for whom lines like 'your lack of ego offends male mentality' *and* 'your beauty and virginity used like toys' *could have been written.*

You write a long heartfelt letter. You tell her what the song is about and why you admire her. You tell her you've never seen one of her films, but you've read the press cuttings. You even tell her about your first experience of pornography, age ten in Paul Winters' house, and how it made you feel nauseous.

You tell her that it doesn't matter if she can't sing because you can't play guitar either.

Then you pass it on to your people, who pass it on to her people and the next thing you know she's in London, in the crowd for your end-of-year show, then in the studio with James the very next day.

*

Of course he wants to talk. About the weather, himself and the bloody rugby, a game I know so little about it's laughable. I know that there is rugby union and rugby league, and I know that rugby players regularly get cauliflower ears and sometimes their opponents try to pull their knackers off, but other than that – nothing. Which makes it all the more strange because that is what everyone seems to want to talk to me about these days.

Talking about the weather and sport though evokes a sense of false camaraderie within the cabbie. But I'm stumped when he starts talking tactics and asking questions about who should play where, so I grunt and cough and evade his questions to such an obvious extent that he is eventually forced to stop talking and instead turns on the radio to fill the awkward silence that now sits between us.

I feel bad, but not *that* bad.

*

That Nirvana song is everywhere. Everywhere. It has followed you for the past three months. On the radio, on the tour bus, on MTV, in record shops and before and after every show you play, the provincial DJs cranking it out as the kids go nuts to that guitar riff in their ripped jeans, their lank unwashed hair flailing just like the new favourite singer's. It's a great pop song and for the critics and dusty custodians of the hallowed halls of rock there is a new entrant into the pantheon, but you can't help wonder where this is all going.

He seems like an odd guy to be the biggest rock star in the world, Kurt Cobain. He seems funny and playful but troubled too. A typical broken-home small-town boy.

Every interview he gives is dripping in sarcasm and disdain for the schematic he is now a part of. The Business. You and Nick actually enjoy giving interviews – it's part of the reason you're in this bloody band in the first place – but Nirvana don't seem to want it. It's hard to tell what they want.

Watching him play is interesting too: offstage he's even smaller and frailer than you are, a bag of bones and an unshaven face hiding behind a dirt-blond fringe. But onstage, plugged in, he becomes the music, his frame thrown about by the volume as if the electricity is surging not through his Strat, but through him. In contrast his beanpole bassist is unfeasibly lanky. Taller than Wire, even.

And all across the globe the process of emulation is now in full swing.

If the papers are to be believed apathy is in – they're calling it slacker, or 'Generation X' after the Coupland novel – but you resolutely fail to hear anything apathetic in Kurt's strangulated howl. There's nothing lazy about playing two hundred shows a year. Apathy is settling for second best. Apathy is never having a go.

He's a star – so why does instinct tell you no good can come of this?

The guy looks doomed, basically. Like he's heading towards disappointment or much, much worse. How can this song be topped? Nothing this huge can be sustained and already his best moment has passed; his band's career has peaked.

Their zenith is behind them.

*

For the past four weeks a novelty Swedish Europop act called Rednex has been number one with a techno-country version of the old American line-dancing song 'Cotton-Eye Joe'. Everywhere I've been I've heard the same repetitive beats, sampled fiddle and hysterical chorus.

It is the type of song that you hear in your head during a fever, on an endless loop. Maybe you're on your death-bed, or perhaps you've contracted something exotic. You can't eat or sleep or take water. All you can do is lie back and wait for it to end. And while you lie there, all you can hear is 'Cotton-Eye Joe'. It is also the song that knocked East 17's 'Stay Another Day' off the top spot.

I liked that song a lot. I admire East 17 and can't help but think that our bands have something in common, mainly because we're both publicly derided for the stratum of class we were born into. Because we're underdogs and derivatives of other things that have gone before. Because we don't give a fuck. We never expected to get this far in the first place.

But according to the radio that the taxi driver has turned up way too loud, it's all over for the Rednex. *They* have been toppled by French-Canadian knee-trembler Celine Dion – a whole other kettle of crud.

These are the records the British public like to buy today. The musical Big Macs – here today, burped out tomorrow. Rednex. Pato Banton. Baby D.

These are the artists they deem most worthy of their attention – or, more importantly, their money. Because purchase power is everything now. We vote with our credit cards. Democracy rules the art form; products are dictated to by the whims, demands and tastes of the mindless majority.

Our last single – a single promoted by a piece-of-shit, clichéd-riddled video that we were all too tired and jaded to even bother questioning – went in at Number 25.

Like Kurt's band, it's clearly over for us too.

*

The studio is tiny. Inside they herd the small crowd of teenagers like cattle.

1992 begins with your debut appearance on that staple of BBC scheduling and the British television institution that everyone loves to hate, Top of the Pops.

The biggest surprise is that the entire afternoon is a thoroughly underwhelming affair and not half as much as fun as live TV, or for that matter, children's television. Though a shirtless and ripped-looking James sings live, the rest of you mime and feel like complete frauds, not because it's uncool to mime – you couldn't care less – but because the song sounds so muted, so flat.

They make you run through it three times. The first time all you can think is, look at me, I'm on Top of the Pops. *The second time you concentrate on jumping about, but it feels contrived and the music is just too damn quiet to get properly into it, even when Nick drops to his knees and licks James's strings. On the third occasion, when the damp-squib low-budget onstage pyrotechnics go off, you're already thinking about television's power to distort the truth. You're thinking about the hundreds of episodes of this show that you watched as a kid, and how back in James's bedroom in those late-night discussions you all agreed that* Top of the Pops *was definitely the pinnacle.*

But now you're here you feel let down. You feel like you've seen too much. You think about Dorothy and the journey down that yellow brick road to the Emerald City and how there's no magic and there's no wizard; how it's all a smokescreen, an illusion. Because you've seen behind the curtain and it's crap there too. You think about how your innocence was shattered way back when. At twenty-five you feel stupid for even feeling this way, but you know you'll never be able to trust the telly again.

But still. Three days later when you all gather round

to watch it, it's hard to remove the smile from your face. When all is said and done, it is Top of the Pops, and that tiny fragment of you that is still a child glows with pride.

*

I'm beyond caring what the cab driver thinks of me, so I have a little lie down in the back of his car. But the seats smell of stale smoke, a burnt peppery smell, and I imagine all the arses that must have sat there over the years. Fat arses, drunk arses.

I sit up again, ask if I can smoke, light one up, offer him one, pass it to him when he says yes, then sit smoking in silence as we drive down unfamiliar roads.

'Maybe just a bit further,' I say.

*

February. You're back in London for tour rehearsals and they put you up in the Columbia Hotel on the Bayswater Road.

— All our bands stay there, says the girl from Sony. It's kind of a tradition. Plus they give us extraordinarily cheap rates.

Nick and Sean have gone home to Wales. Nick is back with Rachel and Sean is deep in domestic bliss with Rhian. Years those two have been together. Years. Though he never says as much, you know that Sean needs that other life to go back to, away from this. Nick too. He freely admits it. He even said so in a Sounds *interview.*

— I'm happiest when I'm back at home on the sofa at my mum and dad's with the dogs.

So it is up to you and James to keep the party flame alive, but even then you're opposites. James likes long hard drinking sessions. Beer, mainly. He's a pub-crawl kind of guy, but not a brawling kind of guy – not offstage, anyway. A sensitive guy with muscles, he's a series of contradictions, is James. Always has been.

You, though. You choose to go it alone with your books and a bottle of something low-calorie.

Up in your room, getting drunk in the half-light.

Sometimes you have company, but you're often relieved when they leave. Because you're never happier than when you're alone, avoiding the confusion of sex, avoiding declarations of undying love.

Up here in your room.

Drunk in the half-light.

With your books and your pens and your writing.

You write poems and letters to girls. You write songs. You stare at the walls to pass the time.

You order more mixer from room service, replace the receiver then pick it up again and dial.

— Hello. Blackwood 261753.

You love the way she answers the phone the old way. Her voice takes you back there in an instant. Back home. The smell of the house. Snoopy in his basket. Dad pottering about in the back garden. The possibility of rain.

You take a sip of your drink.

— Hi, Mum, it's me.

— Hi, Richard. How's it going, love?

*You also love that unbridled sense of enthusiasm.
Enthusiasm for everything. Always seeing the good in
everything, in everyone. The endless possibility of the
positive. You wish you could feel that way. Or even if
you couldn't, you wish you could fake it. But you know
you're far too selfish for that.*

— Great.

— *Me and your dad saw you on the telly last week. We
stayed up to watch it.*

— What did you think?

— *Well, we thought the programme was awful, but
you boys were great, just great.*

— Thanks, Mum.

— *My son – a pop star on the telly.*

— Well, we're not quite there yet, Mum . . .

— *As long as you don't forget your mum and dad
when you're rich and famous. Where are you now then,
love?*

— In London.

— *At Askew Road?*

— No, we don't stay there any more, Mum. I'm in a
hotel.

— *Lovely. Do you have to pay for that?*

— No, the record company pays for it.

— *And you don't have to pay them back?*

— No, it's free.

— *Brilliant. We're very proud of you, you know.
What's this hotel like, then?*

*Muffled voices in the background, then your mum
again, quieter.*

— No, he's in London. In a hotel. Sorry love, it's your dad. He wants a—

— Hi, son.

— Hi, Dad. How are you?

— Can't complain. We saw you on the telly, you know.

— Yes, Mum said. What did you think?

— Good, very good. Didn't think much of that tit Terry Christian, though. Where did they get him from?

— From Manchester, I think.

— They should have bloomin' left him there. I could do a better job than he could.

You smile into the phone.

— Anyway, save your news. I'll get it from your mother. I'll put her back on. Nice to hear from you, son. Say hi to the boys, will you?

— I will, Dad, you take care.

Mum comes back on the line.

— I'll not keep you, Richard. I know these hotels charge a fortune for phone calls.

— It's all right, Mum. The record company pays for that too.

— Well, still. So when are you next on telly?

— I'm not sure. But we're going on Radio 1 this week to promote the tour.

— That's exciting. Be sure to let me know when, so I can record it for your dad if he's not in. When's the album out, then?

— Next month, Mum. The 10th. I'll make sure the label send some copies to you.

— No need for that, love. Me and your dad have

already been into town and ordered copies from HMV.
One each, one for your sister, one for your gran and a
spare copy, just to have, like. Oh, I've just remembered,
I saw your friend Keith Wotsit when I was down
there.

— Keith from junior school? Keith Pisspants?

— That's the one. He's a solicitor in Pontypridd now,
you know. You should have seen the car he was driving!
It must have cost him a bomb. I always thought he was a
bit touched, that one. I still picture him crying when they
made him take off his sandals in the swimming pool at
your birthday party. Remember that? It just goes to show,
doesn't it?

— I suppose it does.

— Jean next door said he's getting married. To another
solicitor, apparently. Anyway, listen to me rabbiting on.
You better get going, love.

— OK, Mum. I'll call you next week. I'm not sure
when because we're away but I'll give you a bell. Give
Snoops a hug from me.

— I will, love. You look after yourself. Love to the
boys.

— Bye, Mum.

— Bye, Rich.

And then you're alone again. Alone and teary, the
bottle empty.

A knock on the door rouses you. You wipe your eyes.
The mixer has finally arrived.

*

215

When I see a sign to Blackwood I have the taxi driver turn off at the next exit and drive me there, but then on the edge of town I have a silent freak-out and change my mind.

I can't do it. I can't go into Blackwood. In light of what has happened and what is still to come it is as painful and insane as it is pointless.

What are you doing?

I don't know. Let's just keep driving.

He recognises you, you know.

No, he doesn't. He just thinks I'm weird.

See, that's the thing: you're not weird at all. You're actually painfully boring and meaningless. You're really unremarkable. And you're just delaying things again.

I know, I know. But now is not the time. I'm freaking out right now. If I could die this very second I would do it. Oh, Christ, what the fuck have I done?

You've not done anything other than run away from your problems, as usual.

Don't, please. Not now. You're drawing attention to me. See: the driver is looking at me strangely in his mirror.

Not my problem.

'You have got the money for the fare, haven't you?'

The driver's question interrupts this infernal internal dialogue and pulls me back into the moment.

'Yes.'

'It's just we've been driving for half an hour now and I get quite a few what we call runners, you know. I'm not saying *you* are one . . .'

Yes, you are. Cheeky cunt.

'. . . it's just that, you know, I'm actually self-employed
. . . and . . .'

And what?

'It's all right, I understand. How much are we up to
now?'

'We're just over thirty quid.'

I reach into my pocket, pull out the roll that has been
warmed by my thigh and peel off two twenties.

'Here you go.'

The driver's eyes flicker towards the mirror again. I
know he thinks something is up. You can tell, you can see
it in his gaze, but the customer is always right and he's
seen my roll of notes, and he's human and he has a mortgage to pay, so he signals then pulls out into the fast lane.

*

*Preceded by two Top 20 singles in four months, on 10
February 1992 the Manic Street Preachers release their
debut album. At eighteen tracks in length and clocking in
at seventy-three minutes it is considered by most critics a
grossly ambitious, egotistical and deeply flawed piece of
work. Most reviewers note that it could easily be trimmed
by half. Most also comment that it won't sell anything like
the sixteen million copies that the band had promised.
Worst of all, most reviews neither love nor hate it; they
almost all hedge their bets: it is a failure, they say, but not
quite the bold career suicide those daft Taffies threatened
it would be. It has its moments.*

You defend the work by saying it is what it is: twenty-

*five years of life in the provinces condensed into one com-
plete package, and that flawed is always more beautiful
than perfection, ambition more potent than apathy. Anger
more revolutionary than despair.*

*To mark this transition – partly to absolve your family
of any guilt or embarrassment and partly to distance yourself from the 'Richey Manic' moniker that the press have
tagged you with – you change your name to Richey James.*

It says so on the sleeve.

*

It's times like these that I am envious of the relationships
that Nick, James and Sean have outside of the band.

If I was like them I'd stop this nonsense right now and
head home with my tail between my legs. I'd buy flowers.
I'd apologise.

I'd take a hot bath.

Yet somehow I've never been able to commit to a long-
term relationship, let alone a marriage. Attaching yourself
limpet-like to someone for life is an alien concept to me,
one destined to fail. I suppose it's ultimately because I am
selfish and jealous and narcissistic and I seek perfection in
places where it can never be found.

I don't know. Maybe I've just not met the right person.

*'The right person'. There is no 'right person'. You're
talking like someone who believes in fate and destiny and
all those other amorphous concepts.*

Who are you to say the right person isn't out there
somewhere?

Right. So *you're just going to sit there waiting for this right person to come along and show themselves, are you? Pathetic.*

No. I'm just trying to understand why it hasn't happened. Why I haven't found love.

Because you know fine well that love is just another philosophical construct – one based on sexual desire, insecurity and a deep-rooted fear of lifelong loneliness. Therefore to fall 'in love' is denying what you already know. And in denying what you know, you are somehow selling yourself out. And besides, there is no 'right person' out there for you. You're too boring and jealous and self-obsessed.

Maybe you're right.

Your ideal woman would be a mirror. A mirror with a brain, but no mouth.

That's not true. I've always got on with women better than men.

You just can't commit to one.

Right.

Because you're fucked in the head.

Right.

And you're talking to yourself right now.

Right.

*

Day two of the tour and you're curled up in the back seat of another splitter van, your fake leopard-print coat doubling up as a blanket, a beanie hat pulled down low.

Last night's set still ringing in your ears.

February, March, April and May are already mapped for you and though you should be daunted by the thought of some fifty or sixty shows – including your first proper international dates – you take a strange sense of comfort from the laminated spiral-bound itinerary that you are each handed. You know where you are going to be every day. There is a purpose and structure to your movements.

There are people to drive you and people to fly you. People to wake you in the morning, people to help you to bed at night. People to tune your guitar. And there is a smattering of people there to lavish praise upon you each night, just for showing up.

All you have to do is give yourself to the motional tide. Let yourself be guided from city to city, hotel to hotel, and you will be fine.

Because these are the good times.

You keep reminding yourself of this every day: these are the good times. You'd say it was the best job in the world if you had ever had one to compare it to.

Meanwhile out in the real world away from the steel bubble of the tour van and the silent hum of the British m-way things are happening. You read about it all in your copy of The Times *while sucking on a sugar-free Ribena:*

BOUTROS BOUTROS-GHALI
NEW UN SECRETARY-GENERAL.

EU FOUNDED; MAASTRICHT TREATY
SIGNING THIS WEEK.

NIRVANA NO.1 – COBAIN TO WED
ROCKER FIANCÉE LOVE.

And you? You are driving to Warrington to perform in a nightclub called Legends. Ticket price £5. Doors open at 8 p.m. Capacity 120.

The van heads north.

*

'Am I?'

'Are you what?'

The cab driver eyes me suspiciously in his mirror again.

'Sorry. Nothing. I was just thinking out loud.'

You're not doing a very good job of disappearing, are you?

Shut up.

We're driving through a small town that I don't recognise. It's more of a large village or suburb and it looks like every other large village or suburb in South Wales: one long high street featuring a pub, chip shop, Spar, estate agent, off-licence, newsagent, pub, pub. Everything the modern human being needs, all under one gloomy sky. It could be Sebastopol or Llanhilleth or it could be the edge of Cwmbran. It could be any number of places around these parts.

'Wait – can you pull over for a minute?'

The driver sighs, then pulls over. I think I've just decided something.

'It's OK, I'm not going to do a runner. Here, have some more money.'

I pass him a £20 note, pull my hood up, climb out of the car with my joints creaking and then walk back down the street to the off-licence where I buy a ten-glass bottle of Smirnoff and forty fags, gum and a Mars bar. I pay and am just about to leave when I turn back and buy another packet of fags for the taxi driver.

I put the bits in my pockets and carry the bottle by the neck. It feels good in my hand.

It'll be the first drink I've had in months and I know that the real beginning of the end starts here, right now.

Or maybe it started when I left the Embassy Hotel. Or maybe outside that hotel in Germany. Or maybe when I got clean. Or maybe when I first went to hospital. Or maybe when I joined the band. Or maybe when I first cut my arms. Or maybe when I first had a drink. Or maybe when I left home.

Or maybe when I first opened my eyes.

Or maybe when I left the womb.

Who cares about all that. It's party time.

No, it's not party time. This drink is for you. This drink is to drown you. I'm going to kill you.

How many times do you need telling? You can't kill me. I am you.

Then I'll die trying, prick.

I climb back into the taxi and pass the driver a packet of Benson.

Then we're off again.

*

Recoupable advances . . . mid-week chart positions . . . micro-marketing strategies . . . multi-formatting . . . buy-ons, residuals and forthcoming AGMs . . .

You're in a meeting with the band accountant.

Three of you are wearing sunglasses as he bombards you with music-business terminology and jargon, all of which you understand, but really don't care to think about. You're having too much fun to get distracted by that.

You're in Cardiff for a show tonight and all you want to do is go home and see your families, take a shower, eat some food. Curl up in front of the TV with Snoopy.

It might be your only chance to as the next four months will be spent out on the road, but you can't because you need to see the accountant instead. 'It is imperative we meet,' read the fax.

Yesterday the album officially debuted at No. 13. Creditable enough, is the word that comes down the record-company line, but nowhere near good enough to justify the expenditure. Eight months into your record deal and already it looks like your days are numbered. Eight months. Less time than it takes to make a baby.

So here you are in a day room in the Barcelo, sitting on the beds, the chair and the floor, you hiding your eyes, your necklace between your teeth, your forefinger scratching at the cuticle of your thumb as you wish you had got more sleep last night.

— Unfortunately your projected sales of sixteen million don't quite tally with the label's predictions, says the accountant with the faintest of smirks. So the next choice

of single releases will be crucial. We're also going to have to rely on high merchandise sales to offset the expenditure of a four-month tour. Each show is costing us about a grand at the moment. What I mean is: the label is not prepared to spend indefinitely. Not without hits, anyway.

But you're already zoning out, wondering if there'll be any familiar faces there tonight. People from the past. People you don't want to see. People claiming to be old friends.

You zone back in again.

— Singles are just loss leaders. So we need to get you straight back in the studio as soon as this tour ends and start work on album number two. I'm assuming you've already been working on new material?

— Oh yeah, says James. We've got tonnes of new songs. And our independent market research tells us that 63.4% are bona fide Top 10 hits.

Sean smiles at this, then clears his throat. Nick crosses then uncrosses his legs.

And you. You're wondering about what to wear, what time to start drinking and whether your band have already peaked.

No. 13, you think. Typical. Unlucky for some, but some-how perfect for the notorious Manic Street Preachers.

*

Of course I've thought about it.

Disappearance is not something you commit to without any forethought whatsoever, I just hadn't quite planned it this way. In fact, I hadn't planned it at all. It seems to have just happened.

Maybe if I had been able to get a decent night's sleep just once during these past few weeks I wouldn't be here, lost in a land that is so painfully familiar to me, and I would be back where I am expected to be: talking about myself into a Midwest microphone.

Of course I've thought about it.

Didn't I always tell interviewers that my ambition was to reject society and go and live in a concrete bunker just like J. D. Salinger? Hadn't I made a point of reading books about the concept of disappearance – Virilio and the like? And hadn't I always joked about 'doing a Reggie Perrin' – the false paper trail, the pile of clothes on the beach. Or was that Nick who used to say that? The way our thoughts used to intertwine, it is so hard to remember now.

Nicky Jones. Part brother, part unconsummated lover, but mainly best friend and fashion-crime partner. I'm sure he'll cope. He has the support network and the will to cope with anything. What with his endless ailments he might make out like he's soft, but he's a tough bastard really. He's the only person I know who has simultaneously offered one hundred thousand people out for a fight.

Because he's iron-willed and mentally tough. So is James. And Sean. That's why they are where they are right now and I am here – in the back of the taxi to nowhere about to unwrap this beautiful glass bottle, discard the paper it is wrapped in, unscrew the metal cap and take a heroic swig.

Unlike any other time before this, however, I can say with great confidence that this will be the last drink I will ever take.

*

How much bad poetry does one need in one's life?

Nicky and you joke about how you could put out a whole collection of work after each tour, the amount of stuff you are handed from fans.

While record sales might not be huge, a discernible hardcore fan base is swelling daily. A fan base of Nicky and Richey clones.

— Every day is like Valentine's Day, he beams.

You sit in his hotel room one night in Nottingham when you've had enough of the usual aftershow on-tour shenanigans and sift through the latest batch that your smiling and ebullient publicist Caffy brings you by the armful, dividing the poetry and fan mail into piles that you then categorise and grade by both content and presentation.

There's the 'Little Baby Nothings', who form the bulk of the contributions: teenage boys and girls who offer their unconditional love for you, undying hatred for themselves, and cover the pages in glitter and cheap perfume. They're an articulate bunch.

There are the 'Triple XXXers', who send you their explicit sexual fantasies accompanied with anatomically accurate illustrations and/or Polaroid pictures of themselves. Sean is the subject of a surprising number of these dark scenarios actually and as the most reticent and dead-pan member of the band – not to mention unavailable – he is quite disturbed by the content of these letters, especially the one that has his head superimposed on the body of Kate Moss.

There are the 'Geeks & Freaks', who write to ask inane questions about things like set-lists and record catalogue numbers. They're collectors, mainly. Completists.

Then there's the 'Green Crayola' pile, also known as the 'Blunt Instrumentalists'. Fans whose handwriting erratically lurches from side to side. Fans whose letters occasionally come with the stamp of an institution on the envelope. Letters written in red ink that doesn't look like ink, but instead something altogether more sinister. Letters that set alarm bells ringing. Letters that make you consider hiring bodyguards for the first time.

These form the smallest pile and are, increasingly, almost all addressed to you and you only.

— The fans for whom the Cult of Richey is just not quite dark enough, Nicky drily observes. Look what you started. Scary. Bloody scary.

And though you're flippant about it all – James to the point of sarcasm and disgust at some fans' willingness to practically degrade themselves for you, while a soon-to-be-married Nicky is bemused – not one of you would take the piss out of these troubled young souls who wait for hours at the stage door each night, who buy you flowers and chocolates and books you might have once said that you'd like to read, who sport still-healing scars in the same places on their bodies as you do on yours; you *and your management and even the guys in the crew all implicitly know that these young men and women are not to be laughed at.*

Because in amongst all the sub-Sylvia Plath poems, the copycat haircuts and the queries about how much the 'Feminine Is Beautiful' seven inch is worth, you recognise something.

You recognise the fact that it is these kids who buy your records and T-shirts and travel across continents to see you jump about onstage for an hour. It is they who allow you the luxury of this lifestyle and provide occasional respite from the loneliness of it all.

But more importantly than any of that, within them you recognise versions of yourselves. Your young, hopeful, naive, beautiful selves.

You only hope you're not going to let them down too dramatically, as all your heroes let you down.

*

My problem – one of them, anyway – is I have nothing left to say. Nothing new. Nothing that hasn't been said before. I have no original thoughts left in me – only recycled quotes, like the one from Kierkegaard that said something about how people can be divided into 'those who write and those who do not write', and that those who write represent despair, while those who read disapprove of it because they believe that they have a superior wisdom – yet if they themselves could write, they would write the very same thing. In other words: we are all equally despairing, yet some of us have the opportunity to achieve success through our despair.

This is how I have always viewed the limited success that my band has enjoyed. Not by monetary success, nor even by the inconsistent chart positions or critical acclaim, but through the ability to connect with certain people, the idea that we have taken what fuelled us when we were younger – despair in its various manifestations – and put it to positive use. And also the idea that if we, four flawed individuals whose strength is in our four-cornered creative configuration, can do it, then they have a chance too. Anyone does. Despair has always been our muse, our currency.

But what does one do when one despairs at despair itself? When it becomes so intolerable that any sense of creativity is deadened then destroyed beyond all repair?

It was bound to happen, I suppose. You can only exist on despair so long before it eats you alive and reminds you what it is really about.

Payback time.

Trading in despair is like – if you'll allow me the clumsy and painfully obvious rock 'n' roll allegory for just one moment – Robert Johnson selling his soul to the devil. He'll give you songs. He'll give you success. But when he comes knocking at your door for payment you cannot ignore him.

*

War mode.
A few shows in and you're in war mode.

Attack, attack, attack!

Show no mercy, take no prisoners.

Kill on sight.

Maybe it's the perceived failure of the album that has given you all a boost. The notion that you have even more to prove than ever. Or maybe it's the strange mixture of adoration and hatred that flavours the air each night. There's two factions to the crowd – the loyal hard core and the curious cynics who've seen it all before. They still want to shout abuse, throw plastic cups and lit cigarettes. They're the ones who sneer at Melody Maker, *but believe everything they read about you in there, all the same. But the tide is turning and the cynics are being replaced by panda-eyed kids.*

These shows become the most exciting you have played as a band.

The threat of violence follows you everywhere, so much so that the masochist in you begins to enjoy it. Wire is the same. He invites it. He wants to provoke a reaction as a means to get into people's heads. And James too – though for very different reasons. He just wants revenge on the big bastards who bullied him for being a skinny kid with a lazy eye, or the thugs who broke his jaw. Physical retribution.

You joke that you are the mistreated dogs that ran away and formed a pack. And now you're back, feral and hungry for blood.

Though you don't speak to them much, the support band, a bunch of unwashed Geordie drug-guzzlers called The Wildhearts, are good people to have around. Their lives are far more chaotic than yours and they ingest more narcotics than you ever could. You get drunk just looking at them. They're like something out of Viz.

More often than not though, trouble, when it comes, is not from the crowd but the venue's security guards, who seem more concerned with working off a bit of their latent aggression than protecting either band or crowd. The Steroids Boys, you call them. The ones who have been cursed with over-active pituitary glands.

All they know about your band is that you have big mouths and you are 'trouble'.

But then you see their posture and facial expressions change when you lot roll into the venue.

'Is this them? *These feckless drips?'*

Silent Sean, with his long lady's hair and baby face.

All five feet five of James.

Gangling Nicky griping and moaning about his bad stomach, bad knees, stiff back and the lack of decent shower facilities.

And you.

You with your hair getting bigger and blacker by the day, your foundation getting whiter, your mascara thicker, your frame slighter.

Nine stone straight in your stocking feet. An apparition who stalks the shadows of the stage. 'Johnny Thunders on the Rosemary Conley diet' is how James describes it.

That's the look you're cultivating, anyway.

*

And now there's no escape. I've read all the books, watched the films, seen the world, fucked the girls, spent the money, experienced the sensations, ridden the roller-coaster of emotions and at the end of it I feel blank. I've heard the echo of thousands of people screaming my name and it has left me feeling more empty and more worthless than ever. I've seen the disappointment on their faces when they meet me in person. No one wants to be let down by their heroes, but that's what I am. A let-down, a fake. Because the version of me they think they know is exactly that: a version. It is not the me that screams inside. Somewhere back there I made myself into Richey Manic and in that first vain rush of fame and success forgot about Richard Edwards. I got greedy. I forgot about the real me. Let him whither in the shadows, away from the flicker of the nightly strobe lights.

And now there is nowhere else to go but down.

So let's drink to that, you and I. Let us not mourn. Let us instead celebrate this slow phthisis.

One for the road?

One for the road.

*

Nicky wants to throttle you when he sees you having a spliff with a couple of the crew.

— What the fuck's that, Edwards?

— Chill out, maa-aaa-aan, you chuckle. Haven't you heard? It's peace and love for the Manic Street Preachers from here on in.

He shakes his head.

— If it was smack I wouldn't mind. At least some great songs were written about smack. But weed? It'll rot your brain. Turn you into a Levellers fan.

— Here, have a bit, you say, waving the big biffter in his face.

— No chance. It'll be the undoing of you, mark my words. And if you even think about growing a beard you're out the band.

He walks away shaking his head.

— Fascist wanker, you shout after him.

— Hippy cunt, he replies without looking back.

*

And then I'm drunk and I'm talking to another one of *them*. One of the fans. I've met hundreds just like him these past few years. Undernourished, over-serious and hanging on my every word. Such devotion to or expectation from me can come to no good, but they never seem to believe me when I tell them this.

'There is no choice,' I'm saying – almost pleading. 'I've tried all the options: fame, money, girls, books, travel. All of them leave me feeling even more spent than before, and now I feel foolish for even trying.'

'There's no harm in trying, though,' says the fan. 'Anyway, think of everyone you've influenced or inspired. There are loads of kids out there who've been turned onto new music, new books and new ideas because of you and your band.'

'You should never trust people in bands,' I say, my head lolling a little and the words rolling around my mouth like marbles in a sink. 'You should never trust anyone, but especially people in bands. And yourself. You should never trust yourself, either. I mean, how can you know what you're going to do? I certainly don't. I never know what I'm doing. I have no idea what I'm doing right now.'

'You're lost, that's all,' says the fan.

I close my eyes and sigh deeply.

'I'm not lost,' I say, curtly, then take an arrogant swig, my vanity pathetically propined. 'I'm hiding. I'm running away. Lost is not knowing where you are. I know precisely where I am: a living hell. It's what to do about it that's the problem.'

'Self-destruction isn't the key.'

'You think I don't know that already?' I hear myself snapping sarcastically from behind my closed eyelids. 'You think I haven't heard this from the band, my family, my friends, everyone at management and the label, the journalists, from the doctors and psychologists and counsellors and sponsors? And the letters too. All those letters that people send me telling me that they've cut their arms so that they can share my pain.'

'But, Richey,' says the fan. 'Maybe some of these people can identify with you. Or maybe some of them just want to help you?'

'Well, they should think about their own lives. They should look out for those they know and love, rather than some idiot who can't even play his guitar and steals all his best lyrics from writers far better than he is.'

'You're tired, that's all. You've pushed yourself too far. You just need a holiday, that's all.'

Then I hear a voice singing. Oh God, it's my voice. Am I actually singing in public?

'*Didn't we have a lovely time / The day we went to Bangor . . .*'

'Yes, I'm quite beyond help now,' I say, my voice slurring again. 'I mean, look at me. Just out of rehab and I'm drunk. My first drink in months . . . all that work undone. Hey, what is this place, anyway? Where have you brought me?'

Silence follows. You ask again.

'Well, what is this place? Where am I?'

You open your eyes and you are sitting in your car, back at the car park, back where the cab driver dropped you off. Darkness surrounds you. Darkness and silence. An empty bottle sits in your lap, your chest is tight, your breath short. You are scared. In the silence it feels as if you are in a coffin beneath the dirt. You are in a coffin and no one can hear you. They will never find you. You are buried too deep now. All resolutions are forgotten and the burden is back tenfold.

Then in the far, far distance you can see lights twinkling through the night. You stare at them, cling to them as a sign of life. An anchor. A sign that you are not dead yet.

Instead you switch on the radio but you no longer feel like singing.

*

There are seven letters about the band in this week's
NME. *Five in* Melody Maker. *Even the metal press are*
starting to cover you now. Kerrang!, Raw, *that lot. In*
fact, after overcoming their initial scepticism, it is these
publications who have given Generation Terrorists *the*
best reviews. But you all get the most fun out of reading
the Letters pages. The best missives come from those who
hate the band.

Dear NME,
    I had the great misfortune of going to see the
Manic Street Preachers last night in Sunderland and
can report that they were COMPLETELY SHIT.
You couldn't even hear Ritchie (sic). In fact,
I don't think he was even plugged in, which just
goes to prove that the daft sod can't play a note.
They should probably do us all a favour and
FUCK OFF BACK TO WALES AND DIE.
    PS – Their album is shit too.
Bobby Gillespie's Dealer
Darlington

*

And then all of a sudden an invisible force is grabbing at
me like a hand and pulling me back. My brain scrambles
and it takes a few seconds to process the information.
To recognise the softly spoken voice with the accent like
mine on the radio to register.

Dad.

'. . . obviously everyone in the family is concerned, and we just want to get in touch with him to know that he is OK. We've phoned all his friends and all the acquaintances that we can think of . . . nobody seems to be in touch with him at all. The lads in the band are all very concerned also.'

Dad.

'All I'd like to say is, Richey, if he's listening, please get in touch, just a phone call or a postcard just to let us know you're all right. If he needs time to be on his own, then that's OK with everybody, but if he does have a problem that we can help with, he'll have a strong support from his family and also from the band, Nick, James and Sean . . .'

Then cut to: news. A UN tribunal has charged twenty-one Bosnian-Serbian commanders with genocide and crimes against humanity. A rugby friendly between England and the Republic of Ireland at Landsdowne Road after a Combat 18-led riot. Sixty-four people burnt to cinders in a fire in a karaoke restaurant in Taiwan.

I start to sob uncontrollably. I sob until my face aches and my eyes hurt. My temples throb and my stomach flexes. I am ill, I am sick and I am all alone.

I sob so much that I move out of myself. I rise out of my body, out of the car, and I hover over the car park, looking back at myself from a distance, and I see myself bent double, head in hands, no longer sobbing any more but my back silently shuddering.

*

After reading a review in the Observer *and being given a copy by someone – a fan, maybe? – you devour* American Psycho *in about two days. And for those two days you become Patrick Bateman. You crawl through his mind and see the world through a curtain of blood, but mainly you think it is hilarious; molasses-black humour and a flawless satire on the whole Wall Street yuppie-excess era. Reading it, you find yourself laughing harder than you've laughed at anything in a long time. In fact, you can't remember when you last laughed. Perhaps it is his fascination with the banal that gets you, that you can relate to, that makes you see a little of him in you.*

You pass it on to Nicky, who in turn passes it to James and soon American Psycho *becomes the tour read of choice and the new favourite cultural cornerstone. A new entry in the Manic Street Preachers' pantheon of the elite.*

You find yourself quoting chunks of the text to each other, at first in jest, but soon it becomes the norm.

'I don't want to get you drunk, but that's a very fine Chardonnay you're not drinking.'

and:

'You'll have to excuse me, I have a lunch meeting with Cliff Huxtable at the Four Seasons in twenty minutes.'

and:

'I have to return some videotapes.'

*

It is not a nightmare and it is not a dream. This is very much happening.

Is it, though?

Yes. I think it is.

Can you be sure?

About what?

About anything.

I don't know how to answer that. I mean, I know I am talking to myself. I know that is real. But I also know you do not exist.

Yes, I do.

No, you don't. You're something – someone – I have conjured up.

Not true. I'm here of my own volition.

You're just a voice, that's all. A by-product.

A 'by-product'? I think I'm actually offended by that. A by-product of what, exactly?

I don't know. My own disintegration. Psychosis. Depression. Mental breakdown. Delusion. Hallucination. The withdrawal from the medicine.

I was here long before you stopped taking those pills and you know it.

I don't know. All I know is you won't shut the fuck up and give me a minute's peace to think.

How can I shut up when you keep having conversations with me? You just told me it was you in control here, not me. You created me.

Fine. Then I'll stop talking to you.

Please yourself. But you and I both know that's an impossible task. Don't we?

I said, don't we?
Don't we?

*

A few weeks in and chaos becomes the norm. It's actually very liberating.

A strange cocktail of fatigue, adrenaline, routine, illness, alcohol anxiety and corporate obligation conspires to keep the band on the edge at all times.

You begin to behave the way in which people expect you to behave. You become a cartoon version of yourselves; an eight-legged fuck machine programmed on terminal auto-destruct.

You enter your Sex Pistols phase. Your dumb Sid-Vicious-with-a-thesaurus phase.

You give them what you think they want.

And there is fun to be had, for a while.

Every day there is a new challenge. Flu, tonsillitis, hepatitis and herpes pass through the ranks. A combination of pills, pastilles and tinctures circulates continuously. You get your drinking down to a fine art, making sure you are at least a bit pissed for every waking minute after sundown.

Even Nicky falls with a slump and whimper from the wagon from time to time, as much out of boredom as anything. He misses his girlfriend and his slippers but he can't tell the world that. So instead he grabs the mic and he bellows the most non-PC thing he can think of, then breaks things. So does James. He breaks his guitars with more fury and invective than you have ever seen him muster. Stripped to the waist and smashing his guitars, you make sure to get out of his way. The murderous look in his eyes tells you to.

Your own attempts are pathetic in comparison. It takes ten minutes for you to meekly dismantle your black Telecaster, partly because you're a weakling and possibly because you do it with a sense of irony.

Or do you?

Out on the road it's hard to tell any more.

Either way, the others joke that it's the most noise you have ever got out of it.

This is the Manics reverting to type and reality increasingly becomes distorted.

More people stare and point when you stop at service stations or sit in the lobbies of regional radio stations. Others laugh as if you are invisible. As if somehow an extravagant haircut and face they might recognise suddenly make you impervious to criticism.

You find yourself in increasingly absurd situations: sitting at a Sony-bought table at an Irish music awards ceremony, pouring salt from a shaker on Wire who has passed out at your feet; vomiting in airport toilets in front of tut-tutting businessmen; spurning the advances of one of Right Said Fred backstage at Top of the Pops; getting another tattoo in Liverpool . . . or is it Bristol?; bruising your knees and knuckles after a fight with a bouncer; postcards to people with nothing but 'SOS' written on them and signed 'Patrick Bateman'; dancing to disco songs on sticky dance floors; sex in hotel rooms with kohl-rimmed girls, sometimes two at once; endless visa applications; more meetings with more marketing men; meetings with video directors touting their treatments, radio pluggers, your agent, your accountant, your lawyer, your managers.

Laughter. Incredulity. Long silences.

Last night's set ringing in your ears.

You forget to send birthday cards to people back home. You max out a credit card on books and clothes and shoes. You send flowers to your mother. You meet 2 Unlimited, Blur, Norman Whiteside, Black Francis, Ian Woosnam, some guy who may or may not be Daniel Day-Lewis.

You can't remember if you only imagined sending flowers to your mother, so you send more. You travel the length and breadth of Britain. Then you do it again. You stop eating. You stop caring. You come loose from your moorings.

You get pissed. You destroy everything in your way.

And then you go to Europe.

5

'The time is out of joint: O cursed spite,
That ever I was born to set it right!'

(*Hamlet*, 1. 5)

BORED OUT OF MY MIND

I'm sick and hungover and cold and hungry and guilty and alone and I'm almost 100% certain that I want to die.

You're not alone.

I just want to run and never stop but I don't have the energy.

Hearing Dad's voice made me realise that I am beyond repair. Completely, utterly and totally. I have to want to get better and the desire to live has gone. I can't just go back and say 'sorry' and then continue like this never happened. Not now. Not the way I'm feeling. I can't cope with the kid-gloves treatment any more. I don't think I could stand everyone tiptoeing around me – the silent disappointment and frustration in the boys' eyes. I refuse to be a freak show.

So that's it.

I'll take this car and I will use it as a weapon. I will drive and drive until I am far away from all that is familiar. I will drive and drive until the petrol runs out and on that very spot I will take decisive action. I'll just go.

You can't even say it, can you?

Say what?

You know what. Death. Departure. Dissolution. Demise. Extinction. Passing. Parting. Whatever you want to call it. Self-slaughter. Seppuku. Oblivion. Quietus. Curtains. And do you want to know why? Because you're still scared of the finality of it all. You're still clinging to a tiny fragment of your old, stupid, pathetic, worthless coward self.

I'm not.

You are.

No. I'm really not.

Show me.

Maybe I will.

I wipe the tears from my eyes, put on my seat belt, light a cigarette. I turn the key.

Nothing happens. Not so much as a judder, a cough or a cold morning splutter.

I try again.

Nothing. Absolutely nothing.

The silence of the static car is deafening.

It is a void and I am a cipher within that void.

A non-entity.

I am a useless, worthless, pathetic null.

The bloody battery is dead.

*

Boredom.

Boredom punctuated by bizarre incidents that in past times would have provided a talking point for weeks but are now part of the norm. Part of being a band. Part of this persistent motion; this continual state of borderline delirium.

You zip across Europe in nine blurred days, crossing invisible borders in darkness.

In Paris you sound like shit. Utter fucking shit.

In Brussels, gripped by an anxiety attack, you refuse to go onstage until you've vomited up every last drop of bitter bile that lines your stomach.

In Amsterdam you do what every British man does and wander the red-light district, agog at the clinical nature of the women in the windows, the ubiquitous waft of skunk weed hanging heavy.

In Germany, somewhere on the autobahn, a woman rams your bus before blocking two lanes of traffic just to get your autographs.

In Copenhagen a group of humourless anarchists try to entice you back to their squat in an old military compound to sell you a kilo of heroin.

In Sweden the girls really are as sexy as they say they are.

Then in the mismatch of the century you first open up for a guy who used to be in a band called Van der Graaf Generator and then later for a punk band whose name translates as The Dead Trousers. They remind you of the Toy Dolls or something. When James asks them if they're going to play 'Nellie the Elephant' that night, they say, in characteristically frosted Teutonic tones, 'You are mistaking us for the Toy Dolls, but in the spirit of international relations we shall learn and play this song for you, our English friends, provided you join us.'

You decline their kind offer and don't bother pointing out that you are, in fact, Welsh.

They tell you that it is cheaper to fly into Canada and then travel south of the border because for all their whistles and bells, the US wing of the label is much less inclined to squander money on an unknown entity like you lot. Some of them have barely heard of Wales, much less Hanoi Rocks. They're also inherently suspicious of anything that has been hyped to high heaven in the UK music press. They're smart; they've had their fingers burnt before. Dozens of bands better than yours have failed to make a dent in America – what makes you chumps any different?

They might have a point.

But you're still excited. It's America. America! For four modern culture-vultures who grew up hungry in the valleys, it's the dream. Just to be here feels like the start of something.

You fly in over Newfoundland, the clouds parting to reveal icy terrain as far as the eye can see. Flying is still new enough to you to make you feel humbled. From up here even the mountains look small, like tiny frosted patterns on a pavement.

All you can do is put your trust in the pilot and hope his wife didn't leave him this morning.

*

Then it's just a series of linear events that I seem to observe from a distant, detached position. I watch from afar as a twisted sense of organisation kicks in: you need to go from A to B to C to D.

And don't dilly-dally on the way.

A is the service station.

B is the phone box.

C is the taxi that picks me up outside it ten minutes later.

D is the bridge I cross for the final, final, final time. And so on. Z is anywhere: I no longer care where.

Are you sure about that?

I told you: all my discussion with you is over. You are, as they say, a dead man walking.

How exciting. So what does that make you?

*

In Toronto a TV crew interview you and the Wire playing miniature golf, of all things. Even here the questions remain the same: the hype, the punk revival, the scars on your arms. You're happy to kiss the arses of those who count in order to get ahead; happy to slag off your homeland. Why not? You feel little pride for Britain. Not when success in America is so much more important to you.

— The 1980s in Britain were so dead and empty yet the British media is so influential and important, you tell them. They're so obsessed with avant-garde and original music that anything outside of that is deemed worthless and impossibly boring. And that's the saddest thing about British culture; that's why it's so washed up.

You keep going.

— We're typical twentieth-century kids. Our attention-spans are limited, flicking through channels, radio stations, records, comic and books, just scribbling things down. We can't concentrate. That's why our lyrics are so confused.

Then you say something about Jesus being the greatest fake symbol the planet has ever known, that AIDS is the most significant cultural event of your era, then Nicky chips in that he's glad Freddie Mercury snuffed it.

Off camera your North American TV plugger goes pale and wonders what he has got himself into.

*

The car is gone. It has slipped away for the final – *final*, *final* – time. And so has all its contents: my tapes, the half-eaten chocolate bars and rotten apples, my road maps, the odd book or two, my photos. I've left it all behind in the immobile car.

Objects in the rear-view mirror may appear closer than they are.

All I have with me as I sit in the passenger seat of the taxi with my hangover pressing against the window and my breath forming and dissolving on the cold glass is my hat, water, cigarettes, lighter and money.

I am resolute in the decision that has been made for me, and as if by way of signalling this breakthrough, the weather seems to have adjusted itself accordingly.

There's no muted fog or low-lying clouds cloaking the bridge today, no swirls of vapour drifting around its quivering suspension cables – no solitary droplets falling down into the dank darkness below.

Today the air is clear and the view is stunning in both directions. The Severn is still in some places and shimmering in others, as if its surface is being broken by shoals of tiny fish.

But that is all quickly behind me as I head inland, back into Wales, feeling strangely indifferent to the prospect that I will never return to England again and that, like it or not, I am now in the laps of my forefathers and, to some extent, my fate shall be their encumbrance. I'm a pox on every person I meet, anyway; and every town, city or country I visit too. I might as well go back to where it all started.

Complete the circle.

*

You've not even played a single note on American soil and already you've made major concessions over the album. By the time you fly into JFK on a red-eye flight from Montreal, the changes are done and dusted. Songs are dropped because their titles are deemed too depressing ('Spectators of Suicide') or too profane ('Damn Dog'), the spoken-word interludes that Nick's brother Patrick – who flies in from Illinois, where he has been living – recorded are notable by their absence, as are the literary quotes that you selected to accompany each song on the sleeve.

This is what upsets you the most – the notion that literature will work against the band. No one from the US label actually says it outright because you don't meet any of the spineless fuckers until it's too late. But the message that trickles down from LA is: intellectuality doesn't sell.

And inside, a small part of you dies.

And finally, in a move whose irony is bile-bitter, they even remove your most tempered and calculated song, the song that is your most blatant and unashamed attempt at a US rock radio hit, 'Motorcycle Emptiness', from the record. They deem it 'too middle of the road'.

So everything you suspected about America turns out to be true. Everything has a price. Everything is for sale. Everyone can be bought. Wealth is all that matters.

Looking out from your hotel-room window across the Manhattan skyline it becomes obvious that the selling of your souls to Sony has barely even begun, and to conquer this country you'll all have to bend over and spread your cheeks to let The Man fuck you hard over and over and over again.

*

I'm thinking of all the people I have known.

I'm thinking of all the people I have known and all the people I have lost.

People taken by death. Nigel. Gran. Granddad. Philip.

And others. Many others. Not just people, either. There was Snoops too. Poor Snoopy, still fresh in the soil; as missed as any human. Maybe more so. Snoopy, whose death hit me in ways I never could have predicted.

I can't forget the moment Rachel and I lowered his

body into the ground. Into the frozen dirt. A layer of frost covered everything that morning and the grass crunched beneath our feet as we took a step back, our eyes wet and our breath just hanging there.

And there are others who have faded from view like old Polaroids left out in the sun. People who are ash and dust.

They're with the worms now and all that remains are the memories of them, memories kept barely alive in the minds of the living, soon to be gone themselves – and with them, all the memories of all the people they ever knew.

People always said I was morbid.

You are – you're talking in the past tense about yourself.

I'm not so sure, though; I think it's just that I've always been acutely aware of life and its limits, and how can one contemplate thinking about life without thinking about death?

Yes, I think about it a lot. Too much, even for a Joy Division and Smiths fan. And yes I dwell upon it. But how can I not, when it surrounds me like this.

So I'm sitting here preoccupied by velvet-lined coffins and funerals and the thick, thick clay that sticks to the gravedigger's spade.

And, naturally, my thoughts vainly progress towards my own passing and things like how I will be remembered, if I am remembered at all. And what will my headstone say?

('*Here lies a dickhead*'.)

No. There will be no headstone. I won't allow it.

I won't let it get that far.

All these years of contemplating death will count for something. There can only be a headstone if there is a burial and there can only be a burial if there is a body and there can only be a body if that body is dead and laid out for all to see.

You can't beat death, but you can beat the whole rigmarole that surrounds it.

*

— Hey, do you want to buy some lobsters, man? They're fresh out the Hudson this morning.

The guy with the greying trucker's whiskers sitting along from you at the bar doesn't look like a typical Manic Street Preachers fan, or, for that matter, a fan of the types of industrial goth bands that the venue is famous for hosting.

He reaches down by his side and lifts up a canvas holdall.

— They're monsters.

— No, thanks.

— What about some blow, then? You look like you like to party. And, no offence, but you look like you could use a little booster right now.

Oh. That's why he's here.

Is there anyone in New York who isn't trying to sell something?

— No, thanks.

— Hey, where are you from buddy – Canada? No – wait. England, right?

— Wales, actually.

— Wales! Awesome. But that's in England, right?

You don't need this right now. All you want to do is slowly drink your way through the sleep deprivation and jet lag that seem to have increased your anxiety and nervousness ten-fold. You knew you should have stayed backstage.

— It's next to England.

— Awesome. Like France and shit. Like the Queen of England and shit.

— Yeah.

— Awesome. So what brings you here, man?

Take a hint, you're thinking.

— Um, music. My band is playing here tonight.

— See, I knew that. As soon as I saw you walk in I knew you were a musician. Are you in Blind Melon?

— No. I think Blind Melon are supporting us tonight.

— So who are you guys, then?

— We're called Manic Street Preachers.

— Manic Street-what?

— Manic Street Preachers.

He pauses for a moment, draws on his cigarette, then screws up his face.

— You might want to think about that name there, pal. I don't know. I mean, don't take it personal or nothing, but it ain't too memorable. I mean, I've forgotten it already. You want to go for something instant. Something that punches you in the throat, you know? Something like Extreme, maybe. Or Ratt. Those guys knew what they were doing.

You zone out. Your head feels fuzzy from the sensory overload of downtown New York and the drink isn't helping.

Outside mirrored buildings stretch defiantly to the sky like middle fingers raised to a God who said capitalism could never work; plumes of smoke billow from the underground air vents and in Times Square the blinking neon is never turned off lest the people forget their purpose in life is to spend, spend, spend.

It really is like being in a film here: only you're disappointed to discover the film is tawdry and plotless; you've seen it all before and the over-sugared popcorn makes you feel nauseous.

Meanwhile the drug-dealer guy has shifted his bar stool closer to you and is still yakking away. Your head feels heavy and numb like a copper band is being tightened around it. Dead air hangs between you.

Your temples throb and the beginning of a panic attack washes around in the juices of your stomach.

You've really grown to hate such pointless small talk in recent months. Incessant chatter with strangers depresses you; it leaves you feeling spent. Already, one day into your inaugural trip here, and it is evident that Americans excel at talking in platitudes and banalities. They've taken it to a whole new level.

Or maybe you're just tired and jaded already.

Worryingly, the club in which you are to make your all-important debut – a showcase gig in front of a bunch of 'key industry movers' (the label rep really does use this phrase) – is in a converted church and you all remem-

ber what happened last time you played a converted church.

Generation Terrorists *posters adorn the walls.*

The guest list exceeds paying customers.

Anxiety rises, and with it comes your old friend self-doubt.

You wonder why on earth you chose a 'career' in this most sociable of fields, entertainment. The question what were you thinking? rolls around in your head like a ball-bearing.

You don't need to be here. You could have been a lecturer or a poet.

You could have been a lighthouse-keeper or a librarian. You'd like that, spending all day in a room where noise is prohibited and words line the wall. Cups of tea and a small electric heater to keep your feet warm in the winter. Your dream job. Long walks with Snoopy in the countryside at the weekend. A Sunday roast at Mum and Dad's. A girlfriend, maybe.

What were you thinking?

(There's still time to change it.)

Joining a band like that.

(But you can't let the others down.)

Being a rock star.

(You've come this far.)

Travelling the world.

(Give it six months. Just six months.)

What the hell are you doing in America, though?

(Don't panic.)

Stay calm.

(Take a deep breath.)

Everything will be OK.

(Just get through today.)

— Hey, are you sure you don't want some coke? You can try a bump or two before you buy.

The old guy breaks your train of thought, but not your increasing sense of panic.

For a brief moment you actually think about buying everything he has, proceeding straight to the toilets, snorting it all in one go and then seeing what happens.

An overdose an hour before the door opens for your debut American showcase would be one way to get out of it (Ian Curtis didn't even make it across the water).

But you know you're not going to do that – not least because a cocaine death would be so clichéd you know you would die from embarrassment before the actual cardiac arrest.

And the fact you've never even taken cocaine before.

No, instead you're going to get up from your stool and you're going to go and find the others to get them to help persuade you that you are not a worthless piece of shit who can't even tune his guitar, that you're a crucial member of the team, that you're not going to die – not today, anyway – that everything will be all right.

— No, thanks.

You stand up and go in search of the dressing room.

— Hey, he shouts after you. If you don't want lobster I got crawfish too?

*

I time it perfectly.

The taxi pulls in two streets away from Newport bus station, which gives me just enough time to cut across the concourse, get on the bus, buy a ticket and take the back seat. Hood up all the way.

You said you would never come back here. Back to Newport. Back to the bus station. You can't even get that right.

And then the doors are closing with a compressed hiss and the bus is lurching forward, and it smells of stale smoke and there are a dozen black marks burnt into the plastic of the seat in front of me.

Pathetic.

The window has been scratched repeatedly with a knife or a key or a pointed object of some description.

I sit chewing what's left of my fingernails. I feel neither tired nor hungry, just strangely blank, as if my physical and emotional faculties have gone into shutdown. I don't need to piss or shit or even smoke.

I breathe out and for a moment everything falls silent and for the first time in days I can sit and simply let myself be as Newport disappears, and with it goes my distant past. Beyond Newport sits the car with the flat battery. I imagine it to be there in years to come.

Maybe the service station will have been extended and the car park redesigned, but the car will still be there. Its wheels will have gone and rust will speckle it like blotches on a rare and delicate egg, and maybe it will be up on blocks, where it will sit immovable, a totem of glass and metal overlooking the Severn.

But then I realise that this is just more vain thinking on my part. Soon – sooner than I probably realise – the car will first be ticketed, then clamped, then finally winched up onto the back of a flat-bed truck and driven away to be impounded.

As the band's car, it will be Martin or one of the boys who will have to pay the fine to prevent it being crushed into a tiny geometric cube.

I wonder if it's possible to turn a person into a tiny geometric cube?

*

— *The only good thing about America is you killed John Lennon.*

You do your best to rouse the industry crowd from their corn-fed white-bread torpor, you really do. Wire gives them his best lines. You provoke them, you goad them and you try to look poised and beautiful and brilliant and threatening in your new clothes, bought this very morning in a variety of thrift stores.

You're all dressed for America, and present a united front in your bleached-out denim jackets, shades and matching black boots, plus a variety of chains, laminates and rosaries hanging around your necks.

Together you are one; your sum is greater than your parts.

Gestalt psychology.

Halfway through the set, in an effort to physically rouse the somnambulist crowd, you turn your amps up, but the soundman turns the stage sound down. Riled, James offers the front row out for a fight – a nice idea, were it not comprised of just two hippy burn-outs stood twenty feet back – and you catch a jet-lagged Sean yawning into his bass drum as he bends down to adjust his kick pedal.

Someone lights a cigarette. Someone throws an empty plastic cup.

You're not used to merely being 'the entertainment'. You're used to abuse and sometimes adoration but rarely the type of indifference that is exclusive to the cynical and the urbane; the people who venue-hop their way across Manhattan for a living five nights a week. The people who make the decisions: who is happening, who will sell, who will rule the airwaves.

Not since the earliest days of the band have you felt like this.

Your body has never felt so lifeless and useless and difficult to rouse; your guitar a plank of wood in your hands.

Your limbs are heavy and your sound is transparent.

And you've never felt so bored.

*

You're doing it again.
What?
Thinking about it.
About what?
You know what.

I can't help it. I was only imagining what my obituary would say. Everyone does it.

So what does it say, then, your obituary?

I'd like to think it mentioned my accomplishments with the band . . .

Wait, hold it right there. Accomplishments? What accomplishments would they be?

My lyrics . . .

Your lyrics! Christ. Then you're even more deluded and fucked in the head than I thought you were. Listen, my friend. No one gives a shit about the lyrics these days. A melody they can whistle along to, that's all people remember. Something that sounds good on the radio.

Well, there's my interviews too . . .

Yesterday's chip wrappers. What else?

My degree.

Well, that's hardly going to fill a half page in the South Wales Argus, *is it?*

Do you think it would only be half a page, then?

You'll be lucky. It's not like you've done something important, like play rugby or star in a film like that Catherine Zeta-Jones.

But I'm known, though.

Yeah, you're known. *Amongst certain types of people. Fuck-ups, junkies, mental cases, mainly . . .*

Those are my fans.

Yeah. And it's them they'll write about, not you. It's them who'll be your legacy. 'Edwards gained a small but devoted following of adolescents with bad skin and terrible social skills . . .'

That's not true.

Isn't it?

No, not entirely. Some of them have great skin.

Well, it's good to see you're finally developing a sense of humour.

Gallows humour, they call it.

So what else will this obituary say?

I don't know. Maybe something about how I was a nice person . . .

Look, I'm going to have to stop you there. You know, newspapers have better things to do than write obituary pieces about someone because they were 'nice'. They'll mention where you were born, what school you went to, they'll mention one or two of your minor hits, and that'll be it. Nothing else.

But . . .

The thing is, and it almost pains me to say this – almost – the thing is, you're just not that important.

I am to some people.

A few people, maybe, But nowhere near as important as you think. Your judgement is skewed from all the drink and the pills and the books and the therapy. You've totally lost your way. Basically, you've made the classic fatal mistake.

Which is?

You've fallen for your own hype.

*

A drive north up to Boston.

Then a drive west back across the border to play the Opera House in Toronto.

The next morning, you move south down through Michigan and around the lake to Chicago, Illinois.

Then west across six states to San Francisco to play some hippy-run club.

Then north again through Oregon and Washington, up to Vancouver.

Then south down to Los Angeles to play the famous Whisky a Go Go.

On the first glance you think it is a travel itinerary designed by a sadistic travel agent in collusion with a record label who have misunderstood the term 'breaking a band' but you soon realise otherwise. In fact, this is what is known as a whistle-stop tour. It's the three- or four-month-long tours undertaken by bands like Aerosmith and Def Leppard that you should fear. It's just that coming from Britain you've been spoiled. You're used to half-day drives between town and cities. Even Europe is easy to 'do', France, Belgium, Germany, Austria and so forth all practically huddled in a cluster, their capital cities rubbing up against one another, compared to the vast sweep of America.

Here, though, everything is big. Even bigger than you suspected. You have to recalibrate your senses and your spatial understanding to cope with it. The skies are wide and so are the waistlines; it even smells different. America smells of sugar and salt and vanilla essence.

The freeways hum quietly with six lanes going in either direction.

And everything is so alarmingly new world. The cities have a uniformity and a lack of architectural imagination that is both unnerving and depressing. Billboards guide you through the land. Buy this.

Eat that.

Wear these.

Then die.

It doesn't seem real.

Then you land in Los Angeles in the middle of a riot.

Six days ago a jury of twelve found four LAPD officers not guilty of assaulting a black man with clubs and tasers. The incident was captured on tape and beamed around the world for all to see.

But now white America has closed ranks and looked after its own. White America has sent a message to black America: you are still enslaved. We still own you. We will beat you. Know your place.

Know your place.

Riots erupted and now federal troops stalk the streets downtown. The state guard has been deployed, curfews put into place and National Guard soldiers called upon as Los Angeles is burnt, smashed and looted for near-on a week. For six days Molotovs have lit the sky and sirens split the night with their screams.

Until today, when you arrived in a city where broken glass still crunched underfoot.

But you see none of this as you're driven from LAX

down La Cienega Boulevard in a people carrier laid on by your employer, one of the world's biggest corporations.

This isn't your battle. It's not your riot.

You are one of the privileged, perfectly detached as you observe the aftermath from afar, from the freeway that takes you right on through to West Hollywood.

You are strangely silent, as if you dare not even comment.

Wire tries to engage the driver – a bulky black man – in conversation about what just happened but he simply shifts his big frame awkwardly, then shrugs.

— All I know is, only idiots loot their own communities. It's nothing to do with me.

And then he's silent again.

You drive onwards and the streets become wider and cleaner. The faces whiter.

In the distance the hills of Hollywood loom from the brown haze like the walls of a great castle in the sky.

A castle for the wealthy rulers of this corrupted fiefdom.

*

The fog has lifted in more ways than one, and with it comes a sustained clarity of thought.

I feel pretty good as the bus follows the road northwards towards the southern end of the Black Mountains. I feel free. And the further north I move – away from England, away from Cardiff, Swansea, Newport and Blackwood – the more intense those feelings become.

My persistent headache has gone and I can actually breathe without my chest fluttering. My hangover has subsided and been replaced with an inexplicable sense of euphoria.

As the bus tilts and coughs, I'm not even thinking about the implications of anything any more. I'm beyond that. Closure has already begun. In my mind, my flat has been sold, the band has split and all our records have been deleted. Obituary writers the world over are uncapping their pens.

Westwards, in the distance, I see a town, nestled low between hills and mountains.

*

Time change. In the blink of an eye you are in Osaka. You are in Nagoya. You are in Kawasaki.

You are on trains, in restaurants.

You are in saunas, you are on balconies.

You are in Kawasaki, wandering through weird little markets, lost on your way back to the hotel.

And you are followed by a small coterie of acolytes everywhere you go.

Everywhere.

Wherever you go. Outside the venue. In the hotel lobby. Whispering at your door.

Whispering behind hands folded over their mouths. Whispering and giggling. Whispering and giggling and moaning, their eyes averted, gazing at the floor, the sky – everywhere but at you.

They stare without looking. They are hissing shadows.

You turn and try to catch them but they're too quick for you. They look away or close together into small huddles, still whispering and giggling behind the hands that they draw up like veils.

— It looks like the Cult of Richey has truly reached the land of the Rising Sun, sniffs James, and you can't tell if he's perturbed that as frontman, guitarist and songwriter, he's not getting as much attention.

Which isn't to say he isn't getting any attention – he is. Plenty of it.

They love, love, love you in Japan. Love you. Love all of you.

They even chase Sean down the street when he's out buying Sony Walkmans and TVs that fit in the palm of your hand. Sean loves it here. He gets to be a rock star and he gets to feed his insatiable appetite for gadgetry. He gets attention too, but when he's had enough he asks them to leave him alone and they politely recede.

But it's you they reserve the special gifts for.

With Nick avoiding the chattering squall and retreating to his room with his crosswords and his rugby results, it's left to you to appease the crazy girls whose voices stalk your broken sleep and whose palms press against the window, leaving oily prints behind.

*

You remember coming here as a child.

Yeah, I know. I remember Abergavenny as an adult too.

It was the summer. You rolled in some dog shit.

I don't remember that.

Mum had to throw away your anorak.

I don't remember that.

You remember the market, though.

Vaguely.

Mum and Dad bought you some trainers. It was the first time you had seen Velcro.

They were green, weren't they?

And the castle. You remember that too.

Oh yeah.

Did you know Rudolph Hess was held in Abergavenny after he was arrested?

Really?

Yes. They held him here before the Nuremberg Trials.

I didn't know that.

But we're not staying in Abergavenny.

We're not?

No. Too close to home. You might as well say your goodbyes now. What do you think this is, a holiday?

No. I know what it is.

Good. So we'll keep going until we drop.

OK.

We'll make sure no one will ever find us. Find you.

OK.

*

There is a different kind of darkness in Japan. It is there in the increasingly alarming letters that arrive at your hotel. It's there in the news stories of death cults and gas attacks. It's there in the way the walls whisper at night.

Nothing is quite what it seems; everything here is transparent and it is just as Mishima portrayed it: a country with a fucked-up psyche where violence simmers just below the still surface. It's a place where the young are fetishised and girls' panties can be bought from vending machines. A place at odds with itself, a place torn between the traditions of old and the external, foreign influences that have only recently – and begrudgingly – begun to be accepted.

Masks pass you on the street. Market traders and rickshaw drivers with bad teeth draw on their cigarettes and silently observe you, the gaijin. *People continue to recognise you.*

Or maybe they don't recognise you at all. Maybe they're just pointing and staring at the pale foreigner with the jet-black hair who is effeminately dressed, like a kabuki performer gone hideously wrong. Maybe you're just paranoid but when you get back to your hotel after a late-night post-show walk more gifts await you at reception.

Books, traditional masks, art prints.

Kimonos, videotapes, snacks.

And more letters.

There are three fine-ink drawings of the 4 Real photo and one disturbing drawing of you with wings and ribbons where your legs should be. It looks like you're flying over the Eiffel Tower, which appears to be on fire, though it's hard to tell exactly.

You carry the letters and gifts into the elevator and watch as the city slips away below you.

Only when you leave Japan behind do you realise the full extent to which the country with its crazy cults, stalkers, sex trade and underlying, unspoken sense of violence has affected you.

You were able to immerse yourself.

Lose yourself.

Re-create yourself.

*

In the Dutch novel *The Vanishing* a young holidaying couple pull into a service station. While the man puts petrol into the car his girlfriend goes to buy supplies in the shop and is never seen again. She simply walks around the corner and vanishes.

Her disappearance haunts the man for years: how can someone just disappear like that, without warning? He knows she hasn't run away, so what is the other explanation – abduction?

I saw the Dutch version of the film a few years ago, and the thought has stuck with me ever since; the notion of someone being erased like that.

In the end, the young man finds out what happened to his girlfriend when a sociopathic stranger called Lemorne approaches him and reveals that he knows what happened to her, and that in order to find out the man must go through the same experience. He agrees, and after

271

drinking drugged coffee, he awakes to find himself in a dark confined silent space. He is in a coffin, underground. He has been buried alive – just like his girlfriend.

Although this image of the young man frantically scratching at the inside of the coffin lid, the flame from his Zippo lighter fading as he realises that his girlfriend suffered the very same fate, is a horrific one, it is the notion of disappearance that fascinated me the most.

The perfect disappearance is very different, though; the perfect disappearance could only be perfect if the disappeared was the only person complicit. With them goes the story, never to be told – only guessed at.

*

Summer in England. Summer in London.

The days are yours and at first you find yourself feeling guilty. You're not used to having free time stretching ahead of you. But then you get used to it, spending long lazy hours reclining on the sofa, reading, watching films, working on new lyrics. You fill your notebook with ideas for the next record.

You write down things like: 'Exile on Oxford Street meets Metallica on meth', 'We need to first go to war with ourselves – MSP are our own worst enemies' and 'When Baghdad is razed, this should be the record they prise from Saddam's death-grip'.

Nevertheless, welcome obligations punctuate the early summer months: the odd press interview, photo shoot or

TV appearance. And then there are the festivals: appearances at Belfort in France, Belga Beach in Belgium. The Tanzbunner festival in Germany.

One-off shows like these are so much easier than being on tour. It feels like a holiday, all the boys and small crew together, for a day or two away, on bills where your sets are kept short and the sound is shitty, but you don't mind.

The pay is good but it all goes on getting you there and back in one piece.

*

The bus pulls into Abergavenny station and I alight. I'm gasping for a cigarette, so smoke two in quick succession, wondering: what now?

Keep going.

Where?

It doesn't matter where. Just keep going.

Am I insane? I don't feel insane.

How do you feel?

Pretty weird. But sort of happy. I feel lighter than I have in a while.

They say that a period of happiness is sometimes evident shortly before the end.

I'm talking to myself again, aren't I?

So long as you do it internally, no one will notice.

Do you think they know where I am?

Who's they?

Anyone.

I don't know. You're the expert on disappearance –
you tell me.

I've not been very careful.

No. Wandering around Newport was probably not the
best idea. But no one knows you're here yet. That's why
you have to keep moving.

OK, I will.

Good.

Richard?

Yes?

Thanks.

For what?

For looking out for me.

You can thank me later.

*

Maybe it's because you were too broke and too geo-
graphically detached – and keen on basic hygiene – that
you never went to festivals as kids.

That's why you got on so well. Because your disdain
for the rituals and routines of your peers united you.
Festivals were for the kids with money and railcards.

You'd take a book and a bath over a sleepless weekend
of watery noodles and bongos any day.

Only James made it to a festival – to Womad in
Berkshire. When he reported back it merely confirmed
everything you already suspected: that these places were
the domain of the suburban rebels for whom rebellion

and subversive activity was going barefoot for the week-end.

As you approach you see them all, the walking dead, wandering the road from Reading train station to the festival, sleeping bags over their shoulders, crates of crappy lager underneath their arms. Bad hats, bad hair.

— Quick, wind up your windows, laughs Sean, his sleeve over his face. Before the stench consumes us.

You can spot your own fans a mile off, though.

Your fans make an effort. Fur coats, heels, T-shirts customised with slogans, bad dye jobs, tight jeans, bouffants, tiaras. And that's just the boys.

The fact that they are so obviously the most impractically attired fans for a festival is a point that fills you all with pride. With them on-side, it feels like you might just take this festival.

You put on your new silk turquoise blouse, apply another layer of corpse-white foundation then finish off with some outsized Ray-Bans.

By the time you've got through the traffic, the crowds, the security at the back gate, into guest parking, registered and then walked into the backstage area you're already running late for a TV interview. You repeat the conversation you've just had in the van: festivals suck, the crowds stink and everything is overpriced.

And then you're onstage and the sun is going down and Wire is telling the crowd how much they fucking stink.

Fifty thousand of them are watching the band, maybe

double that, but it feels like they are staring at you – the weird guy who cuts himself. It's as if they're waiting for something to happen.

Even though there is a chasm, a void, between you and them, you can smell the crowd, you can feel the warmth emanating from that many sunburned bodies. You give them music. You give them the songs they want to hear, loud and at double speed.

But they want more.

They've been drinking all day. For two days.

No food, no showers.

Just cider, beer, vodka, whisky.

Spliffs, speed and LSD.

So you give them more. You give them something to talk about.

Wire whips off his guitar and hurls it into the crowd. Only the crowd is fucking miles away and it doesn't even make it halfway across the void, because Wire is a weakling and he never thinks before he acts, never thinks before he opens his mouth, and that is half the reason you love him.

Instead it lands squarely on the back of the head of a big bruiser of a security guard. You later find out it has cut his head open and broken his arm.

Approximately three minutes later you're back in the van heading into town, panting and laughing, zooming through the walking dead still clutching their jugs of cider and their blankets. Fleeing for your lives, fleeing back to civilisation.

You were right: the festival was yours. You took it.
And now – for a while at least – it is over.

*

The notice in the window of the office at the station says there are tour buses leaving for Hay-on-Wye via 'the picturesque Black Mountains' every hour, on the hour. The company is called Day Trippers, like the song.

Do it.

It's twelve minutes to.

Yes. Do it. Buy a ticket, then get on that bus and go.

The bus is already in its bay.

Do it. Do it now.

Yeah. Some fresh air might do me good.

*

You take the train from Paddington back to Blackwood.

Dad meets you at the station.

He's pleased to see you, and so is Mum. You've barely seen them in the past twelve months.

The house seems smaller but your bedroom is just as you left it and Snoopy greets you by leaping up and scratching at your crotch, his eyes wide.

You spend a quiet week doing regular things, which you somehow invest with precious new meaning. They take on a magical, almost sacred, quality and it's then that you realise that everyday acts like walking the dog, taking long baths or getting the shopping in have become alien to you. The last year has changed you. You have been living within your own distorted world.

Your own bubble. You're not sure whether this is a good thing or not, but you do know you feel more relaxed than you have in months.

Your appetite, which is meagre at the best of times, returns.

At night, though, stone cold sober, you find yourself unable to sleep.

So after Mum and Dad have gone to bed you sit in your bedroom with the curtains open watching the silent street.

You think of Osaka, Nagoya, you think of LA, New York, and you wonder if you have even been there. You wonder if the past year really happened. For a few fleeting seconds you think you are sixteen again, and you have woken from a dream, a projection of the future.

The silence of this quiet street in Blackwood howls in your ears so you read by lamplight for hours and hours – a biography of Van Gogh, a Tanizaki novel, the selected plays of Tennessee Williams – and you write.

The words finally come and all you can do is keep going. Keep writing. Keep learning from your mistakes and hope that something good will come of it.

And when the screaming silence of night finally abates to a barely audible whisper on the wind you finally fall asleep.

*

I don't know anything about Hay-on-Wye, other than that it is full of bookshops, and that I will never visit it. I buy a ticket anyway.

Then I buy water, cigarettes, a Mars bar. I think about making a phone call.

To who?

To anybody.

I thought we'd discussed this.

You're right.

Let it go.

I have. I am.

I smoke a cigarette and wait for the bus to show.

*

Your first Top 10 single and it's not even a song by your band. Doubt is automatically cast over the record's success and the status of the band because it is not only the theme tune to a highly popular and much-loved TV show, but also a record from a charity album that was put together by the NME.

With that in mind, says your label, it should really have gone Top 5.

And besides, they add, The Shamen just sold two hundred thousand copies of a funny little dance song about ecstasy and spent a month at number one. All you Manics – you supposedly sexy, subversive and daring Manics – can muster is a soft-rock rendering of a song about suicide.

But still, you all tell yourselves.

Top 10.
Top of the Pops, *again.*
More airplay. More magazine covers.
Smash Hits *and the* Sun.
All of that.
You live to fight another day.

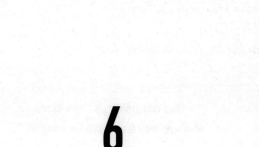

6

'God has given you one face,
and you make yourselves another.'

(*Hamlet*, 3. 1)

SCARS – DEAD – HATE – VOID

I'm sitting on the bus and watching as two couples get onboard: an elderly Welsh couple and a slightly younger couple who sound like they are American or possibly Canadian but almost certainly tourists.

A couple of minutes later the driver arrives. He gets onboard, and then addresses the five of us in a manner that is far too formal for such an undersubscribed outing.

'Hello and welcome to Day Trippers Buses. We'll shortly be leaving Abergavenny and taking the scenic route through the Black Mountains to the historic town of Hay-on-Wye. You will then have two hours to enjoy the sights and foods before we return.'

As an afterthought as if answering a question yet to be asked, he adds: 'Unfortunately there is no toilet on board this bus today.'

Then he squeezes himself into his seat, starts the engine, lets it tick over for a moment and pulls out of the station.

*

They keep sending you back to Germany.

They tell you that after the UK and the US it is 'the biggest market share'.

They tell you that to 'crack' Germany is 'to gain a foothold in Europe'.

And so like good little servants you do what you're told.

You're actually glad of the distraction from yourself. You're glad of the three or four weeks of daily routine.

And so you fly back into Germany for a more comprehensive assault.

On places like Frankfurt.

Stuttgart.

Munich.

In an attempt to banish the recent bouts of self-pity you give yourself tasks to make each day more bearable and to get the best out of the experience that has been afforded you.

So you shop for mementoes of each town that you visit because you know you will never remember them otherwise.

In towns like Karlsruhe.

Tier.

Bremen.

You read only German authors for the entire trip.

People like Goethe.

Schopenhauer.

Hesse.

You punctuate your heavyweight bunk-bed reading sessions with trashy gossip magazines and European pornography, of which there is an abundance in all the service stations.

Porn mags like Busen.

Busen-Extra.

Busen Lesben.

You continue your regime of sit-ups and press-ups – what you call your 'jail cell' workout – and take swims and saunas to ease the hangovers. You veer from one extreme to another within hours: from exercise to oblivion.

In towns like Essen.

Sollinge.

Hameln.

You eat a lot of fruit during the day and drink a lot of vodka at night. You even grow to quite like the stiff malt breads and cold meats that you hated so much on the last tour. You exchange pleasantries with the American bands you find yourselves sharing cramped graffitied dressing rooms with.

Bands like Afghan Whigs.

Babes In Toyland.

Jawbreaker.

And by the time you fly back into Gatwick your suit-case is rattling with tacky trinkets.

Key-rings.

Bavarian beer mats.

Jars of unidentifiable pickled vegetables.

You dump them all in the bin outside the Duty Free shop before you've even left the terminal.

*

We leave Newport and are soon heading north, up towards the mountains.

The Welsh couple have a flask of tea out and the American couple are excitedly taking photos of the passing landscape from the window – photos that will almost certainly contain, at best, nothing but a washed-out, indistinguishable blur of sky and landscape, which I am sure is not their intention. Also their flash keeps going off so they'll be lucky to see anything other than the reflection of the white flash. But I don't tell them this. It is their business. It is their mistake to make.

Just as this is mine.

I have my forehead against the window to cool the beginnings of another nagging headache and I watch the sky slide overhead. From here it does not look real; it's an impression of a sky, like a painter's attempt to evoke quiet foreboding and its rolling, swirling potential.

The bus judders over a pothole and my head bangs against the glass with a deep thud.

It looks like rain.

*

Autumn comes and Sinead O'Connor tears up a picture of the Pope on live television and inspires a wave of death-threats. You are all immediately jealous that you didn't think of it first, especially Nick, who excels in these matters.

Elsewhere the Church of England finally allows women to become priests.

America gets a new head of state, Bill Clinton. They call him 'the first black president' and 'the rock 'n' roll president', even though he is neither. Such a country would never vote a black man or anyone deemed remotely 'rock 'n' roll' as their leader. Not in your life-time.

Windsor Castle is ablaze.

And you. You spend each night in a different British city.

From Glasgow to Exeter, Newcastle to Bournemouth you make a final assault on the UK for the year.

More than half of the shows are sold out, ticket prices have increased, the dressing rooms become cleaner and roomier, the rider more elaborate. Finally it feels like you are playing to your people.

Gone are those who came to hate you and abuse you. Instead, familiar pale faces fill the front rows.

Each of you has your own following now, identifiable in different sections of the crowds. To stage left are the girls who think they have a chance of getting on Wire's big penis and those who smile and laugh at his increasingly ridiculous onstage declarations and rants.

In the centre are those – boys mainly – who crush themselves up against the barrier to study James's guitar parts up close so they can go home and replicate them later in their bedroom – a blatant substitution for masturbation – and the girls who sing each and every word back at him, their eyes closed, heads tilted back to the ceiling, their delicate white throats exposed.

Over to your side, stage right, are the clones. The

thinnest, quietest and fiercest girls, usually dressed in clothes similar to those you wore on the last tour or, for those particularly fastidious fans, replicas of whatever it was you were wearing in the last NME shoot. Flowers fall upon the stage. Faces press against the tour-bus window. Their attention to detail and willingness to hang on your every move is unnerving. Flattering.

Disturbing.

But you enjoy these shows.

You enjoy these shows because you understand your role now.

You enjoy them because you just have to turn up and let the noise of the crowd and the band spur you on. You're living on adrenaline alone.

The only downside to this tour is the perpetual cold.

— Why do we only ever tour in the British bloody winter? you ask, backstage at the National on Kilburn High Road, before your ninety-fourth and final show of 1992.

— It's your fault, Edwards, smiles James. They think we like pain.

— Yeah, Edwards, says Nicky, one long leg crossed over the other as he picks at his bare feet. They think we actually enjoy suffering. I tell you something, though – Christ – they've obviously never experienced the pain of chilblains.

You laugh and pour the second of your required three pre-show drinks, your breath hanging there in the air.

*

And then we're out into Wales – the real Wales. The Wales of the Thomases – Dylan and R. S. I remember reading both at school for my O-levels where I learnt that in no other medium but poetry has my country been so successfully portrayed for what it really is: a beautiful country made ugly by the burden of the past, and by the brutality imposed upon – and perpetrated by – its people. A land of pride and pity.

R. S. Thomas said it best: '*There is no present in Wales / And no future / There is only the past / Brittle with relics / Wind-bitten towers and castles / With sham ghosts / Mouldering quarries and mines; / And an impotent people / Sick with in-breeding / Worrying the carcase of an old song.*'

And this is where I differ from my average fellow Welshman: I can recognise that this mess of a life is all my fault, and my fault alone. I refuse to blame God, Wales, the English, my heritage, my history or this bold and brutal and brutally beautiful landscape. I blame no one but myself.

No. We all must be accountable for our actions; without culpability we are inhumane and though I am many things, inhumane is not one of them.

*

It must be the idea of someone at the record company because it sure as hell isn't yours: stick them in the priciest studio around and they're bound to strike gold. Throw enough money at them and something will happen.

It has *to.*

So here you are, wandering around the gardens of a fourteen-bedroom Elizabethan house in deepest, grandest Oxfordshire, the place that belongs to that producer guy from Buggles. The one with the glasses. You've not met him.

It is bedecked with Tudor panelling and ornate fireplaces and has stone-floor rooms for better 'resonance'.

James bloody loves it here; he's like a kid let loose. With his cut-off sleeves and pumped-up pecs he's even starting to look like The Boss. He's letting his hair grow out.

When you leave them, James and Sean – who is wearing a furry Russian hat and tracksuit – are huddled in the corner, conspiring about multi-tracking, middle eights and other things you have no concept of. Wire meanwhile is practising and perfecting his trick shots over and over, the click-clack of balls emanating from the games room; his tall frame folded double, legs spread, tongue hanging from his mouth. He doesn't even need to be here. In fact, tomorrow he'll be gone – back to Rachel, back to the house for the week, back to his hoovering, his videos, his crisps, his domestic bliss.

You leave them to walk through the gardens where you stop to smell a flower, check to see no one is watching and then pluck it.

From the studio you hear the sound of cheering. Nick has just done something remarkable with the cue-ball, the black and a pint pot.

There follows a burst of feedback. A strangulated guitar riff. More cheering.

It's probably time for a drink.

You walk back across the lawn.

*

The bus is climbing now. The driver works down through the gears in order to tackle the curves of the road that keeps cutting back upon itself as it rises from the valley floor.

It's nice out here. There's room to gain a wider perspective on your surroundings that the city just does not offer. In London – or New York, Paris or Berlin for that matter – you can never see beyond the immediate street or two. Here though a complete recalibration of the senses is needed to fully appreciate the space that surrounds you so comprehensively. Large boulders that would dominate a city street lose their proportions in this broad landscape. Hills higher than any building in Wales look insignificant next to their older, taller siblings.

Perhaps this is where I need to be. Perhaps perspective is what I seek. Perspective and silence and solitude.

Perhaps I need to fully appreciate my own complete and utter insignificance – to feel lost amongst these ancient sleeping giants – and acknowledge that life is short and pointless and everything I have ever said or done is worthless.

You already know that.

I don't know. It's worth a look.

You won't find anything out here but rain and rocks and grass.

Maybe that's all I need.

For what?

. . .

I said, for what?

Now it's my turn to stay silent.

*

Strange dreams.

Dreams of a barren rocky outpost, like how you imagine Iceland to be. Nothing but rocks and water. No trees, no grass, no people, no birds. Just rocks and water; the sky pressing down on you. Dreams about Brad Pitt naked at the end of your bed, tugging at his cock, which turns into a swan's neck in his hands. Dreams about Flavor Flav giving birth to a hundred little Flavs, all of them running around with miniature clocks around their neck, squeaking, 'Yeah, bwoy-ee!'

Dreams about Snoopy. Dreams about being buried alive.

Dreams about home.

Anxiety breeds compulsive behaviour and you become increasingly obsessed with your appearance. No, not your appearance – your physiology. Appearance is cosmetic; you can hide it beneath clothes. It is your naked physical shape that bothers you.

You worry constantly that your drinking will physically manifest in that enemy of the rock god: the beer gut.

You'd rather never have your picture taken again than be seen as fat and past it. You can't play guitar, but the very best you can do is deliver the lyrics and look good.

So you do your sit-ups, ten at a time. You count them out. Then you do them again. And again.

Ten crunching cycles of ten.

Your head to your knees, morning, noon and night.

You become addicted to the numbers, addicted to the dull throb in your abdominals. You lift weights too. Nothing heavy, just dumb-bell reps to gain a little definition.

Morning.

Noon.

Night.

You eat out only for practical reasons. You eat to gain energy to do your sit-ups, your weights and to stay alive.

You get it down to one late-afternoon meal per day. An omelette, or a baked potato, maybe a salad. A banana as a treat.

Then after that you consume nothing but vodka and water and cigarettes until the same time tomorrow, a regime that you continue for the duration of the making of the album.

Morning.

Noon.

Night.

Then drunk in the darkness of your room at the studio you lie back listening to mixes of the album on the huge and indecently expensive headphones you bought in Japan.

You lie there, your stomach cold and tight as if a rock is sitting in it.

What you hear on your headphones is a grungy sounding rock record with half-finished lyrics.

No, no, no, you think.

This is all wrong, you think.

There still might be time to change it.

To change it all.

To burn the tapes and start again. To start over. Right from scratch.

You throw off the headphones and leap off your bed but a head full of Absolut throws you lurching to one side. You bounce your head off something solid – the wall – and a dull pain clangs around your skull. Nausea fills your mouth and you have to squat down and catch your breath. Your ears ring and your temples throb.

Standing again, you feel your way along the wall to the light-switch. You turn it on and though your panic subsides, the pain in your temples does not. You put your fingers to your scalp and feel the beginnings of a bump. A big cartoon bump.

In your boxer shorts, T-shirt and unlaced boots you leave the residential annex and cross the gravel forecourt to the studio in the main house.

It is a cold, clear night.

The stars are out.

Beyond the building you can see the silhouette of distant woodlands scratching at the sky. A monkey-puzzle tree looms out of the darkness – tall, alien and foreboding.

You reach the house but the side door is locked. All the lights are out.

You bang on the door. You shout James's name, but your voice sounds disembodied, stupid, lost in the night.

Small.

You walk around to the front of the house, your feet sinking on the soft lawn now.

The studio is a dead entity. There is no life in there.

The house is asleep.

The world is asleep.

Only you are awake.

As you stand there shivering in the moonlight it's as if you have just woken up, as if you have been sleepwalking. The anger you felt only moments before has passed and you are suddenly woefully, sorrowfully sober.

Your head aches and you are shivering.

You wonder what you are doing here. Then, as if on cue, a cloud passes over the moon.

You are all alone.

*

We leave the dual-carriageway behind and it doesn't take long before the B-road begins to take a steeper incline. I see the hills and peaks of the Black Mountains ahead of me. They don't look real. They look like a film set.

It occurs to me that I now no longer have anything on me other than the hat on my head and what remains in the pockets of my anorak; everything else has been shed. In hotels, in woodlands, in the car. I conduct an impromptu inventory: water, cigs, lighter, gloves, money. A Mars bar.

There is little by which to identify me, other than my tattoos and my many, many scars, some of which have long since healed into barely discernible silver lines, while others – the more recent ones – are pink, keloid and swollen, fat like earthworms after a rainstorm.

Though I'm sure my paper trail of possessions means I could probably be tracked quite easily, I know by the time they find me it will be too late.

By the time they find me all that will be left will be bones in the dust. I will make sure of it.

*

The album is finished.

You don't know how you feel about it, but you know it is not the pride that a father feels for his newborn child.

It is called Gold Against The Soul *and it feels like it's neither one thing nor the other. Maybe time will demonstrate otherwise, but to your ears it sounds like a rock record. A bit punk, a bit metal. A bit poetic, a bit vexed.*

But mainly just *a rock record.*

Or maybe even an unintentional parody of a rock record.

Only it is not a parody, it is the new album by the Manic Street Preachers and it is your job now to go out there and talk it up, when all you want to do is start over. Or just scrap it. To get drunk and forget about it.

The sad thing is, you're not angry, just deflated. Disappointed in the band. Disappointed in yourself.

Because you have done what all the bands who have ever let you down did before you, and which you said you never would: you have compromised what you had. Already.

You have tried to appease those clueless fuckers in Soho Square, in LA and in New York. In giving them what they want, rather than what they need, you have committed a cardinal sin. You have diluted your bile, dampened your fire.

You have delivered the clichéd difficult second album.

You are clinging to your careers like City brokers as a recession hits.

And that's the worst thing of all – you have become careerists. Game-players.

Hit-chasers.

Cocksuckers.

*

Just as I'm nodding off, my head still against the cool glass, the twists and turns of the climbing road making me feel nauseous again, the driver slips a tape into his cassette player. There's a few seconds of crackling before the sound of a male-voice choir emanates from the speakers.

It is slow and quiet at first – nebulous, almost. But then the voices commingle to create something powerful and mellifluous, something so irrevocably *Welsh*, that when combined with the stark landscape around me and the bruising of the sky overhead, it causes tears to swell in my eyes.

This music – goodwill songs to be sung to the Welsh communities during the harshest and most impoverished post-war years – is utterly celestial. Cutting straight to my emotional core, it's music that is beyond analysis and approximately one million times more powerful and meaningful than any song I have ever had a hand in writing.

Through it I hear Wales for the first time.

I see Wales for the first time too and it is enough to convince me that I am doing the right thing, because this is the music I want ringing in my ears for all of eternity.

*

You go to see Mike Leigh's new film Naked *at the Curzon – alone, back in London fulfilling pre-publicity obligations.*

And there he is – twelve feet tall in a trench coat. 'Johnny'. The perfect personification of the modern young man with too much on his mind. The lost boy. The vulnerable one.

He's Mark E. Smith, he's Jimmy Porter – and he's you too, if you were Manc, acerbic and brassy. If you were motivated by anger and hatred rather than riddled with anxiety, possessed by doubt.

'What if God just put us here for his own entertainment?'

David Thewlis' Johnny leaves you dumbstruck; Johnny

as moralist, Johnny as rapist, Johnny as Christ figure, Johnny as victim, Johnny as plague, Johnny as parasite. Johnny as the only living soul in the city capable of screaming.

'Have you ever thought, right, that you may have already lived the happiest day in your whole fucking life and all you have left to look forward to is fucking sickness and purgatory?'

The film is so fucking perfect it makes you want to give up writing immediately. It makes you want to curl into a ball and roll off the roof of the nearest high rise. Because you know nothing you could ever say, do or write could come close to capturing this bleak era – this empty pit of a life – like Naked *does.*

'You don't want to fuck me. You'll catch something cruel.'

Later: you know you are drunk and it's too late yet still you're dialling.

You're dialling because your head is humming and you're drunk and you're alone and that film – that character – has got under your skin.

You're in the Columbia again. The one they always put you up in when you're in town because the bar stays open and they don't mind if you spill ash on the crappy carpet. Because it's the done thing, the industry way, to put their mid-level rock bands here. Because the music business is big on tradition and fearful of change.

You call the first number that comes to mind. The Wire.

It rings for a long time before you hear a muffled voice.

— *Hello?*

— *It's me.*

— *Rich? Is everything all right?*

— *Have you ever thought that you may have already lived the happiest day in your whole life and all you have left to look forward to is sickness and purgatory?*

A sigh comes down the line.

— *So you've seen* Naked *too, then?*

— *Yes. How did you know?*

— *I saw it last week.*

— *Oh, right. What did you think of it?*

— *It was great. What time is it?*

— *I don't know. About three?*

— *Where are you?*

— *The Columbia.*

— *Are you pissed?*

— *A bit pissed, yeah.*

— *Right.*

— *Where are you?*

— *You know where I am: at home. You just called me here.*

— *In Wales?*

— *Yes, of course in Wales.*

— *Why aren't you here in London?*

You hear a muffled noise, a hand over the receiver, a voice in the background. Tones of reassurance from Nick.

— *Because I don't need to be. It's you and James doing the interviews for the tour, remember?*

— Oh yeah.

You remember your day: repeating yourself in a room in the Hall Or Nothing offices to journalists who laugh at all the wrong parts and take the funny bits seriously. James was there too, chain-smoking anxiously.

— Nick . . .

— Yeah?

— I love you.

— I know you do, you daft sod. But you're only saying that because you're pissed. Is James there?

— Remember when we used to share a bed at Philip and Terri's?

— How could I forget?

— Well, there's something I never told you about that time.

— Go on . . .

You take another sip of vodka. It tastes like paint stripper. You wish you had some ice.

— Well. It's a bit awkward, actually.

— Go on . . .

— Well . . .

— What is it, Rich?

— Well, it's just that your feet used to really fucking stink.

— Gee, thanks.

— Yeah. It was a sort of horrible sweetness, like rotting meat. I think it was that pair of Green Flash that you always wore.

— Oh yeah. They gave me athlete's foot, they did. We burnt them in the end, didn't we?

— *Yeah. The thing is, Nick, I never minded. After a while I almost found it comforting, in a strange sort of way. The amount of nights I fell asleep with that stench in my nostrils.*

Nicky laughs at this. Says nothing. You take a sip of your drink and carry on.

— *It was a good time then, wasn't it?*

— *Fucking hell, Edwards. Don't get all nostalgic on me.*

Your eyelids are getting heavy, your head lolling. The brown carpet of the Columbia is a swirl of colours like looking into a tub of Neapolitan ice cream on a turntable. The curtains swirl as if they're billowing, but you know they're not. The mattress sags in the middle from all the bodies that have lain there.

— *It was, though, wasn't it?*

— *It still is. It still can be.*

— *I don't know.*

— *You're drunk, that's all. You always get like this when you're drunk – you did back then too. Don't you remember? We had the same conversation then as we're having now. You used to sit there, all pissed and sloppy, pining for our bedroom days in Blackwood. And before that, before you even started drinking, you'd sit in James's bedroom, saying how you wished you were a child again, how it all turned to shit when puberty hit. You were probably saying the same thing in your Mum's womb: 'Oh, woe is me, life used to be so much better . . .'*

You drain the glass and suddenly feel really tired. Exhausted.

— Well, I think I'll go to sleep now.

— OK, Rich. Let me know how the interviews go tomorrow. I'll see you Thursday, anyway.

— Nicky.

— Yeah?

— Sorry for waking you up.

— That's OK.

— And sorry for waking Rachel up too.

— That's all right.

— And Nick?

— Yeah?

— You feet don't smell any more.

— That's good to know.

— Night, then.

— Night.

*

Ahead, where the road levels out, I see a passing point, a circle of gravel worn into the green thatch of grass that slopes down from the valley's flanks on either side to a brief horizontal. Beyond that the valley forms a perfect uphill U-shape that the road continues to follow while the damp green mountains tower on either side.

I rise from my seat and using the backs of the chairs to steady myself against the rocking of the bus and my own light-headedness, walk down the short aisle to the bus driver. My hood is up.

'I think I'll get off here.'

'What's that?'

His voice comes over his shoulder, his eyes on the road.

'I said, I think I'll get off here. At this next stopping point.'

'Get off? Why? You're in the middle of bloody nowhere.'

'That's OK. I just fancy a bit of a walk.'

'I'm not meant to drop people off along the way – this is a round trip to Hay-on-Wye.'

'I appreciate that. But I think I'll get off here.'

The driver slows down to pull over and as he does he turns his head to glance at me, even though I know he has been watching me periodically in his rear-view mirror anyway.

'Going walking are you?'

'A bit of a wander, yes.'

'I'm not going to pick you up on the way back, you know.'

'That's fine. I know the area well. I'm actually meeting a friend in a little while.'

He lets out an exaggerated sigh of exasperation just to let me know that this twenty-second diversion from his usual protocol is far from desirable.

Behind me I can hear the whispers of the two couples who are also reading me up and down. I can feel their eyes on me.

The bus pulls to a halt and the door opens.

'Thanks,' I say. The driver just shakes his head.

I step down onto the tarmac.

The bus drives away.

The door closes.
I'm alone.

*

No way are you ready to tour again. No way.
No fucking way.
You're in no fit state. Neither physically nor mentally.
No way.
The dead time spent in expensive studios has softened
you, distracted you. It's deceived you into thinking you're
something you're not.
The Sony people are enthusiastic – too enthusiastic.
But only because they want a hit record. They certainly no
longer trust your opinions; everything they loved about
you – the hyperbole, the cynicism, the grandiose declara-
tions – they now hold against you. It's like they genuinely
believed Generation Terrorists *would sell sixteen million*
copies. A bloody debut record. It's as if they feel hood-
winked and humiliated, though of course they don't say
that. They say the new one has 'commercial potential'
and that two or three of the songs have 'hit written all
over them'. Their talk is dull and full of unrealistic expec-
tations about Radio 1 playlists, marketing campaigns –
and America. Always America. They're fucking obsessed
by the place.
There's talk of thirty-, forty-date US tours. Talk of
remixing the record for 'American ears'. Talk of James
overdubbing more and more guitar solos; talk of support
slots with grunge-lite bands too awful to comprehend.

The information filters down through Philip and Martin who tactfully only provide you with the edited highlights. You all react differently. James is stoic, Nicky sardonic, Sean ambivalent.

And you. You're filled with horror.

Horror.

But before any of that, Britain still needs to be broken, though deep down you know that it is you who will break first.

You can feel it in your bones.

In your bones.

Your brittle bones.

Still. You get to choose your own supports for the tour. It's your agent's one concession to sending you round the darkened grief-holes of Britain for the zillionth time, playing venues that undermine the profile you've built in the press.

And therein lies the problem. One of the problems, anyway. The way they write about you and the way you talk about yourselves far outweighs the dull reality of a semi-popular rock band playing to a few hundred people on a dark damp weekday in Northampton or Dundee.

Crawley.

Hull.

You only have yourselves to blame.

— Maybe we've shot our load, says Nick, and maybe he's right, though none of you want to think about that; not when you're meant to be enthusing about Gold Against The Soul *to anyone who asks. And they do ask.*

That's one thing you've got right. People are still inter-
ested.

People are interested because there is nothing that the
British – the Welsh – like better than to see the failure of
one of their own. They're interested because they want to
be there to watch your downfall.

Schadenfreude.

They want you on the cross and you might just climb
up there for them.

But first: tour business. You compile a list of bands and
collectively pare it down to two who you think will do the
business, without blowing you away. Both have frontmen
called Matty. Matty Hanson and Matty Blagger. They are
both endearingly enthusiastic about the tour in ways you
never could be.

You meet them both for the first time at a London
studio for an NME cover shoot. It's just the three of you,
closed in tight.

Matty Hanson is a black kid from the Midlands who
raps as Credit to the Nation and is currently riding high-ish
off the back of a recent single that unashamedly samples
that Nirvana riff. He's instantly likeable, though smokes
way too much weed for your liking. You feel stoned just
being around him. Matty Blagger fronts Blaggers ITA, a
left-wing anti-fascist/anarchist collective born out of the
squat scene. He used to be a fascist until reading Orwell
turned him. And now the Blaggers have signed to a major,
and face having to do what all you other bands do: run the
treadmill. The hamster wheel of touring and promotion.

And compromise.

Compromises at every turn.

You don a leather jacket as the flashbulbs flash and you stand there sandwiched between the two Mattys, thinking about the conversation that the four of you – Nicky, James and Sean – had back in James's bedroom only three or four years ago, about how if any cover shoot were to happen they would only ever feature the four of you.

'The four of us or nothing.'

Another compromise.

And you feel nauseous just thinking about the tour.

You pass the time thinking up ways to get out of it.

*

Judging by the litter bins and tyre tracks and the convergence of a number of footpaths, the turning point appears to be a regular stop-off or meeting place, though as it is a soon-to-be wet weekday there's no one else here but me.

It is not yet raining, but it will. The air has that heavy feeling to it and my head hums, my vision briefly flickering from colour to sepia and back again in such a way that I'm unsure whether it is my eyes or my imagination playing tricks on me.

Or maybe it's neither.

I light a fag under my hood where there is no breeze.

What now?

Mountains surround me. Ahead the road climbs up the pass beyond my line of vision, but I don't intend to take the road. In fact, I don't intend to do anything other than keep moving, so I impulsively opt to take the path that veers off up the left-hand side of the valley; the side of the valley that is not in shadow.

The shadow of the valley of death.

Standing among the mountains, it's easy to see why man felt the need to create God. Or Gods. And if these mountains are the product of him, then I think I finally believe, and it is only now that I realise the subtext of this journey: to be closer to him.

*

The others call you Narcissus, the amount of time you spend staring into mirrors. And that's coming from a bunch of vain bastards.

It has gone beyond merely 'putting on your face' and fixing your hair before the show. It's gone beyond functional purpose and crossed over into self-obsession. One more manifestation of this fixation you have. This endless attempt to understand yourself.

You think of Narcissus as depicted by Caravaggio. The beautiful boy who spurns lover after lover to instead become enraptured by his own reflection. You think of Narcissus, pure and porcelain-skinned, his hair parted and his mouth open just so. Only when he tries to kiss the reflection does he discover that the boy staring back at him doesn't exist.

Some readings say he took a sword and killed himself. Others had it that, unwilling to disturb the perfection of his reflection, he died from thirst right there on the banks of the spring. This is the interpretation that you prefer.

Sometimes you can look at yourself for minutes at a time. You stare yourself out, but you always blink first.

You always lose.

Other times you scour your face. It is as if you are trying to look beyond the outer cosmetic layer in order to see inside yourself, to get inside the real you, for only the eyes are capable of telling the truth. You stare into mirrors – dirty, cracked mirrors of different sizes, in different dressing rooms and public toilets and in pocket-sized compacts too, in the hope that you will find something more. Something beyond your own sad self; an entity you are already bored with. But you always seem to come up short. All you ever see is an ordinary blank face; a face in need of a shave.

Sometimes you barely recognise the man staring back at you.

It's like your own lyrics say – and what can be more Narcissistic than quoting your own lyrics? – 'I need a reflection / To prove I exist.'

When Narcissus died, his physical form turned into a flower as beautiful and delicate as he was.

You wonder what will become of you.

Rebirth as a flower would be perfect, but you doubt such a thing is possible.

*

Walking along the lower side of the valley, I pass stone-walled plots and silage sumps. Dirty water topped by a floating film of the colours of the spectrum sits in a series of old ceramic basins now used as troughs for sheep that are arranged across the hillside above me. Long-limbed pond-skaters break the surface rainbows, only for them to reconfigure again.

After half an hour or so I come across a sign that points to Offa's Dyke, the pathway separating England from Wales. This was the boundary that ran from north to south to divide the two warring nations. Legend has it that Welshmen found on the English side would have their ears cut off, while lost Englishmen would be hanged.

Today on this stretch there is no one but me, a Welshman wandering the Welsh Marches, alone and definitely lost as I teeter along an invisible frontier of land and sky. A frontier of mind and body.

Life and death.

As I continue along my chosen path I start to murmur 'Land of my Fathers', before the rising wind takes my words away.

*

The hangover has you incapacitated and you want everyone to know about it.

You're moaning and groaning and whinging. You're all on a train leaving Manchester, heading south. Gillian, your new publicist at Hall Or Nothing, is there. So is a label guy, and a journalist. It's early and you're scattered around the carriage in that barely awake state that seems to define touring.

You're all sipping teas and coffees from plastic cups.

Gillian is Scottish and high-spirited. She can out-drink any of you and she won't tolerate your bullshit. For someone in the music business she's refreshingly straight-talking. She's a good person to have around.

— *What's wrong today?* she asks, *sitting down beside you and prodding you in the ribs.*

— *Nothing.*

— *Well, what's with the face?*

— *I don't know. I just feel empty.*

— *Empty? With the amount you put away last night?*

— *No, I mean, spiritually empty. Maybe not spiritually . . . I don't know. I suppose I'm tired and bored and my own worst enemy.*

— *Aren't we all, though?*

— *Maybe. I suppose my problem is I can't stand myself.*

— *You have a victim complex. Which is weird because half the girls I know fancy you.*

— *I'm just continuously addled with self-disgust, Gill.*

— *Self-disgust? It sounds like self-obsession to me, honey.*

You can't help but smile.

— *Maybe you're right. But that thought just makes me feel even worse. That's a great quote, by the way. I might have to use it.*

— *I know I'm right. And you can have that one for*

free. She jabs you in the ribs again, then turns it into a tickle. I want a writing credit, though.

*

The path runs alongside a brook for a way. Though it is only about ten feet across, the noise from it is deafening as it winds over and around the smooth rocks. Half of a fallen tree lies prone in the water, its limbs charcoal-black and part-petrified.

I stand and watch it for a while, then pull myself out of the trance that the water put me into, then I follow the stream uphill for a mile or so, carefully stepping from rock to rock like a mountain goat.

The rocks are wet from the spray and swash of the beck and some are covered in a film of algae that becomes more and more and more treacherous, so at some point I veer to the left and onto a path that follows a steeper incline, up towards a sky of increasing portent.

*

It's hard work playing the new songs. There are new chords that you have to remember how to play and the guitar hangs around your neck like a dead thing. For half the show you don't even pretend to play it. It just swings there, bouncing off your hips, bruising them, the strap like a noose of your own making.

You feel no shame, though. No shame whatsoever. You'd prefer it if the guitar wasn't even plugged in.

In fact, you'd prefer it if you didn't have a guitar at all. Instead you could just stand there, drinking your drinks and watching the crowd watching the band watching the crowd right back.

You begin to wish you could just do two- or three-song mimed sets, like proper pop stars. They don't even call them gigs. Public appearances, they call them. Three songs on a stage in the middle of some crappy shopping centre, then into the van and on to the next one. You could cram an entire tour into about four days.

Christ, you wish you were a pop star. The best fun you had recently was when Smash Hits *asked you to review the singles. That was fun.* Smash Hits *pisses on all the other rags who try to intellectualise.* Smash Hits *understands that it's all one big joke, so let's have some fun with it.*

Apart from the most ridiculous metal bands who exist to create a sense of escapism, rock music seems like such an outmoded concept today. Verse-chorus-verse-solo-chorus-long-drawn-out-ending-thanks-you-guys-are-the-best.

It's all fakery. Pop stars don't even pretend to be musical. They just do what they're told for a bit, sell three million records then retire.

Kylie doesn't have to pretend she can actually play an instrument. Give me Duran Duran over Led Zep any day; Andrew Ridgeley was always far cooler than Joe Strummer. It's just that it has taken you until now to realise this.

Ridgeley had it right, actually: mill around looking

pretty. Keep your mouth shut then leave with a girl on each arm. Ridgeley never blew his cool by trying to make solo records. That was beneath him. It should be beneath you too, just like bothering to learn to play a guitar at this stage in the game is beneath you.

Why bother? You've got this far.

So that is the new outlook you adopt – you will celebrate your ineptitude. You want to end the fakery.

You even lobby the band about it.

— Let me go out there without that bloody thing, you say to James, nodding at your pristine new black Stratocaster.

It's ten minutes before you're due onstage in – where? – Newcastle? Yes, Newcastle. The Toon. You can tell by the accents of the voices in the corridor.

— But what will you do?

— I don't know. I'll wing it. I'll just wander about looking bored, or confrontational. Go on – it'll be a statement. The last honest statement in rock 'n' roll.

— You're off your rocker, Rich.

— But it'll be brilliant, you counter, warming to your own idea. Everyone knows I can't play it anyway.

— It'll mess with the symmetry. How will I be able to concentrate if you're lolling about the stage, all pissed and sloppy?

— Yeah, Edwards. Do a bloody day's work for once in your life. Lazy work-shy get.

This from Nick, sitting in his jockeys in the corner.

— How about I don't go on at all, then?

— How will that work? asks James. Are you going to do a mime or something like that bloke Howard Jones used to have onstage?

Sean snorts at this.

Your pour yourself another drink and twist up your face.

— Hmmm, I don't know. Maybe I could just mingle in the crowd.

— Doing what?

— I don't bloody know. Just being myself, I suppose. Shaking hands and that.

— Shaking hands, guffaws Nicky. Get her. Like the Queen or something. Queen Richard of the principality of Fuck-Up. I'm all for it. I'd join you myself but you know how I hate the public . . . so dirty . . . so many germs.

A head appears around the door.

— Two minutes, lads.

You knock back your drink.

— Come on, your majesty, says James fondly grabbing you in a headlock. You'll be all right. Everyone knows you're the best worst guitarist of your generation.

— Now that, you manage to say through the choke-hold, that is very true.

*

I never learnt Cymraeg. Never saw the point, really.

Sometimes you have to accept the modern world and look forward; sometimes you have to follow the consensus and the consensus is that whatever you feel about the country, Welsh is a marginalised language. It's kept alive by historians and patriots and academics but it serves no real purpose other than to remind us of what went before. Of what we have lost.

Everyone knows monoglot Welsh speakers are virtually extinct creatures, so it remains a language kept alive by those who speak English too – an irony I have never been able to get my head around.

Besides, I have never looked to the past to learn my lessons, I've discovered everything that I need to know through experience. Through going out there and seeing it for myself.

And what a lot of good that did you. All the things you've seen and done and here you are, wallowing in your own little self-created cesspit.

Actually, I no longer see it as a predicament.

Oh really? So what do you see these mad wanderings as?

A solution.

A solution.

Yes. It's what you wanted, isn't it? It's you who's been telling me to stop whinging. It's you who's been telling me that I need to disappear and never come back. And it's you who's been torturing me for months and months now.

Fine – but I didn't expect you to bring us on a fucking hike.

Who cares? Who cares where we're going? I don't. I no longer care. I just want to keep walking and walking.

And then what do you plan on doing, exactly? You're not even dressed properly.

And then nothing. You're missing the point: I have no plans. Plans hold you back. I'm living in what few moments there are left. And I'll do that by keeping on walking until I meet the horizon, or the earth falls away, or I drop. The point is, from now on I stop thinking. The intellectualising is over. The arguing with myself is over. The worry ends. Because guess what? I no longer care. I. No. Longer. Care.

I'm half dead already.

*

Your second album gets worse reviews than your first, but enters the charts at No. 8, a rise of five places from the debut. So you are officially a 'Top 10 band'.

As your label are quick to remind you, however, it's a quiet week, they've spent over a hundred thousand on marketing alone – including wallpapering London with the cover image – and some cowboy called Garth Brooks is out-selling you ten to one.

But the band is too busy enjoying this tour to over-analyse things. You're just glad to be touring during the summer months for once, glad to have the band's tight circle of friends out with you.

For the first time you appear as a five-piece, with Producer Dave playing some keyboards onstage, his long blond hair flowing behind like some sort of '80s soft-focus/soft-porn AOR dream.

Nick's brother Patrick joins you to man the merchandise stall. Philip and/or Martin come to most shows and are finally able to relax and enjoy some of the rewards from the three years of work they have put into your band. Gillian, Terri and Caffy come along too and you realise you need these people. You need these people to pull you back from the mirrors, the broken bottles and the shadows. You especially need women around you; women are cotton wool made flesh.

You need them all because onstage, or in interviews, or being mobbed by fans outside the venues, you are someone else. You are the withdrawn rock star. The tortured guy.

That 'Richey Manic'.

That dickhead.

Not you.

Him.

That dickhead.

*

I keep thinking of a remote quarry high up in the hills. It's about a hundred yards across and it's been a long time since it was active. It's so remote that even the tracks leading to it are now buried beneath heather that now houses nesting grouse. Scattered all around, composite machinery parts rust like retired fireballs and huge rocks nestle in the dirt and weeds that nestle around them. The whole thing feels like another planet, like no human has ever been here.

I pick up a stone and throw it at an oil drum and the quarry explodes with tiny flashes of white.

Rabbits. Many rabbits scatter in all directions, their white tails bobbing. Across the shale, over rocks, down their burrows. I feel like I have been here before, only I haven't because the quarry does not exist in physical three-dimensional form, instead I have carved it from my own imagination and allowed myself to wander deep into it.

So deep into it, in fact, that it feels like there is no way out. And one phrase keeps repeating in my mind: *a good place to find your God.*

*

Each member of Bon Jovi has their own dressing room; you have a dingy Portakabin to share between the band and crew. Forty-eight bottles of lager, sandwiches and a fruit plate tucked in the corner.

You don't care, though. When they offer you the support slot you nearly bite your agent's hand off.

You're just bemused to be here.

You're bemused because this is a slice of the big time. Bemused because even your own fans will be confused by this contradiction, this major act of selling out.

And you're bemused because Bon Jovi represent everything that the Manic Street Preachers hate about rock music.

You hate them because they sing crowd-pleasing songs about girls and cars and cowboys riding steel horses off into the sunset.

You hate them because their singer wears lifts in his shoes and has caps on his teeth.

You hate them because they are still living in an MTV-imagined version of reality.

But mainly you hate them because they have the worldwide success that eludes you.

How shallow you are.

A couple of weeks later, during your first time off in months, in the final days of summer, Nick marries Rachel.

He grins all the way through the service.

This was always going to be the way for Nick, your twin in glamour, the light-hearted yin to your troubled yang, the least rock 'n' roll man – and therefore the most rock 'n' roll man – in this sordid game. Nick who enjoys hoovering and dusting, and who doesn't care who knows it. Nick who likes telly and crisps. Nick who loves domestic bliss. Nick who would rather stay at home than tour. Nick who has found love and happiness. Nick who has a fulcrum to his life, where you only have chaos.

On the day, at the ceremony, you are simultaneously insanely jealous, ecstatic, sad, nostalgic, embittered, enamoured and suddenly, perhaps for the first time, in love with the idea of a life partnership.

Two days later it is business as usual as you're back on Top of the Pops, *your roadie Paul donning a Mickey Mouse mask and taking the honeymooning newlywed's place stage left.*

7

'My words fly up, my thoughts remain below:
Words without thoughts never to heaven go.'

(*Hamlet*, 3. 3)

FUCK ME AND LEAVE

Trudging onwards and upwards I keep my head down to watch where I am putting my feet, periodically stopping to cough and hack up the phlegm that seems to be coating my lungs. Walking this way gives me a new perspective on my surroundings. In the city you walk with your head up to allow yourself to be impressed by the dreams of architects, or you stare straight ahead to avoid the gaze of your fellow man who dares to try and make a connection by catching your eye. But here it is different.

Here I scour the ground and I see lichen patterns forming on the damp stones like the tiniest flowers clinging to the rock face. I see small huddles of spiraea gathered together in the nooks between rocks, their pink-plumed heads nodding nervously in a cross-breeze. I see many, many sheep turds.

Suddenly the countryside seems to vibrate with colours as life and death do battle everywhere I look. A gentle rain chips away at the ground. The beck carves through the land, submerged rocks knocking against one another like cannonballs on its bed. A flower blooms only to be torn away at the stem by a rabbit with chisel teeth. A lone tree cuts the sky like a knife. And all around me: life and death and life.

Life.

And death.

*

Germany again.

Autumn again *and you've not seen daylight for nearly a week and when you do it has been through sunglasses, a hangover and a dark veil of anxiety.*

Frankfurt and Nuremberg.

Munich and Stuttgart.

Essen and Hamburg.

Bremen.

Hanover.

Cologne.

Afterwards all you remember are the spaces in between each town or conurbation and the efficient, clinical hum of the Führer's Reichsautobahnen.

You were here two weeks ago to play a festival and now you're back again. Only this time the weather has turned. It is clear and crisp and you feel the cold constantly. You pile on layer upon layer of clothing but it doesn't seem to make any difference; you can't get warm.

And the food looks disgusting again; the thought of putting any of it in your mouth repels you, makes you nauseous. You pick at pieces of hard, dark bread and cheese, but little else. You can't face it. You drink a lot of strong black coffee. Sometimes you forgo milk for vodka.

You have no appetite. For food, drink, conversation, any-thing. Behind a slurred veneer you find yourself sinking into a dark, dark place.

One night someone offers you a cigarette so you take two. By the end of the week you're getting through twenty a day, which increases to forty after a couple of weeks. You smoke incessantly; it's disgusting. The nicotine kills what little appetite you might have had and stains your fingers yellow.

Of course it's self-destructive. That's why you do it.

— Get them fags away from me, says Nicky, flapping his hand dramatically.

And even though he's joking, and even though James has smoked for years, you know he disapproves too. They all do because the smoking is symptomatic of something else, something bigger, something wider. A problem that won't go away.

A problem no one wants to talk about, least of all you.

Meanwhile, for convenience's sake, the band's thirteen-song set list remains unchanged for weeks. It has got you through the entire summer as you stalk the stage in the shadows each night and James carries the weight of the band on his shoulders. Each night he is exhausted, each night his voice becomes a little hoarser from the shouting. Germany greets you with vague interest and Gold Against The Soul *fails to chart.*

In time a general oppressive mood permeates the Manics' camp and you become paranoid that it is emanat-ing from you, though you can't be sure. Everyone in the crew certainly treads lightly around you for most of the time, making sure to give you a wide berth, and even Wire's shark-smile has become a rare commodity. James is similarly distracted and spends most of his down-time with the roadies and the soundman, discussing guitar pedals and muso stuff, or else hammering the strong German beers in the bars of each town. He's like a sailor on shore leave, whereas you feel like the ship's rat.

Diseased and hated.

Sean, as usual, glides through it all with his head buried in his Game Boy, or staring off impassively into space with headphones clamped to his head. You have no idea who or what he listens to. In fact, you have no idea what he actually thinks about anything.

For the first time in years you feel like four separate entities crawling around in the darkness, which hardly helps your paranoia. Sometimes it goes quiet when you walk into the room. In your bunk during the overnight drives you're sure you can hear your name being whispered so you keep a little flask of vodka by your feet and stick as close to a routine as possible in order to get through this thing in one piece. Sleep. Hangover. Reading/writing. Interviews.

Drink.

Show.

Drink.

Sleep.

*

The ridge of the hill is like the spine of a great reptile that lies half-buried in the earth, its neck bent and head held low as it turns away from a world it no longer recognises.

I follow it.

*

You see some of Germany beyond the bus and the sub-zero backstage rooms, and afterwards you almost wish you hadn't. Because it's only later – much later – that you realise you left part of yourself back there in Belsen and Dachau.

Most bands either cut loose or rest up on their days off. Not your band.

Not your band.

Your band goes to see death camps. Your band takes taxis to the places where thousands upon thousands of people were erased, their twisted emaciated corpses piled high, all watched over by avatars of evil.

Dachau is by far the worst. You go there the day after the Munich show and are dumbstruck by what the guide tells you. Like how when they liberated it US troops found sixteen hundred people to each barrack designed for two hundred and fifty. How they were so horrified by what they saw, they shot some of the guards there and then, without trial. A trial was unnecessary. They had seen it with their own eyes.

Dachau stays in your head long after you leave. And though you should feel glad to be alive and free, you don't. Instead you feel trapped in a world that could allow this to happen.

You sink deeper into the dark place.

That night, with no show to play, no focus for the day and your own hotel room, you get drunk on vodka and stub out a cigarette on your arm. You actually hear the flesh crackle as you do it. It leaves a perfectly circular white blister, which over the next few days will turn red, and then become raw and begin to ooze pus.

*

The beck is far away below as I continue along the reptile's spine. It is nothing more than a grey wound in the earth, a meandering fissure in the earth's crust, the car-sized boulders that litter its banks reduced to jagged dots lifted down the valley during the last days of the ice age some twenty thousand years ago and randomly deposited at the beck's side – itself the last trickling traces of a glacier that must have once covered South Wales with hundreds of miles of creaking, shifting, landscape-sculpting ice.

Where the beck snakes downhill, miniature oxbows have formed amongst the rocks and small shelves where the earth has been sluiced away by the flow, revealing red-peat cross-sections from which tangled roots protrude and earthworms gamely attempt to wriggle back into the wet loam.

Across the other side of the valley, patches of flattened bracken are patterned across the hillside; great brittle burnt-orange swathes, poised for fossilisation. I realise I am walking through one such crop now, a mirror image of what I can see a mile away as the crisp branches and dead leaves crunch underfoot like a frost.

I am tired and keep coughing but I will keep walking, even if it kills me.

*

The cold sake tastes like nail polish, but you knock it back all the same while pushing at the untouched squid rings with your chopsticks.

Tokyo again. City of vending machines. City of the soiled panties. Germany is a shadow on the memory.

You – band and crew – have the night off and take turns suggesting what to do after the meal.

Someone thinks you should all go to a lesbian sumo-wrestling club they've heard about.

Someone else dismisses the idea.

Your head feels hot and heavy; your skin puffy. Blotchy.

Japan again. Jet-lagged again.

Drunk and depressed again.

Still down in the darkness.

You get into an argument with James about football, but halfway through making a long and convoluted point you forget what you're arguing about, and start laughing.

Then you're in another bar. Some ridiculously tacky and clichéd karaoke place that one of the crew recommended.

More drinks.

Nick disappears. Sean gets sarcastic. Someone knocks over a drink.

James meanwhile clenches his teeth and stoically drains his bottled lager. He is becoming as unhinged as you are, in his own quiet, brooding, macho way.

In such alien landscapes, you all revert to type.

Many more drinks later and you are falling onto your bed at the palatial Miyako Hotel.

It's only the next morning that you're told that an earthquake measuring 7.1 on the Richter Scale shook the hotel for a few minutes in the middle of the night.

Blissfully drunk, you slept right through it.

Gifts.

There are gifts wherever you go.

Game Boys, toys, books, flowers, dolls, comics, pornography, letters, cards. It's a gift-giving culture.

You spend three weeks here.

Three weeks flitting between Osaka and Fukuoka. Hiroshima and Tokyo.

Nagoya.

Sendai.

Sapporo.

In and out of hotels. On and off trains. In and out of consciousness.

Smoking and coughing. Smoking and coughing.

Unknown Pleasures *on your Walkman to block out the silence of Japan in autumn. The pink chrysanthemum blossom of a lovelorn, wine-drunk Li Po poem and azure watercolour sunsets. The mist on the distant mountain-tops.*

A solitary cigarette on a station platform.
Then back to the city.

*

Rain falls as the opposite side of the valley gives way to a thick forest of alpine trees planted in near-perfect lines. The trees are tucked in tight and are of the darkest green. There is something very comforting about the regimented pattern as well as the consistency of nature.

I stop and sit on a rock in a slight hollow to drink some water and catch my breath. Then I light a cigarette. When I have smoked it, I use my heel to dig a divot in the soil, drop the butt end into it, then cover it up again. I read somewhere that it takes sixty years for a fag end to biodegrade. Or maybe it was six hundred years. I forget which.

What does that have to do with anything?
I was just saying.
It's a bit late to be worrying about your impact on the planet you're intent on leaving behind, don't you think?
Don't.
They'll be looking for you, you know.
I don't want to think about that.
They'll be tearing their hair out.
Please don't. I thought you had stopped. I thought you were going to leave me alone.

I don't remember that conversation. You and I both know I will only stop when you make me stop.

Oh, I will.

Saying isn't doing.

You'll see.

*

Smoking and coughing. Unknown Pleasures *on the band ghetto-blaster that you've commandeered for the small party in your room after the show. It's a two-person party.*

You and her.

More drinks, more cigarettes. Barefoot in your room.

Smoking and coughing.

Giggling and swaying. 'Shadowplay' *on the ghetto-blaster.*

— *Wait, wait, wait. You've got to listen to this one. I mean* really *listen.*

You rewind the intro and turn it up.

You close the curtains, banish Tokyo for the night, drain your drink and swallow hard. You'll never get used to the taste.

From the speakers, the compressed kick-drum beat pounds in your head.

She's on the bed.

Martin Hannett, you're thinking. Martin Hannett. How did you do it?

You remember her from the UK tour – she flew over and followed you for a few shows. She was more forthcoming than most of the Japanese fans; more Westernised.

She had travelled, read books, was unafraid of conversation. She wasn't a wrist-cutter, just someone who was interested in you. You had a little kiss and a cuddle, then parted ways. Never to meet again.

But now she's back, up in your Tokyo room with her shirt buttons undone, lipstick on her teeth.

You drape a scarf over the lamp and it casts a strange green hue across the room. Green and black.

Ian Curtis had the right idea. Ian Curtis never got old. Never wrote a love song. Never took a bad photograph.

You light a cigarette, inhale, then balance it on the lip of your Coke-can ashtray while listening to guitar lines like rivets being pulled from steel plates.

Then you're on the bed and things are happening in the murky green light.

Ribs against ribs, teeth colliding. Her hand against your chest momentarily pushing you away.

— No.

— Are you sure?

— No.

Her eyes are wide and black and bottomless. You come together again and Ian Curtis sings in his bone-dry baritone.

Hands walk under waistbands and faces are buried in necks in this black green night, the burning cigarette sending grey ribbons dancing to the ceiling like kite-tails. You fumble in your wallet with wet fingers; drunk and urgent, the beginnings of a headache are sighing in the back of your skull.

Teeth, nipples and fingernails.

Tongues, hair and flesh. Two bodies joining together as the music gets louder. A shadow on the wall: a hideous two-headed, multi-limbed monster.

The bass line, the bass line. Mechanical and automated. The monster on the wall. Clicking and hissing like a piston.

Like a piston.

A piston.

A piston.

Cold and metallic.

Functional and unfeeling.

Like a monster.

Like a piston.

A spitting snarling thing.

A monster.

*

My heart pounds in my ears and when I stop walking it takes minutes for my breathing to return to normal. My blood flows, my muscles scream and all my senses are heightened.

I am entering a stage of delirium from this hunger, fatigue and the continued withdrawal from Prozac. And other things. Darker things that are harder to define.

I half expect to wake up in a bed in London, or the flat, or maybe even Mum and Dad's, and for this to 'all be a dream' like a cheesy film that has written itself into a corner but the way my body is aching, and the sweat is cooling on my back and making my T-shirt stick to it, and the little toe on my right foot feels like it's had the skin rubbed right off it, tells me that what I am experiencing is very real.

*

They say you've lost weight. They say you've been at it too hard, for too long. They say you're not looking good – but then you knew that already.

So as soon as the tour is over and you make it back to Britain, they send you to a health farm for the best part of November. Listless days are spent drinking water and picking at fruit. You have dry heaves but you also have cable TV, and you walk around the wooded grounds feeling like a prisoner waiting for parole.

The label foots the bill.

You know what the accountants and the lawyers are thinking. And the band too, probably: thank God we signed to a major. No indie label would ever have the budget to keep patching him up.

And then Philip dies.

Just like that, he slips away.

Philip.

Your manager.

Your man on the inside.

Your friend.

You were warned but you never actually believed it. None of you did. You didn't think it would actually . . . well, you just didn't think. Not Phil. No.

Not Philip.

When you hear the news you all clam up and fall silent. For once, no one has a thing to say. There's no group hugs, no emotive 'sharing'; just a vast, vast silence.

Cancer.

Cancer took ebullient, indefatigable, brilliant, brilliant Phil. Stolen away at thirty-four.

Phil your mentor, your saviour, your surrogate – what? Surrogate nothing. His role was beyond definition; he was more than any manager. He was a one-off, never to be replaced. He was the Manic Street Preachers' earth-bound entity and representative. He was the man who said yes when everyone else said no.

The man who gave you a home and the shirt off his back. The man who gave you hope.

The man who proved you wrong about London, about the music industry. The man who dared to believe. Him and Martin. Both of them. Fucking saviours. Fucking great, great guys.

Gone. Just like that, leaving behind him an impressive legacy, an impeccable reputation and a massive hole in all your lives.

Suddenly nothing really seems to matter.

December 1993.

Merry Christmas.

Piss on the earth and goodwill to all men.

*

I slump and slowly fall to the ground where I lie flat on my back beneath God's great awning. My chest rises and falls. My sallow face is streaked with dirt as one hand grips the ground and pulls out a fistful of heather. I separate a sprig that is topped by minuscule purple flowers and bring it to my nose, then inhale.

It makes me think of the gypsies that used to come knocking at doors when I was younger, selling tiny bouquets of 'lucky heather' held together in twists of tin foil: it makes me remember how we were warned to keep away from the gypsies, told how they would put a curse on us, or that they kidnapped children, yet I only ever thought that they were exotic and exciting for these very reasons and envied their itinerant lifestyle.

I wonder if this heather will bring me luck, then smile at the naivety of such a superstitious thought and the realisation that, no matter where we go or what we experience in life, a large part of us all remains in childhood.

I sniff the sprig again, then put it in the pocket of my coat.

'Just in case.'

Then I close my eyes.

*

You're driving around Cardiff with Nicky in the passenger seat, his chin on his knees.
— How do you move this seat back?
— The handle. Pull the handle. The one under the seat.
— I can't bloody reach under the seat, can I?

— You know your problem, Wire?

— No, go on then, tell me what my problem is.

— You're all legs, that's what. You're a pair of legs with a smile on top. And a bad attitude.

— Bad attitude? This coming from the Dark Knight himself. Mr Infernal Abyss. Mrs Sillier Plath. I suppose I should take that as some back-handed compliment . . .

You both smile sideways at one another, thinking the same thing: listen to us. Two old biddies.

— Seriously though, Nick, you should think about having a leg reduction. Look at them, they're ridiculous.

— A penis reduction, maybe . . . I could send a couple of spare inches your way if you like. I've seen your Walnut Whip many a time, remember?

— Funny.

— You love it.

Then you're down by the docks. Down by the water. The gateway to Cardiff.

Regenerated Cardiff.

You didn't even know you were looking, but you find yourselves being shown around a showroom flat by an estate agent who discreetly asks for your autographs at the end of the viewing.

— Not for me, he says. For my daughter.

It's a third-floor new-build overlooking the water.

The flat is white, clean, pure, new. It smells of paint and is untainted by humans. It comes part-furnished and has lots of shelf space.

The elevator moves silently and the car ports are empty.

Cardiff Bay stretches out before you. The water below your window.

The sky.

The seagulls.

— I'll take it.

A week later and you have a flat, a mortgage and a toaster.

But you don't have time to immerse yourself in this new-found Wire-esque domestic bliss entirely, however. Not when there is a new task at hand: the making or breaking of the Manic Street Preachers.

Because it is make-or-break time. The second album sold less than the first and your last single – a multi-formatted affair that featured numerous turgid dance remix interpretations and reeked of desperation – stiffed. You all know that this may well be your last chance, and that critical praise means zip to the money-men.

Last autumn you handed James a folder of your most realised set of lyrics yet. Lyrics culled from notes written in Germany, in Japan, across Britain. Lyrics now filtered through the death of a loved one; words left out to rot over a cold, bleak winter.

Lyrics that read like a last will and testament.

Yes. Your best work yet.

So here you are, reverting to the workmanlike routine that is in your blood. With a sense of necessity and purpose re-instilled after the opulent surroundings and flatulent sounds of album number two – the album whose title you don't even want to say out loud – you reach the collective decision to go back to basics. Right back, to a small room in a cheap studio on a nowhere street down by the docks here in Cardiff. Here where the prostitutes tout for business and middle-aged men crawl the kerbs. Here, where the sky always struggles to sustain its own weight.

You become workers in a factory of your own choosing: clock in and clock out. Put in the hours, reap the rewards.

And it works. It actually fucking works.

As designated driver your responsibility is to round everyone up, run the errands and keep the machine running. Then and only then do you allow yourself a drink.

Day in, day out the routine stays the same. The boys commute and converge to record these strange new compressed sounds that James has conjured in order to breathe life into your words, your songs.

Songs of death and exploitation, songs of horror, songs of despair.

Songs that strangle and asphyxiate.

You are so ruthless in your self-editing that all the fat has already been trimmed by the time your songs reach the studio. There, you listen to PiL and Nirvana and Joy Division to put yourself in the headspace, but otherwise rely on little in the way of external input. It's all there on the doorstep anyway: the sea, the sky, the city, the prostitutes in search of punters, their faces deranged and desperate like Goya masks.

There are no interviews, no travelling, no gigs. Just driving and working and drinking and sleeping.

Over and over, against a backdrop of grey familiarity.

And then each evening, when your work is done, Sean and Nick depart and you're off into the red-light night. Either down St Mary's Street with James, or back to the flat for solitary films and smokes and books and bottles. You never have so much to drink that you can't get yourself up in the morning for work, though.

No. Because this is make-or-break time.

And here in your new home town, with your backs up against the wall, the album that you dare to call The Holy Bible *is birthed.*

*

The sound of coughing wakes me and for once it's not my phlegm-coated chest, but something baritone and distant.

It gets closer.

I open my eyes and see nothing but the sky. I am shivering.

The coughing is followed by the sound of rustling grass and the tramping of feet. I slowly sit up and see stars, tiny flashes circling around the peripherals of my vision; shapes I can't quite pin down before they are gone.

It takes a few moments for me to focus but when I do, I see a bearded man with a staff. He doesn't seem surprised to see me. He simply raises a hand, then walks towards me.

*

It's morning and you're at home when your hear the news on the TV: America's greatest – and only – decent living rock star Kurt Cobain is no longer living.

Suicide.

They say on the news he shot himself at home, alone and on the run after an aborted attempt at rehab.

He was born in 1967, like you. He was ill at ease with his role in the world, like you. And now he has erased himself, his brains across the floor, a smoking gun at his side.

A suicide note.

A wife and a child.

The phone starts ringing but you ignore it. It rings all day but you don't want to answer it. You don't want to talk about what just happened. You don't want to talk about what just happened because you're scared about what you might say. What thoughts may be triggered. About what thought processes might be set in motion.

You don't want to think about it at all.

You just want to drink, then sleep.

And with no recording, no obligations, no appointments, that is what you do.

Meanwhile, with candles still burning in Seattle parks, the British press have already found something to fill the gap, something insidious and cheap and so crushingly calculable that it borders on parody.

Britpop, they call it – a ridiculous recreation of a golden, mythical era. Only it's not Britain they're recreat-

ing, it's London – and a Mary Poppins London at that.
That's why Britpop will have little lasting impact upon
Britain, let alone the rest of the world.

And who wants to wave the flag, anyway? Flags are
for burning.

*

'Now then,' says the bearded man with the staff.

'Hello,' I say, then make as if I am about to stand.

'That's all right, son. No need to get up.'

Embarrassed to be caught napping in the heather, I shakily get up onto my feet.

The man's beard is long and grey and makes it very hard to define his age. He could be forty, or he could be twice that. He's also wearing an old tweed jacket and a pair of glasses that have a piece of Sellotape on one corner of the frame.

Despite the shock of seeing him here, his presence is a friendly one.

'Nice day for it.'

His accent is indistinguishable. It doesn't sound Welsh, though.

'Yes.'

'Bird-watching, I mean.'

'Oh. Yes.'

'I just saw two red kites back there,' he says, jerking his thumb back behind him. 'And a buzzard. Or maybe you weren't bird-watching at all.'

I don't say anything.

'It's all right son,' he smiles. 'I couldn't give a tinker's tit. You could be on the run for all I care. You look like you could use a cuppa, though.'

'That would be great.'

He takes off his backpack and gestures to the ground. 'Do you mind?'

'Be my guest.'

The man sits down in a cross-legged approximation of the lotus position, opens up his pack and pulls out a flask. It's an old-fashioned, tartan-patterned one. He unscrews the lid, pours a cup, then passes it to me. It's coffee.

'It's black, I'm afraid.'

Close up I see that his beard comes halfway down his chest like a thatched grey waterfall and around his mouth it's yellowed from nicotine. His face suggests that he is very old, but his bodily movements are light and nimble. His hair is piled up into a woollen hat that he's pulled down low over his ears, and his eyes sit deep in his face, giving him the look of a permanent squint. There is something solid, immovable and elemental about him. Something timeless. He looks as much a part of the landscape as the grass, the heather and the bracken.

The stones.

The beck.

The boulders.

Maybe he *is* God?

No. He's not God.

I take a sip of coffee. It is strong and it is bitter and it is good.

*

346

You are inexplicably, overwhelmingly, surprisingly, staggeringly and scarily popular in Thailand.

After weeks and weeks of isolation in Cardiff you emerge from a Welsh winter into a Thai spring. You expected gifts and fans but what you don't expect is this – something approximating Beatlemania.

From the moment you put on your sunglasses, light a cigarette and walk through customs to the second you return four days later you are treated like gods.

Like gods.

Your second album has sold fifty thousand copies here – more than in the whole of America – so you arrive with an entourage including press people and the head of your UK label, here for no other reason than the fact there's no one to say no to him spending a few grand on a trip out east with those daft Welsh fuckers who still haven't recouped their advance. No one has thought to tell the Thai fans that back home your last single moped into the charts at No. 36, your poorest showing since you got signed. Or if they have, then the Thai fans don't care anyway. They're just grateful you've made the journey.

Three thousand turn out for the signing session alone.

The heat in Bangkok is stifling. It's not like the white burning sun of a European summer's day, where shade provides respite. Here it is inescapable. It grabs you by the throat. It's a damp, clawing heat. Like being wrapped in clingfilm.

You don't want to be here, though; not really. None of you do. You'd rather be at home, avoiding reality, and you're fairly certain that were it not for the band none of you would probably ever have left the British Isles yet.

Wire is the worst traveller. His hypochondria and crippling homesickness flare up as soon as he gets to the airport. His luggage clinks with bottles of pills and potions and remedies and he spends every spare minute in his room, taking long baths, drinking water, eating nothing but crisps and calling his wife three times a day.

In fact, Thailand turns you all into exaggerations of yourselves just as Japan did before it. While Nicky withdraws into his usual fragile and contemptuous state, James becomes a booze-hound lording it up with the NME *guys who join you for a couple of days on Sony money, and Sean refuses to have anything resembling 'fun' on the principle that fun is for other people and that indifference is more his thing.*

And you? You go for a walk, alone.

Soon your trousers are around your ankles and you're sitting there as the woman tugs at your cock, a little angrily for your liking.

The hotel room is a dirty box with paint peeling from the walls and the sound of coughing coming from down the corridor. There is also a fan, but it's not plugged in and its flex resembles a dead snake.

It could be a metaphor for your flaccid penis, which you are willing to get hard in the sweaty hand of this hooker to save you both the embarrassment of failure –

a hooker who is, admittedly, far more beautiful than any street girl back home in Cardiff or London.

Your penis feels detached, though, disembodied. You knew this would happen, but you wanted to find out anyway.

When she smiles at you sympathetically – or maybe with eyes full of pity – it just makes things twice as bad. It's ridiculous. You are meant to pity her, not the other way around.

Useless floppy manhood.

You paid the equivalent of three quid for this, and you intend to give her the same again on the way out. Maybe more.

Or is that insulting?

You just needed to know what it felt like to pay for it.

And the biggest surprise is it feels exactly as you expected it would: blank, boring and businesslike and tainted with regret.

Anyway, does it even count if you don't cum?

*

I take out my cigarettes and offer them to him.

'A tailor-made,' he says, and deftly removes one. 'Lovely.'

Deep down in the valley I hear a screech. Fighting foxes, perhaps. Or a bird.

He leans in and I light his cigarette for him, then light mine.

'Well then,' he says.

We sit in silence for a while, drinking coffee and smoking our cigarettes. The coffee begins to warm me up.

His staff lies beside him. It has an elaborate design around the handle. A hand-carved serpent coiled around the thick end, then finished with a varnish. A leather lanyard has been fed through a small drilled hole.

A couple of minutes pass then he speaks.

'I've seen you.'

*

You're all squeezed into a boat, sweating and steaming your way down the River Chopraya. If the journalist and the photographer weren't here, you wouldn't be either. But there's more to this trip than just playing the gigs, drinking bottled beer or getting wanked off by prostitutes – this trip is as much about showing people back home that you are now an 'international band'. Look, the photos will say: here are those Manics in an exotic location. Here are the Manics being mobbed, just like the Beatles. Here are the Manics being the type of rock stars we always said they were.

It is all about projection these days. Projection of an image; the 'idea' of the band, rather than the sweating, agitated, diarrhoea-stricken reality.

Tomorrow night, before you return to the stage for an encore in the sold-out, airless MBK Hall, you will attempt to puncture that image by taking a knife from the set that sits in your dressing room – a gift from some fan girl – and drawing it across your chest in a series of measured moves. As you do, your skin will tear open and sweat will run into the cuts and it will sting, then the blood will flow, and you'll feel more like yourself again.

Here, back home, and in the band too they'll try to interpret what it means – but you know exactly: it means nothing. There is no rationale that can be applied to this moment; for once it is something beyond intellectualisation.

For once it is simply about the feeling. It's about release.

And in that moment everything is forgotten.

*

My impulse is to stand and run but I know it would be futile, not to mention absurd.

There is nowhere to run to, and I just don't have the energy.

Besides – the coffee is good.

Instead I look at him – this bearded stranger – and nod.

He says it again.

'I've seen you.'

I don't know what to say to that, so say nothing. Articulating words feels too hard right now. I've not had a proper conversation in days.

'Don't take that the wrong way. I'm not following you. I was up on the fells over yonder and I happened to see you enter the valley. We don't see many people up here and I couldn't help but notice the way you were walking. I thought maybe you were drunk at first, but I can see you're not. I noticed you didn't have any gear with you either. Then when I saw you collapse I thought I'd better check and see if you still had a pulse. Not that it is my business.'

'Thanks.'

My voice cracks as I say this and I have to clear my throat a couple of times.

I take another sip of my drink, pull some blades of grass out of the ground and roll them between my fingers. Then a thought occurs to me.

'What are you doing up here? Not that it's my business either . . .'

He smiles at this. He smiles with his eyes. And when he does his whole face lights up.

'Just wandering,' he says. 'Trying to get away.'

I look up.

'Who from?'

'Them lot,' he says with a subtle nod of the head.

I look around and behind me but don't see anyone. I furrow my brow at him.

'People,' he says, and smiles again. 'Just people in general.'

*

Spring is in full bloom and the album is in production when a letter arrives from Daniel, your friend from

Swansea, who you've not spoken to in ages. Probably not since just after you graduated, when he came to see the band in Bristol. He writes to tell you that two weeks ago Nigel, one of your gang at university, hung himself.

Nigel was by far the coolest and funniest person you knew at Swansea and your first instinct is to ask: 'Why – what was the reason?'

That's always the question people ask about a suicide: why?

When faced with such horror they want a simple, digestible explanation, yet how can anyone answer that but Nigel himself? No one can ever really know what goes on inside another person's head and there is no quick and easy answer, for the human mind is a deeply complex and dark entity.

Nigel's suicide sends you into a tail-spin of fear, horror and self-analysis. You guiltily think of all of the band's associations and flirtations with the concept of suicide – 'Suicide Alley', 'Spectators of Suicide', 'Suicide Is Painless' – and how pathetic and offensive they now seem.

Poor Nigel.

Poor, poor Nigel, so alone like that.

Yet for all your sympathy you can't help but turn his death around to yourself and the thought: It could have been me.

You hit the bottle as a tsunami of questions flood your mind. When did he know for sure? What were his final thoughts? What did it feel like, the tightening of the rope? Who found him?

How many people cried at his funeral?

Late that night, drunk and teary and feeling completely destructive, you take a pen and paper and write down a verse from a Wordsworth nature poem.

> If this belief from heaven be sent,
> If such be Nature's holy plan,
> Have I not reason to lament
> What Man has made of Man?

Then you fold the paper into an aeroplane and launch it from the window of your flat, out into the Cardiff night, out to sea.

The night wind takes it and turns it, takes it away, away.

8

'If thou didst ever hold me in thy heart,
Absent thee from felicity awhile,
And in this harsh world draw thy breath in pain,
To tell my story.'

(*Hamlet*, 5. 2)

THERE IS NO CHOICE

He pours me some more coffee.

'It's beautiful, isn't it?'

'Yes,' I say. 'Thanks.'

'I meant the landscape.'

'Oh, right.'

'Do you know what makes it beautiful?'

I look around and I see an empty green valley below us. Behind us I can see layer upon layer of soft rounded hills stretching for miles. I see rocks.

I see trees.

Grass.

Clouds.

I see Wales.

But before I can answer he speaks again.

'It's not what you can see, but what you can't see.'

He pauses and time appears to stand still and it is as if I have been here for days with the bearded stranger. Finally he speaks.

'The beauty is in the absence of people.'

'Right.'

A pause.

'Of course, beauty is subjective. What might be beautiful to me may be inherently ugly to you.'

'No, I agree with you,' I say. 'It's people that I'm trying to get away from too. Well, kind of, anyway. I think maybe I'm also trying to escape myself . . .'

He nods at this.

'And how is that working out for you?'

'Ah – I guess that's the annoying part. I can't escape myself.'

He laughs at this. A big hearty laugh from somewhere deep within his nicotine-stained Santa Claus beard.

He pokes at the ground with the toe of his boot. Then his smile slowly fades.

'The thing is, we can never escape ourselves. We don't have very long in which to try, either. Life is short. And that's the other problem: that constant awareness of our own mortality. The realisation that we have no control over our own demise, only how we choose to spend our time before then.'

A thought swims up to the surface from the darker depths of my memory. A quote.

'*Life has no meaning the moment you lose the illusion of being eternal.*'

'Sartre,' he replies, quickfire.

I'm taken aback. Not by my own pretentiousness – though I should be – but by the old man's response.

'You know it?'

He shrugs in the affirmative.

'Only how we choose to spend our time,' he says again with resignation.

A moment passes and then, as if suddenly remembering something, his face lights up.

'Sandwich?'

*

The band do their best to accommodate you, but you know they don't understand how much you're hurting right now. In an attempt to alleviate any professional pressure, they tell you you're free to walk away from any obligations. Take a hiatus, they say. The band isn't everything.

And then Nicky says something that haunts you for days.

— You're like the Motorcycle Boy from Rumblefish, *aren't you? What's that Dennis Hopper quote about him?*

James interjects.

He says that the Motorcycle Boy is miscast in life. That he was born into the wrong era and on the wrong side of the river.

— Yeah, says Nick. That's it.

— And the worst thing is, though he has the ability to do anything there is nothing he wants to do.

Days later, alone in your flat, your body just sort of gives out. It rebels against you. It takes a stand: fuck you, it says.

Food is an impossibility and you can't sleep. You have a constant hacking cough and saliva dries around the edge of your mouth. All you can eat are your fingernails and the inside of your mouth.

A multitude of thoughts do battle in your head at any given moment, which makes it impossible to read a book or write lyrics. Conversation seems exhausting and any sexual desire you had has disappeared. You haven't masturbated in about three weeks.

All you can do is pad about the place making cups of tea, smoking and watching videos. You watch your old favourites again and again: Apocalypse Now, Naked, Equus. *And you listen to the same records over and over again. It's easier this way; this way you don't have to make a decision.*

You receive no visitors and you don't answer the phone. You don't answer the phone because you choose not to have one. It's one less impingement on your world.

You don't leave the flat for days. Your arms are a mess.

A bloody, scabby, weeping mess.

A disgraceful map of your own making.

Drained of nourishment, you are incapable of exerting yourself. You simply can't be bothered with anything.

And for the first time, you're actually scared. Scared of yourself.

Scared of what you're capable of.

Scared of the feelings stirring within you.

Finally Martin comes knocking on your door and within the hour you are on a ward in the Whitchurch hospital, crying uncontrollably as pale old men in white smocks look on.

*

We chew on our sandwiches – thick brown bread and thick strong cheese – and we drink more coffee, then we smoke another cigarette each.

We do this in silence, high up on the ridge of a hill in a valley in South Wales, Great Britain in AD 1995, me and this man, whose conversation hints at wisdom and whose demeanour suggests a oneness with the elements and the landscape. An oak tree of a man.

Then this oak tree of a man stands and brushes the crumbs from his lap. I feel the question burning in my stomach. I can feel it rising within me. I have no control over it. It is coming from the other half of me. The half I cannot control. I clear my throat again.

Then I look up

'Are you God?' I ask.

He is a silhouette now. A man in profile against the sky.

He squats down on his haunches, then looks away, squinting.

'No,' he says. 'I'm not God. I'm a retired lecturer.'

'I didn't think so.'

I told you he wasn't God.

'But if you're looking for him – and you wouldn't be the first lost young man to wander the mountains in search of answers – you only have to look around you.'

He pauses to smile, then continues.

'Because God isn't a man. If he exists at all, then he is in the dirt and the rain, the rocks and the grass. And if that's not enough for you, then you should give up looking because you won't find anything closer to perfection than this.'

*

They come and visit you. All of them.

You see more people in three days than you have in the past three weeks.

Mum, Dad and Rachel. Martin and the boys.

Their faces are so stern that you try to crack jokes.

— Lighten up, you tell them. It might never happen.

They bring you grapes and they bring you magazines. The kid-glove treatment.

They don't mention it, but you know the boys are wondering what the hell to do, so you make it easy for them. Even though you're blitzed on Librium you make an effort. You feel you owe it to them.

So you suck up the stammer and the drool and try to comfort them.

You try to comfort them.

— It's OK, you tell them. It's OK. I'm not going to fuck this up for us. For you. This album's too good for us to blow it now. I've been thinking that maybe I'm just a hindrance live. Maybe I could, you know, retire from the public eye, but still do my bit. Maybe take a backseat role. 'Creative director' or something. I could do the lyrics and the art. Keep on doing what I've always done, but stay away from touring. Look after my body. Get my head straight. I still can't play that plank anyway.

This is what you tell them and they nod and smile and

are noncommittal. You don't know what they're thinking. What they want.

When you're done talking you walk them out on wobbly legs to the hospital entrance to say your quiet goodbyes.

As they leave, you wonder how long their sympathy and patience will last. These are limited resources and you're not stupid. You're not oblivious to your surroundings either; quite the opposite, in fact. You're hypersensitive. Sooner or later they'll get sick of waiting for you.

This thought gnaws at you for the rest of the day. The idea that you are letting them down. That staying at home while they do all the hard work feels like a cop-out.

So that night you ring James from the phone in the hospital corridor.

With your voice quivering, you ring him and you tell him you're sorry and that you're really going to try and get better. That you want to be in the band. That you really want to do this properly.

You tell him you're going to practise your guitar until your fingers bleed. And you're going to get better. At everything.

At music.

At eating. At sobriety.

At life.

*

The bearded stranger who definitely is not God stands up and makes to depart, but before he does he rifles through his backpack.

'I don't know who you are and I don't need to know,' he says. 'We all have a right to roam the mountains unmolested. But I do know that the weather can turn out here and you look far from equipped. So, here, just in case.'

He passes me the rest of his sandwiches, a bottle of water and a rescue blanket, which is actually an unused orange tarpaulin neatly folded into a flat A4-sized rectangle.

'Thanks,' I say. 'That's really kind of you. But I'll be all right.'

'If it'll make you feel less guilty about it then maybe you could trade me another one of those cigarettes.'

'Deal.'

I pass him the packet, which has six left in it. I have no more. He takes a couple out.

He looks at me again.

'Really. I'll be fine.'

*

After six or eight or ten days – it's hard to tell how long you've been here – Mum and Dad check you out and Martin drives you to London, to leafy Richmond and a clinic called the Priory, near a huge park where the wild deer run free and the summer sun is a thousand shades of orange exploding on your retina.

You weigh six stone.

*

It's only when the man has long gone that I see that he has left his staff behind. I pick it up and look at the coiled serpent: two snakes intertwined to form a kind of wooden plait that follows the grain of the wood. The handle has been polished smooth by the palm of a cupped hand and the bottom tip is dyed dark with peat and mud and the primordial juices of the hills.

I grip the stick in my hand and continue my walk along the ridge of the hill. My breathing is still short and I am soon sweating again. My panting is loud and troubled and my legs are unsteady.

My energy resources are so severely depleted that I have to stop every few minutes to rest and hawk up phlegm and sip water. Once or twice I stumble and fall. The second time I turn my ankle but after a short rest I am OK to continue.

It is then that I realise that I have stopped thinking. About everything. There's a new kind of stillness and silence about me and the babble of the internal voices – the people of the past, the demons of the present and the concerns of the future – are all finally quiet. There is only this moment, the here and now, and it takes all my efforts to remain conscious and moving within it.

It becomes entirely about the repetition of move-ment: put one leg in front of the other. Breathe deep. Keep sending that oxygen into the bloodstream. Stay upright. Watch where you put your feet. Aim for the horizon.

One step at a time.

*

Captive, bored and bombarded with quasi-spiritual jargon and hollow religious clap-trap, being in this place reminds of you being back in the Methodist chapel, only this time you're paying £300 per day for the privilege.

It's no coincidence that this place is called the Priory – 'a religious house governed by a prior or prioress'. All residents are automatically inducted into compulsory AA meetings so you find yourself gently coerced into entering the famed Twelve Step Programme.

You have issues with it right from the off. Step 1 is fine – 'Admission of one's own powerlessness', that's easy – but everything else is problematic. Step 2 is the 'encouragement of a belief in a higher power, while attacking "intellectuality and self-sufficiency"'.

No, no, no, you scream inside. You can take my time and my money but you can't have my fucking mind.

No way.

Not my mind.

You don't say this though because you are willing yourself to get through it. You don't say this because you know you need help. Instead you concentrate on the notions of a higher power. God is out, because he doesn't exist. Something that doesn't exist is not going to pull you through this. Ditto false prophets, icons or dead heroes.

The only worthwhile figure you can think of without bursting into tears of regret is Snoopy, but even he is old and on his last legs.

So you concentrate on the concept of 'nature' instead: nature with all its cruelty and violence, but its constant capacity for regrowth and healing.

Nature matters because it will out-live us all.

So you spend your days smoking cigarettes and day-dreaming of creeping ivy and woodlands and streams and meadows and conducting 'a searching and thorough moral inventory' (Step 4).

You don't know whether any of this is helping, but at least the urge to draw blood dissipates and you finally begin to get a few snatched hours of sleep here and there.

Meanwhile The Holy Bible, *your greatest work both musically and lyrically, is released during your stay but you're too deep in the programme and too lost in your own self-created green heaven to notice.*

*

It is beginning to get dark when I stop for a while and sit and watch the sky. It's breathtaking. Over from the east, working towards me, it is a range of blues, moving from white through pale blue to azure to the colour of a clotted bruise. Then over to the west it is shot through with all the shades of fire – darkening salmon, orange, carmine, cherry, crimson, copper, chestnut. It is a banquet of colours and I want to reach out and touch it, taste it, pierce it and rise beyond it. The sky is so vast and I am so insignificant that it is only this moment that matters. This is what I focus on. Only this moment.

The sky.

Me.

The moment.

Then I start laughing.

I start laughing because I think of all the years of worry and anxiety, of books read in lonely bedrooms, all those thoughts about self-disgust and self-obsession, about art and artists, money and music, of love and loyalty, blood and bandages, of murderers and the murdered, and I think: what a waste of time and energy. All I really had to do was to learn to stop worrying and live in the moment.

But can you ever actually do that without first relinquishing the one thing you ultimately have control over: your body?

I don't want to think about this.

I don't want to think about this because it was too much thinking that brought me here. It was too much thinking that destroyed it all.

And right now I feel too fucking free to go and spoil these sanctified moments by rationalising or analysing them.

My mind is going and my body is going, but in this moment, beneath the sky of a thousand colours, I feel OK.

I laugh as I think all of this and when I stop I can still hear that laughter, braying and honking and cackling and giggling. It is the laughter of a man who has broken through. Or maybe just been broken.

It is the laughter of a madman but I am not scared. Of anything.

*

Six weeks pass. Six weeks of eating and sleeping and talk-ing; all the things you have evaded and avoided for the past however many months.

Six weeks of self-analysis and God-talk. Six weeks of tedious routine that you actually begin to revel in.

Six weeks; your own alternative to the time-honoured school holiday. And now, just as you did as a child, you suddenly feel reluctant to return to what is beginning to feel like work.

In that time your band has released a new single and a new album and played a number of festivals without you. For the first time in five years they have appeared as a three-piece, nothing but shadows and silence filling stage left. They need to, in order to pay your medical bills. It's a big talking point in the press: no one is quite sure where you are and if this is perhaps some sort of publicity stunt. The editorials and letters pages swell with such specula-tion and it's enough to convince you that you need to be back at work.

So, in early September you gather your books and your clothes, the crisp new certificates that say you are a successful graduate of the Twelve Step Programme and a little medal inscribed with the words TO THINE OWN SELF BE TRUE *and you get the hell out of that place. First you go to Mum and Dad's for a day or two of decom-pression and recalibration.*

Then: back to work.

Business as unusual.

*

I taste it first, the blood. It runs down my top lip and into my mouth.

It doesn't taste good. It tastes stale.

Stale blood.

My blood is stale because my body is giving up.

It has received no input, no fuel, and now it is revolting against me. This is one more warning sign, another flashing red light: a smattering of salty rheum and blood dripping from my nose.

I wipe my lip with the back of my hand and a gooey red smear covers it. It is so stunningly red that it is quite beautiful; I never fail to be amazed by the sight of blood. It is like a glimpse into another world – the internal world of the human body.

I start coughing and hawking and there is blood in that too.

*

Noreen the Irish landlady seems to spend all day in the kitchen roasting chickens, baking cakes and steaming great pots of vegetables. You do your best to eat her food to avoid causing offence but can never manage more than half a plateful.

You're ensconced in a converted farmhouse deep in Pembrokeshire, rehearsing for the French tour. Rehearsing the songs you helped write but have never been able to play. Songs that require more than the E, A and D chords that you have got by on this far.

It's nice here, though, and for the first time in ages it

*feels like you're back to being a band again. It's back
to being the four musketeers, back to sharing the same
common goal once again. To promote the album. And for
you to not fuck up.*

*So it's back to the piss-taking and the sarcasm. It's back
to the volume and ringing ears of the rehearsal rooms.
Back to the nightly ritual of watching films together.*

*Back to ignoring the elephant in the room. The skinny,
red-eyed elephant.*

Back to band business.

*The business of phone interviews and group photo
sessions down on the windswept beach. Confessionals to
the weekly inkies and assurances that you're back, back,
back, baby.*

Only this time you do it all sober.

*No whisky, no vodka, no gut-rot sweet white wine. No
late-night books and bottles.*

*Nothing but tea and cigarettes and Noreen's sponges;
long days at the tail of a summer you feel you missed,
and even longer sleepless nights of sobriety addled with
vivid dreams and dark, dark nightmares whose contents
you dare not verbalise for fear they'll send you straight
back to the Whitchurch ward with the old men in the
white smocks.*

*— I had that Take That here last month, Noreen tells
you.*

— What were they like?

*— Just like you boys, lovely lads. Good manners.
Same as you, though they eat more, especially that Gary.
Loved my puddings, that one.*

— Who was your favourite?

— I'd have to say Little Mark. Face like an angel, couldn't sing for toffee.

— Have you ever met East 17?

— East who?

— East 17. They're like Take That, but they come from London, wear silly hats and have better songs.

— No, I don't believe I have now.

*

The staff helps me keep my balance as I continue my ascension.

My feet slip and slide as I clamber over the large damp rocks that lead to the peak of the mountain in this rapidly fading light. I'm breathing in gasps now, the lassitude sending me spiralling deep into a delirious state.

But something propels me forward. Something propels me upwards.

Towards the highest point, marked by a crown of rocks.

Where the mountain meets the sky.

I grip the smooth handle of the staff and use it to take some of the weight as I keep the rocks in sight.

I don't know if it's the light, my mental state, or my erratic, occasionally blurred vision but as I move closer to them and the sun accelerates in its setting, the rocks appear to be in a state of metamorphosis.

At first they look like the heads of a crowd in silhouette – the shadowy, cloying front row of a gig crowd. But then they look like a murder of crows silently sitting on a branch above the valley. Then as I advance still further the crows turn into vultures.

Then they look like the pointed spears of a bear-trap or upended knives stabbing at the sky.

Then they are the fingers of a hand.

Then they are the sharp features of a witch.

Then I have to stop again.

A sip of water. Sweat on my back.

The rise and fall of my ribcage.

The taste of blood in my throat and lungs.

The darkening sky.

*

Paris in September. Paris as the leaves turn brown.

They've never really understood you, the French. They should do, what with their history of existentialism and poetry and reputation for having no sense of humour whatsoever, but somehow the crowds remain small. Twelve hundred people turn out in the capital but the figure diminishes as you head south.

To Lille.

Rouen.

Nancy.

Still, you only have to play ten or so songs per night. It's back to forty-minute sets as this is a joint tour with Therapy?, a hard-rock trio from Northern Ireland who do better business here than your band. Therapy? have songs called things like 'Nowhere', 'Isolation' and 'Die

Laughing', yet are surprisingly happy people. Black-clad piss-takers and party animals. You have known them for a while and though they are good people they are also heavy drinkers, so as James finds himself with some new mischief-making, whisky-drinking pals, you force yourself to pull back away from it all.

You stay in your hotel rooms – a series of them – as long as possible, where you wrestle with the boredom of sobriety. You part your hair and dye it a rich copper colour. You start wearing clothes that accentuate rather than hide your bone-cornered frame. You still can't sleep and eating is no easier.

But the tour continues.

To Grenoble.

Montpellier.

Marseille.

Then it's straight into a UK tour. Another winter tour. Sixteen days covering England, Scotland, Northern Ireland and Wales.

The album charts at Number 6, your highest placing yet, but sales are sluggish. With sales down it's generally far easier to get into the charts these days. It's how many records you sell that matters and so far, The Holy Bible *is* underperforming. You're past caring, though; you couldn't give a shit what the label think any more.

You're just amazed that your last single – a song that the critics have called your most impenetrable lyrical work yet, a song with the chorus 'Lebensraum, kulturkampf / Raus, raus! / Fila, fila' – charted at all. 'Raus' means 'Get outside!', 'Fila' means 'form a line!' and you have just become

the first known songwriter in history to have written a pop
song based upon the orders of Nazi death-camp guards.

And you keep moving.

Cambridge.

Leicester.

Portsmouth.

On and on and on.

Sheffield brings new tattoos. Three in one session: the
eight concentric circles of Dante's hellish inferno from
the first canticle of The Divine Comedy along with the
quote 'Traitors to their Lovers, Traitors to their Guests,
Traitors to their Country, Traitors to their Kindred'.

More blood, more scars, more indelible skin maps of
your own wandering mind.

Then, with bandaged arms, it's on to Leeds.

Nottingham.

Cardiff.

Dublin.

Belfast.

The shows are sold out everywhere you go now but
you really wish someone would just make it stop.

*

I have an overwhelming need to piss so take out my cock
and let go, right there on the shale and the slate. I can tell
by the colour and the burning in my bladder that I am
dehydrated.

It sprays noisily on the rocks and on my shoes.

I look back down the valley that I have walked along

and am surprised by how far I have come. Curving away out of sight, and now cast in the shadow of the opposite fells, I have walked further than I can see. I am nearly at the end of this valley, which peaks at the cluster of rocks just a couple of hundred yards ahead of me at the summit.

I am tired and I am dizzy and I am breathless.

I remember the sandwich, which I take from my pocket, unwrap, then take a bite from, to mask the taste of the blood.

I slowly chew on a mouthful, then put the rest in my pocket.

I don't know how long I can continue for.

*

The simple fact is you shouldn't be doing this.

There, you said it.

You shouldn't be here. In fact, you barely are here. Your frail, ailing body has shown up, but your mind is elsewhere.

Your mind is in Cardiff, Stuttgart, the Priory, Toulouse, Blackwood, Tokyo, Hull, London, Bangkok, Pembrokeshire, New York, Lisbon and Middlesbrough.

Your mind is in 1972, 1983, 1986, 1990, 1993.

Your mind is in purgatory, the inferno, Hades, the underworld, the pit, Jahannam, Dis, Tartarus, in screaming bloody fucking hell.

But your body is on tour with Suede, in the winter, in Europe again.

You are a ghost.

You are a ghost in Switzerland.
Italy.
Spain.
Stop.
In France.
Holland.
Belgium.
Make it stop.
In Denmark.
Norway.
Sweden.
You can't do this any more.
No more.
No.
You can't do this.

*

Then just like that – just as I am staggering up the final stretch of rocks to the top of the mountain that crowns the valley's end – thoughts and memories and faces come flooding back.

It is as if a door has opened. As if something has been unleashed a kaleidoscope of memories crowds my vision. Memories of places I have been, faces I have known. Songs I've sung and films I've seen.

It whirls by, a lurid carousel of colour and noise and emotion. Everything is experienced at a dizzying super-speed. Colours, smells, emotions. Clothes I've worn, girls I've kissed, exams I have sat.

Memories of holidays and haircuts, houses and weather. Books and arguments and aeroplanes and hospitals. Memories of music and motorways, bridges and buses, pills and thrills and tears and screams and smiles.

It all battles for space in my head here on the hillside, exhausted, defeated, half-mad and alone. The summit in sight. Day turning to night turning to day again. And silence.

*

After soundcheck – a perfunctory daily routine in which you are nothing but a spare part consigned to the wings, stage right – you find an upmarket household-goods shop in a quiet Milan side street where, in broken English, you enquire about buying the most expensive meat cleaver that they have. Stainless steel, it's heavy in your hand and when you step into a doorway and remove it from its wrapping, it glistens in the late-afternoon Italian sun.

The chattering in your head is constant now.

The voice won't leave you alone.

Each new hotel room that you enter you hope to find silence, but it's impossible. The noise follows you everywhere. In the shower, sobbing as you cut yourself with a razor; on the bed, naked, trying to muster up the energy to dress and go to the venue; stone cold sober in the backstage corridors of Austria, Sweden, Denmark; onstage as you go through the motions, a ghost with a guitar like a millstone around his neck. Not even the volume of your band can drown it out now. You see and hear the voice in the crowd too, mouthing words at you, pointing, punching, the air, sweating, screaming, crying all your words right back at you.

And then afterwards, as your ears buzz and hum with feedback and static, the chattering gets louder. It's an ongoing argument with yourself. The voice is telling you that enough is enough – it's time to ease the burden, time to do something. It's time to get decisive. It is time to chop off your hands. Bite off your fingers. Cut your veins. Gouge your eyes. Scissor your tongue. Smash everything you can get your hands on. Take all your pills. Set fire to yourself. Locate a bridge and jump off it. Buy a gun and use it. Take a bottle of bleach and drink it. Find an oven but don't light it. Anything. Anything to stop the chattering. Anything to feel better.

Anything to ease the burden.

Anything for some peace.

*

I haul myself up and over the final boulders to the peak of the mountain.

It is nearly dark now. In fact, it is completely dark in the east and the west is following suit. The sky is a dimmer switch, a dying flame – and so am I.

At the summit there is a giant flattened rock whose surface has been worn smooth by centuries of feet. And in the centre is a small cairn to mark the peak.

Gasping for air, I slump down beside it, my back against the crude angles of the rocks.

Isn't it traditional for every walker or climber to add a rock to a cairn, to help perpetuate its growth? I think so.

But I have no energy for that. I can't even lift my body into a more comfortable sitting position.

Because I am a shadow now, a silhouette for all down in the valley to see against the sky, though I expect the valley to be empty now, and for every sane person to be returning to their home, every animal to their burrow or bolt-hole.

Everyone but me.

*

But they don't listen.

They don't listen because they keep giving you work. They still keep giving you tasks to keep you busy. Tasks or tests – it's hard to tell. They still seem happy for you to be out there (but not too 'out there'), spreading the good word of the Manics to the tape recorders and the cameras and the nodding lapdogs of the world's music media.

You surprise even yourself with your ability to hold it together under questioning. There are no tears or break-downs here, boy. Just pure Valleys resolve. Graft. Stoicism. Pragmatism – again. And an unerring dedication to never letting people down.

So when a TV crew arrives at the venue in Sweden in search of an interview, the work is delegated to you. The others have had enough of trying to explain your actions, ailments and illnesses. They're tired of second-guessing your sick mind. It – or rather you – has taken its toll on them in different ways for each of them, Manic Street Preachers has become a job whose daily grind is only barely tolerable right now, though for you it is an incurable disease. You are Richey Manic at all times. He is in your blood. Your bad blood. He is destroying your cells. He is eating you alive. He keeps you awake and he prevents you from eating. He compels you towards pain. He slices your thoughts into tiny worthless strips. He dismantles your jigsaw mind.

He puts words into your mouth and breathes down your neck. He makes sure you are there, in front of the crowd, in front of the camera.

— Every day of my life I feel that I'm not as good a writer as I could be, that I'm not as intelligent as I could be.

This is what you tell them. The telly people. The interviewer from some foreign channel.

— I try and constantly read and improve my mind to get a better perspective on world history.

You say.

— Nobody is going to get good enough to know everything.

And also:

— . . . But I try, which is more than most people do.

You decide it will be your last television appearance.

✳

Exposure.

It will be exposure that will take me.

It strikes me as extremely ironic that I might die from such a cause. 'Over-exposure' might be a better way of putting it.

Over-exposure to the world and all its cruel tricks and false promises.

I smile and then I laugh out loud and think: actually, I'm finally fine with that.

The only thing is, I wish my dog was here with me now. I wish he could be here to curl up beside me so that we might share body heat, so that this dilemma might somehow be shared. Snoopy would make it all right because he's the one thing I couldn't leave behind.

But Snoopy isn't here. Snoopy left last month. Now he's in the ground; this same Welsh ground from which the mountain has been sculpted.

*

Later that day you slip into a complete void. Your ears ring and you become totally numb.

You cannot grasp on to a single coherent thought and you feel nothing.

Even when you're banging your head against the out-side wall of the hotel in Hamburg.

Even when blood is streaming down your face.

Even when small flecks of gravel are imprinted in your flesh.

Even when Nick is trying to contain his sobs as he leads you away by the arm.

Even when the staff gasp in horror.

Even when the blood swirls down the plug hole.
Even then you feel nothing.

*

So. Where do we go from here?

What do you mean, 'we'?

Us. You and me. All of us.

There is no you and me. There is no 'all of us'. There's only me.

Fine. Where do you go from here, then, smartarse?

Nowhere.

So – what? – you're just going to stay here?

I don't know. I don't know anything any more. I don't even remembering getting here. Do you think someone will come and help me?

Is that what you want?

No. I don't know. I'm just so tired. Tired of myself.

*

You decide that 'Stay Another Day' by East 17 is the best single of the 90s.

Granted, it is only 1994, but it is hard to see how it can ever be improved upon.

Back home as you sit around attempting to 'get better' it's all over the radio and the Christmas bells and winter-themed video are sure to send it to number one. You pick up a pile of their CDs when you're in Sony to give away as Christmas presents. You play your copy to death. When you tell people that East 17 are a more credible band than Blur or Oasis, and that Tony Mortimer is the best lyricist around, they think you're taking the piss. But you're not. You're really not. Pop gives you more of a thrill these days. It's cheap and disposable and is not pretending to be anything other than what it is: titillation for young girls. Rock is all about fakery.

And after three weeks off, you are back doing what you have to do. What you do best.

They've booked you in back at the Astoria on Tottenham Court Road. It's two thousand capacity, three nights, all sold out and just down the road from where you played your first-ever London shows in Great Portland Street and Covent Garden over five years ago.

Five years.

Five years is nothing. It's only half a decade. Why then does it seem so long ago? Why, when you think back, do you barely recognise yourself? And why does regret flood these memories?

It's so loud onstage the first night that you and James both suffer nosebleeds after the show. Of course, you get off on this. James less so.

And you play a full-on twenty-song set each night.

Monday.

Tuesday.

Wednesday.

You pull out all the stops: the hits, the obscurities and even the odd surprise from James, with his version of the Watership Down *music and 'Last Christmas' by Wham! (which brings to mind images of George and Andrew and*

Pepsi and Shirley frolicking in the fake snow in their big wool-knit sweaters).

The band let you choose a set list, which you do, writing it out by hand as you have always done and decorating it with salient quotations plucked from your notebooks. You spend a long time deliberating over which quotes to choose. It's important, even if it only matters to you.

Eventually you condense an essay that Ballard wrote entitled 'What I Believe' down to its bare bones: 'I believe in alcoholism, venereal disease, fever and exhaustion. I believe in the genital organs of great men and women. I believe in the inexistence of the universe and the boredom of the atom. I believe all memories, lies, fantasies, evasions.'

And you know what?

You enjoy these shows more than any you can remember in a long, long time. With Christmas around the corner they feel like a celebration.

On these three nights, with the crowds singing every single word back at you, you believe in the Manic Street Preachers again. You believe in noise and music and movement and freedom. You believe in the ritualistic and communal elements of music. And you almost believe in yourself.

In a brilliant and unplanned act of auto-destruction you smash your hired gear at the end. You all do. Ten thousand pounds' worth. Beneath the combat-green military-netting canopy you swing and you smack and you bang and you crash until splinters litter the stage and the feedback from the PA howls like a pack of Carpathian wolves smelling fresh blood.

These three nights feel special.

They feel like catharsis. They feel like emancipation.

They feel like closure.

*

I have dreams like none I have ever had before. They are dreams that take place in that space between waking and sleeping and I find myself drifting between the two as everything becomes blurred.

They are dreams that feature no people, just the elements. Dreams of rock and fire, of lava and mayhem, of the earth torn asunder by lightning and storms and thunder. Biblical dreams. Prophetic dreams. Dreams of a scorched earth. Dreams beyond my understanding.

Dreams of end times.

*

It falls to the floor in clumps, your hair. Henna-red and unwashed.

You draw the clippers from your brow right down to the back of your skull and it feels good seeing it all fall away, fall to the floor around your feet. With it falls away the recent past. The grim Christmas, the autumn in and out of clinics and cold dressing rooms in France.

The sceptre of Germany. The nutty ward in Cardiff. The death of Snoopy.

All of it.

You're aware that something is happening here, something significant, but it is taking place so deep within your subconscious that there is no need for rationality. You're just acting upon impulse.

As the hair falls so too does the last thing you have clung to that makes you 'Richey Manic' – the ever-changing hairstyle.

— Often emulated, but never bettered, you used to joke.

The clippers buzz and scratch at your scalp and you make sure to do it as evenly as possible, though without a guard on the clippers it takes it right down to the bone anyway. Right down to the skull.

When you are finished, standing in a circle of your hair, that is exactly what you see staring back from the mirror: a skull with big black blank eyes.

Now you can sleep.

Now you are anonymous.

*

So it has come to this?

Yes. It has come to this.

*

A day passes. Then another. Three, four, then you get a phone call from London to remind you that you are doing an interview later on in the day.

You don't have to do it, they say. Not if you're not feeling up to it.

— No, no, you say. It's fine. I'm fine.

The writer is from a Japanese magazine and she has flown all the way to London, then driven to Cardiff to do it. You've worked with her before.

She'll be here in an hour.

So you take off your dressing gown and open a new packet of pyjamas. You've been wearing pyjamas for about a week now, a new set each day. They feel comfortable against your skin.

Then, on unsteady legs, you vacuum the flat, put some books and CDs back on the shelves and light a couple of scented candles.

You want to pour yourself a drink. You want to pour yourself two drinks. You want to feel that warm surge in your head and in your stomach, then feel it flush through your cheeks. You want to feel your head loll and your eyes get sparkly and glassy.

But you can't do it. To drink now would be a big mistake. Seven months, you've been dry.

You can't blow it now so instead you take a marker pen and write LOVE across your knuckles. Every time you want to drink, you do this. You do this every day.

Sometimes you do it five times a day. Sometimes even more.

Then you make coffee and you smoke a cigarette out the window while Pantera plays on the stereo. After about two minutes it is completely doing your head in, so you turn it off, but the sound of nothing – or the distant sounds of Cardiff – do your head in too, so you turn on the TV and listen to Henry Kelly ask easy riddles on Going For Gold.

After the interview is over Mum and Dad arrive and you feel extremely emotional but hide it by making them tea.

You want to throw your arms around them and tell them that you love them and that you are sorry for everything, and that it won't always be like this, and things will change very soon, but you worry that this might freak them out, or worry them even more, so instead you busy yourself taking photos of them on the disposable camera that you bought before Christmas.

You tell them you need to finish the film off, so they pose awkwardly on your Laura Ashley sofa, smiling, their arms around each other.

There's more to it all than this, you think. It's about more than just finishing the film off.

And you realise, maybe only truly for the first time, just how much you look like both of them.

They must see themselves in you.

They must look at you and wonder what they did wrong.

And that just fucking kills you.

It's time to go.

*

My skeleton hurts.

It is like cold steel beneath my withered muscles and thin skin. My skeleton hurts and my marrow trembles. My heartbeat is slower than it has ever been.

I am in limbo.

*

This is what you remember: your suitcase sits there in the corner of the room.

You don't want to go.

On the table are your travel documents and your itinerary for the next two weeks. It tells you where you will be at every hour for the next fourteen days. There are even scheduled 'bathroom breaks'.

Beside it, in the ashtray, a cigarette burns. You're sitting on the edge of the bed looking at your reflection in the TV, which is screwed down and not turned on. Below it, the minibar is locked. Outside, London is dark blue and dormant. There is frost on the window and you don't want to go.

You're scared and tired and full of angst and you're reluctant to go to America. Even just leaving your flat was difficult. Travelling to London nearly tore you apart.

You're in The Embassy again. The fifth floor, Room 516. Right now you don't want to see anyone, you don't want to do anything. Ever again.

James calls.

He is only three rooms away yet still he phones.

— Edwards.

— Bradders.

— What are you doing?

— Not much.

— I'm bored as fuck. Do you fancy going down Queensway to watch a film?

— Maybe. What's on?

— I've got it down to two: Frankenstein *or* Pulp Fiction *. . . again. Bobby De Niro with bolts through his neck or the re-birth of Travolta.*

— Yeah. OK, then.

— Which one?

— I'm not bothered.

Half an hour later you pick up the phone and call James back.

— I think I'll skip the film tonight.

— OK. Is everything all right?

— Yeah, fine. I just don't feel like concentrating on anything tonight.

— OK. I'll see you in the morning, then?

— Yes.

— Bright and early.

— Bright and early.

— OK.

— James.

— Yes?

— Thanks.

You hang up.

*

I can see Wales before me. Undulating, hazy Wales. I see valleys and fields and peaks and sedimentary landslides. I see blackened peaks and misty troughs. I see layer upon layer of Wales, great bands of earth and rock like torn streaks of paper on top of each other. In all directions.

Wales.

I take it in then I lie back against the stones and hear my breathing as my ribcage rises and falls. It is heavy, rasping, rattled. My head is hot. My head is swimming. My ears ringing.

I take a deep breath, hold it, then exhale. My breath makes a sound. It sounds like music. The music sings. It says my name.

It says, '*Richard.*'

'The rest is silence.'

(*Hamlet*, 5. 2)

Bibliography & Further Reading

Please note: all chapter titles in this book are taken from slogans on T-shirts customised and worn onstage by Richey Edwards between 1989 and 1994. All epigraphs throughout this book are taken from *Hamlet: Prince of Denmark* by William Shakespeare.

The following texts have also verified facts, provided inspiration or helped in the writing of this book. A special mention should go to *Everything: A Book About Manic Street Preachers* by Simon Price (1999), one of the most exhaustively researched and passionately written band biographies in existence, and an invaluable resource.

Alma Cogan by Gordon Burn (1991)
American Psycho by Bret Easton Ellis (1991)
Ariel by Sylvia Plath (1965)
Bad Vibes: Britpop & My Part In Its Downfall by Luke Haines (2009)
The Bell Jar by Sylvia Plath (1963)
Born Yesterday: The News As A Novel by Gordon Burn (2008)
City of Night by John Rechy (1963)

Complete Poetry by William Wordsworth (2004 edition)

Confessions of a Mask by Yukio Mishima (1948)

The Damned United by David Peace (2006)

Diary of a Mad Old Man by Jun'ichirō Tanizaki (1961)

Everything: A Book About Manic Street Preachers by Simon Price (1999)

Heart of Darkness by Joseph Conrad (1899)

Hellfire by Nick Tosches (1982)

Hunger by Knut Hamsun (1890)

In The Beginning: My Life With The Manic Street Preachers by Jenny Watkins-Isnardi (2000)

Kill Your Friends by John Niven (2008)

The Last Party: Britpop, Blair and the Demise of English Rock by John Harris (2004)

The Last Sitting by Bert Stern (1982)

Less Than Zero by Bret Easton Ellis (1986)

Madness and Civilization: A History of Insanity in the Age of Reason by Michel Foucault (1961)

The Manic Street Preachers: Sweet Venom by Martin Clark (1997)

The Nineties: What The Fuck Was That All About? by John Robb (1999)

The Rime of the Ancient Mariner by Samuel Taylor Coleridge (1992 edition)

Rumble Fish by S. E. Hinton (1975)

The Savage God: A Study of Suicide by A. Alvarez (1971)

A Season in Hell by Arthur Rimbaud (1873)

The Selected Poems of Li Po by David Hinton (1998)

The Society of The Spectacle by Guy Debord (1967)

Songs At The Year's Turning by R. S. Thomas (1955)

The Stranger by Albert Camus (1942)
The Thief's Journal by Jean Genet (1949)
Touching From A Distance – Ian Curtis and Joy Division
    by Deborah Curtis (1995)
Under Milk Wood by Dylan Thomas (1953)
The Uses of Literacy by Jeremy Deller (1999)
The World According to Mike Leigh by Michael Coveney
    (1997)

Thanks to the following publications and websites, past and present: the *Big Issue*, *Check This Out!*, the *Daily Telegraph*, *Drownedinsound.com*, the *Face*, the *Guardian*, *Kerrang!*, *Last Exit*, *Lime Lizard*, *Melody Maker*, *Metal Hammer*, *Mojo*, *Music Life*, NME, the *Observer*, *Q*, *The Quietus.com*, *Raw*, *Select*, *Smash Hits*, *Sounds*, *Spiral Scratch*, the *Sunday Times*, *The Times*, *Volume*, *Vox*.

Resources

Missing People
(formerly the National Missing Person's Helpline):

Website: www.missingpeople.org.uk
Runaway Helpline: 0808 800 7070
Text: 80234
E-mail: runaway@missingpeople.org.uk
Message Home Freefone service: 0800 700 740
Message Home e-mail:
    messagehome@missingpeople.org.uk
If you have seen a missing person:
    seensomeone@missingpeople.org.uk

To report someone missing:
    report@missingpeople.org.uk
To make a donation:
    supporters@missingpeople.org.uk

The Big Issue

www.bigissue.com
To make a donation:
    fundraising@bigissue.com

Acknowledgements

Thank you to everyone who helped with the researching and writing of this book.

picador.com

blog
videos
interviews
extracts